THE
LION OF JUSTICE

ALSO AVAILABLE BY LEENA LEHTOLAINEN

In The Bodyguard Series
The Bodyguard

In The Maria Kallio Series
My First Murder
Her Enemy
Copper Heart
Snow Woman

THE
LION OF JUSTICE

THE BODYGUARD SERIES

LEENA LEHTOLAINEN

TRANSLATED BY JENNI SALMI

amazon crossing

Text copyright © 2011 Leena Lehtolainen
Translation copyright © 2015 Jenni Salmi

Previously published as *Oikeuden jalopeura* by Tammi Publishers in Finland in 2011. Translated from Finnish by Jenni Salmi. First published in English by AmazonCrossing in 2015.

Published by AmazonCrossing, Seattle

www.apub.com

Amazon, the Amazon logo, and AmazonCrossing are trademarks of Amazon.com, Inc., or its affiliates.

ISBN-13: 9781477830284
ISBN-10: 1477830286

Cover design by Laura Klynstra

Library of Congress Control Number: 2014922270

Printed in the United States of America

1

There are no lynx in Tuscany. If you're lucky, you might encounter a wildcat in the southern hills. As I drove southwest from Florence in my gray rental car, the only animals I saw were swallows and pigeons, whose cooing I could hear while navigating the narrow roads.

I could see Montemassi from afar, perched on a hill a thousand feet above sea level. The fortress was awe inspiring, just like in Simone Martini's fresco where Guidoriccio rides into town. The narrow northern tower was long gone, and the roof and walls in the center of the fortress had collapsed. I shifted to a lower gear when the road leading up to the fortress village became steeper. This was my first time in Italy, but when I lived in New York, I went to Little Italy often enough to learn some everyday vocabulary that I was now trying to recall. My Italian classmate at the Queens security academy also made sure I knew the essential curse words.

It had been almost six months since I'd last seen David. He'd sailed in on his boat from Spain to meet me in Kiel. Chief Constable Teppo Laitio from the National Bureau of Investigation, a couple of Finnish politicians and trusted colleagues at Europol, and I were the only ones who knew that he had survived the explosion in the Baltic Sea. Nonetheless, someone leaked the information, and David had to abandon his former hideout near Seville.

David had no idea who was after him, but it was clear to both of us that we were being followed. We had become accustomed to observing people, looking through their masks, noticing objects in places where there should be none. This time, whoever was tracking David had made it clear he was being hunted: the paths outside David's hut were covered in new tracks each morning, and once, when we were out for a walk, the kitchen window had been smashed in. He also received odd phone calls despite changing his phone number frequently. Someone was trying to scare David and force him to make a move.

When David asked me to go back to Finland, we had a huge fight. I needed to visit Finland to take care of some personal business, but I had expected to just drop in and then return to Spain. I had run out of money, so I was planning on selling some of my belongings. I had quit my former job as a security screener at the airport without giving any notice, which foiled my chances of receiving unemployment benefits. I hadn't made any attempts to find another job and instead spent several months being a beach bum in southern Spain. When I returned to Finland, they gave me my old job back; they always needed security screeners.

The week we spent in Kiel was just a short getaway, which made me miss David even more. I hated that my moods were so dependent on hearing from him. He only contacted me sporadically, his e-mail addresses and phone numbers changed often, and sometimes I didn't hear from him for weeks at a time. My brain told me to forget about him, but my heart didn't want to let go just yet.

David had been traveling with a Swedish passport and a new Swedish-Italian identity: Daniel Lanotte. I loved the last name but feared that his chosen first name was too revealing. After all, he'd used his real middle name. David wasn't worried though; he figured there were plenty of Daniels in the world, and at the moment, it was associated with Swedish royalty, if anything. It looked like David had finally found a better hideout, and he felt it was safe enough for me to visit him in southern Tuscany, which drew a variety of foreigners, so a lonely Swede like him didn't stand out too much.

I knew David had made a bold move when he'd gone to see his family in Tartu, Estonia, and I later received text messages from all over Europe: Poland, France, southern Germany. He'd tried to shake his stalker off his tracks and seemed to think he had been successful. He never told me the identity of his enemy; the less I knew, the safer I'd be, he'd said.

David had found Montemassi by sheer coincidence. I don't know where he met Brother Gianni, a monk living in the nearby Abbey of Sant'Antimo, but he'd helped David find a place in the village, right next to the fortress. All four apartments in the building were empty; they'd been listed for a while because the recession in Tuscany had hit the real estate market hard. Brother Gianni knew a real estate agent and had convinced him to rent an apartment to David.

"The abbey is not safe for me," David had said. "Too many people visit the place, and it just seems like an obvious hideout. Instead, I'll be a half Swede who has suddenly struck it rich with stocks and escaped the hideous winter sleet of Sweden to Italy, where he can fulfill his dream of becoming a writer."

Although David had warned me that he didn't look the same as when I'd last seen him in Kiel, I still had a hard time recognizing the man leaning on a stone wall in the central square of Montemassi. During his recovery from the explosion, he had lost some of his muscle mass, and his new stooped posture seemed to add years to his age. He wore sunglasses. His thick, curly black hair was the same wig I'd seen him wear in the lobby of Hotel Torni in Finland. His thin mustache and ridiculous goatee were also pitch-black. His dark-blue sweater and gray jeans were baggy on him, and I was surprised that the back of his hands were covered in black hair. But it seemed that this thin, tall stranger was indeed David.

I parked my car at the edge of the square and got out to stretch. I had let my hair grow enough to tie it in two short pigtails, but otherwise I looked the same as ever. I looked like an impostor in my flowery dress, but it was fitting for a tourist visiting Tuscany in the spring with hopes that the late March sun would be warm enough. I pretended to be curious about an ugly modern bronze statue that looked out of place, and then I moved over to study the tourist information.

I had used my own passport to get into the country, as I didn't see any reason to use forged papers. I was a security professional working outside of official organizations, currently employed by Airpro Inc. Before that I had worked as a private bodyguard, but I gave up that line of work when one of my employers was murdered right after I quit and the other was kidnapped despite the measures I had taken to prevent it. I was happy with my job's easy shifts, and the greatest danger was pompous travelers throwing a temper tantrum. If I was in need of danger, I could always rely on David.

"*Buongiorno, signora,*" I heard a familiar voice say in Italian.

I asked if he knew any English, and when he said yes, we switched languages. We had agreed beforehand to pretend not to know each other; we were just two people who were immediately attracted to each other. A Finnish tourist would lure a local man into showing her the fortress, and it would end like a romance novel or a B movie: love at first sight under the blue Tuscan sky. If the people who were after David had looked into my background at all, they'd know that I wasn't too particular about my companions; if I wanted to have sex with someone, I did. Sometimes even when I didn't really feel like it.

We both knew that if I was followed as a way to get to David, even the best of disguises wouldn't take us very far. Still, I'd chosen to take that chance. I couldn't resist David, and I would have followed him on a much more treacherous road than the one to a Tuscan fortress town.

David wore new cologne, but I could smell him through it. He asked where I had come from, and I answered like any tourist would. We began the climb toward the fortress and walked past a black cat sleeping on a stoop in front of a blue door. A tractor buzzed in a faraway field. It was early evening, and the village was empty.

The Montemassi fortress had only two towers left. The ruins between them that used to have rooms were overgrown with flowers; a tree about my height, resembling a mallow; strange-looking clovers; poppies; a mintlike plant whose dark-purple flowers Uncle Jari would have enjoyed. Although he never deemed it an appropriate pastime for a grown man, he had been a plant enthusiast, and I had learned plant names and classifications through osmosis. Any information that could save a life would come in handy, and when kids in grade school tried to make me eat mezereon berries, I knew they were poisonous. I didn't squeal on them; instead, I carried the berries in my pocket for a while, wrapped up and ready to be mixed into the bullies' lingonberry pudding at lunch.

The fortress opened up with views in all directions, and I saw the rolling hills in the south, widening toward the sea. The only movement down in the village was a mangy dog, carrying a piece of unrecognizable meat.

It was strange to speak English with David, but it was for the best. Our mutual language had usually been Swedish, and only after David disappeared had I learned about his Finnish skills—one of the many things he had hidden from me, despite all we had been through. He had learned Spanish effortlessly and seemed to be at home with Italian as well. Maybe language skills were a replacement for life insurance for David in a world ready to ambush him at any moment.

We pretended to get to know each other. I talked about myself as truthfully as I could: I lived in Helsinki, rented a room from Mrs. Voutilainen, and worked at the Helsinki-Vantaa airport as a security screener. I had never married, I had no children, and I had no pets. David on the other hand was creating his character as we talked. He claimed to be the son of an Italian father and a Swedish-Finnish mother, and to have spent most of his life in Sweden, where he came into some money and then moved to Tuscany to live his dream of becoming a novelist.

"Quite a cliché, huh? As if writing is somehow easier here than in Sollentuna or Småland. But the scenery here is something else, isn't it? Would you like to see the view from my writing room? I could make you an espresso."

It was a classic pickup scene: an Italian man hitting on a tourist—and I said yes. David's place was only sixty feet below the fortress, and the view from there was gorgeous. The vantage point was also handy for keeping an eye on the traffic from the south and the east.

Once we got inside, David asked if I knew any Swedish. When I said yes, he switched languages.

"We should be safe here. I've checked this place daily, and so far I haven't found any cameras or bugs. Still, speaking Swedish is less risky than speaking English—only a fraction of English-speaking people would know Swedish. I've never heard anyone speak it here—only once in Roccastrada, and I quickly moved to the other side of the street. Once I saw a tourist group from Skåne in Sant'Antimo, but they all seemed harmless. Retirees."

"You of all people should know there's no such thing as a harmless group of people," I told him. "A group of retirees would be the perfect smoke screen for an enemy to hide in. And why are you afraid of other Swedes? Do you think a Swede is after you?"

David took a step closer. We had not yet touched. In Kiel we'd hardly made it inside the sailboat before we were pulling each other's clothes off. This time there was an invisible wall between us that we couldn't climb over.

"I don't know who my threat is," David said. "That's why I can't tell you anything. Maybe it's one of the lucky ones who have inherited Vasiliev's place in the hierarchy, and he's upset about the SR-90 isotope being in the wrong hands. Or maybe it's Ivan Gezolian, who delivered the isotope to Vasiliev. Maybe they're actually after the isotope, not me."

David had never told me what happened to the isotope. When I'd learned the previous winter that he was still alive, nothing else seemed important. Only after returning from Spain had I started thinking about all the secrets David was keeping from me. The past year hadn't been enough time to find everything out.

"You have to trust me," he said. "Let's not ruin this time we have together by worrying over nothing. So far I'm safe here, and so are you." David pulled me into his arms, and I let myself go, shutting off my brain and any sense of self-preservation, as none of it mattered then. His goatee tickled my skin, and the rough black hair was unfamiliar under my fingers, but the way David touched me was the same as ever: his kisses demanding, the heat from his now wiry body inviting.

These were the carefree days in late March. Fruit trees were in bloom, leaves grew rapidly. The sun was occasionally so warm that we could walk outside in short-sleeved shirts, although the Monte Amiata peaks still boasted enough snow for skiers. We drove from one small village to another, hiked along the hills, exchanged kisses within the walls of abandoned churches, and marveled at modern sculptures in art parks. Although I was happy, I couldn't help feeling that it wasn't real. I had been cast to play in a movie that David was directing, and he'd never told me the plot; I only knew that surprising twists might be around any corner.

David had two locked drawers, and I had not managed to find their keys despite searching for them furiously on those few occasions when he had left me alone in his apartment. I was sure he knew what I was up to, since we stayed together most of the time.

I'd been in Montemassi for a couple of weeks when David got a phone call. We were having dinner. David had prepared freshly picked artichokes, and their dark-purple leaves covered our plates.

"*Pronto*," he said, greeting his caller, then switched into English. "Yes, this is Daniel Lanotte. Who is this?" He got up and walked into the living room. I heard him ask again, but the caller hung up.

"Damn it," David said in Finnish. His eyes had an odd look to them, maybe even a hint of fear. When the phone rang again, David answered in English. "What sort of games are you playing? Who is this?"

I got up and dumped the artichoke leaves into the compost bin. Our main course, lemon risotto, was bubbling on the stove, so I walked over to stir it. David couldn't go outside to talk, but he wanted to talk as far away from me as possible. I heard him march into the living room and close the thick wooden door behind him, which muffled his voice.

Damn it, I thought as well. But I had to remember that David was not my client to protect—he was just my lover. I could have demanded that my clients let me listen in on their phone calls, even if they didn't always agree to do so. I tasted the creamy, tangy risotto and ground more white pepper into it. I was amused by the way

Italians called a pepper mill *tappomachina*, considering that *tappo* in Finnish means a kill. A killing machine.

David wasn't on the phone for long.

"Who was it?" I asked when he returned to the kitchen.

"My former boss from Europol. Just a weekly routine call to make sure I'm still safe."

"Then what was all that cursing about?"

"Because he interrupted our dinner, *cara*." David smiled, but it didn't reach all the way to his eyes; the eyes I still couldn't interpret. He avoided looking at me. He walked over to the risotto and took it off the stove to grate some pecorino cheese into it with his strong hands. *A killer's hands*, I thought. He grated with determined movements. I quickly grabbed my glass and took a gulp of local wine that tasted bitter after eating the artichokes.

One more lie, or at least, something David would never let me in on. He had never told about the night when he stole the SR-90 isotope and blew up the boat called *I Believe*. He'd said, "It's not something I want to dwell on. I killed four people. I'm not proud of it, but I have to live with it." That was the only answer I'd ever gotten from him. At least in Spain he'd described to me how he floated in the sea for hours and how the freezing cold slowly seeped in despite his wet suit. Once, after downing half a bottle of brandy, he mentioned how the four dead people had hundreds of relatives and friends they'd left behind. Sure, the dead had chosen their lifestyle, but he doubted this was much consolation to those close to them.

After finishing the risotto, we went out for a walk, switching into English as soon as we left. Our plan was to drive to Siena the following day, and David suggested we wake up early to pack for an overnight stay. The tourist season was not in full swing, so we didn't think we'd have trouble finding a place to stay. David wanted to show me the fresco Simone Martini had painted of Montemassi, which hung in the town hall.

"I don't know history well enough to know whether Guidoriccio was considered a hero for conquering Montemassi or not. His role would depend on who wrote the history," David said as we stood inside the fortress, watching the new moon cast a bridge of light across the valley below. A black cat made his way along the stone wall and stopped to meow, which enticed a couple of other cats to join him: an orange and a gray tabby. The cats obviously knew each other well. I wished humans had it as easy as cats; just one sniff and you'd immediately know whether the person was friend or foe. Just then, the tabby hissed at the black cat, who growled back at him, and my theory about cats' flawless recognition system fell apart like dandelion fluff blown off my palm.

In the darkness I wanted to feel physically close to another person, because everything smelled stronger at night, and I was drawn to silhouettes and shadows. As David pressed me against the southern wall and kissed me, I thought about how the hands he used to stroke my neck could easily close around it, too. People of Montemassi had seen a blond Finnish tourist walking around with Mr. Lanotte—surely the body of a Finnish tourist wouldn't later be found inside this fortress. I had to stop myself. Why was I entertaining these thoughts?

As soon as we got back to the apartment, David announced that it was time for bed. I wasn't sleepy, though; my mind was racing. I stayed awake next to David until the wee hours of the morning. I considered taking a sleeping pill, but then I remembered I needed to be sharp for driving the winding road to Siena, watching out for construction crews and detour signs. I finally fell asleep a little after three.

My sleep was rudely interrupted around seven by a rooster crowing below us on the hillside. I had kicked off my blanket. David was already out of bed. I sniffed at the air, hopeful that he had already brewed the first cup of espresso. But the only thing I could identify lingering in the air was David's new aftershave.

I put on my bathrobe and headed to the kitchen. No one was there. The espresso machine stood on the counter unused and cool to the touch. I wondered whether David was in the bathroom. As soon as I splashed my face, I could see better—no one was in the bathroom, either. Maybe he'd decided to make a last-minute run to the grocery store in the village.

I saw David's scooter—he didn't have a car—parked in the yard, so he couldn't have gone far. I went back to the bedroom and opened the closet. All of his clothes were still there. But the jeans, shirt, socks, and underwear he'd hung over a chair the night before were gone, as were his brown leather shoes and jacket.

I told myself he could have just walked to the bakery.

When he wasn't back an hour later, I called him. An automated message said in Italian, "The number you have dialed cannot be reached." I didn't hear his phone ring in the apartment, and I knew he always kept his wallet in his jacket's breast pocket. He must've taken both with him.

I sat around all morning, waiting for him, calling his number every ten minutes. I peeked out to make sure my car hadn't disappeared, too. The black cat from the night before sat on the hood, and I was dead sure he'd seen David leave.

As the church bells rang at noon, it finally dawned on me that something had gone terribly wrong. I doubted David would return. He didn't trust me, so I decided not to care about his privacy. My first task was to break into his locked drawers.

2

The sturdy hutch was made of old wood, perhaps mahogany. It contained four drawers, and the two bottom ones were not locked. I'd used them a couple of times for sorting laundry, and we'd only kept socks and underwear in them. I estimated that David could not have taken more than one change of clothes, if that. The lynx socks I'd bought for him—merchandise for Ilves, the Finnish hockey team, whose mascot was the growling head of a lynx—had not been touched. I'd bought them because of the animal, not because of any team alliances.

The upper two drawers were locked and required a key of approximately two inches in length. I tried to feel for the lock with my fingers, but I could fit only the tip of my little finger in. I grabbed a thin spoon from the kitchen and shoved it into the lock. It seemed like the lock had only two wards inside it. I'd made a couple of futile attempts at finding a key when David had gone out before, but I wasn't sure what kind of key I was actually looking for. Now I had time for a more systematic search, although it was possible David had taken the key with him. The key wasn't essential—I could break into the hutch if I really wanted to with an ax and a saw—but I wanted to avoid damaging the beautiful wood if I could.

I went through David's closets, patting down all of his suit and pants pockets and shoes. I found a hunting rifle bullet in his jacket pocket and a receipt. He'd splurged at a restaurant specializing in truffles in Paganico called Il Tre Canton a week before I'd arrived; the receipt revealed a five-course dinner. He'd had company, judging by the two orders of appetizers and entrées. All of it had been washed down with a couple of pitchers of wine and five after-dinner drinks: either coffee or liqueur. The appetizers must have been something special, as they had cost way more than the entrées. Although David was by no means a small man, I doubted he could've gorged on this much food. He hadn't mentioned this dinner to me, nor had he ever taken me to this restaurant. I tried to rationalize that David had taken his landlord out to thank him for fixing up the place, but I had to admit the idea seemed ludicrous.

The kitchen cupboards had enough dishes for four people. I checked inside the kettle where we had boiled asparagus, and I peered inside the cheese grater. No keys. My default hiding place for the keys to my gun locker was inside a box of muesli or tampons—where no one else would be looking. I assumed David employed a similar logic, so I checked the few boxes of staples he kept in the kitchen. No key in the spaghetti box or the bag of espresso. I sat down at the kitchen table and tried to convince myself to give up. It was obvious by now that David had the key with him.

He had been careful not to let any of his objects reveal too much of himself. The few clothes and items of personal hygiene he'd brought along could've belonged to anyone. That's why I was so interested in the locked drawers, though I knew he wasn't stupid enough to leave anything important inside a drawer that could be pulled apart with tools readily available in the apartment.

I walked back to the hutch, pulled it away from the wall, and turned it around. Then I removed the two unlocked drawers to make the hutch lighter. I began shaking it from side to side. Judging by the sounds and movements, one of the locked drawers held something small and heavy, metallic. It didn't sound heavy enough to be a gun, but it could easily be a knife. I could only hear a faint scraping from the other drawer, like papers sliding on wood.

I inspected the back of the hutch. My dearly departed Uncle Jari, who had taken care of me when I was a child, had been a carpenter, and he'd taught me how to use woodworking tools. The dovetail joints in the hutch were expertly made, but age had weakened them. I was fairly certain I could slide a thin knife between the joints to release them and later put them back together. Although anyone would probably be able to tell that someone had been tampering with the joints, it was still a better option than attacking the hutch with an ax.

The only knife I had was my bowie knife, but its blade was too short and too thick at the handle. A thin file would have been ideal. My rental car had only a small toolbox in it, with a screwdriver and a jack. The nearest hardware store was in Roccastrada, but I didn't know when it opened. I screwed around with the bowie knife until five o'clock when I realized how hungry I was. The only food in the fridge was a tomato, a piece of cheese, and some oranges. Because we were supposed to be on our way to Siena, there had been no point in stocking the fridge. I ate a couple of oranges and took a shower, then hatched a plan. The truffle restaurant was only thirty minutes away, and someone might be able to tell me who had dined there with David.

I had to look like a person who didn't have much time for primping, so I wore a black-and-gray striped tunic, black jeans, a leather jacket, and sneakers and added a touch of mascara. I'd look like a woman unsure of her charms, someone desperately seeking a holiday fling.

I grabbed the key to the apartment off its hook inside the door and locked the apartment. That key certainly didn't fit the locked drawer. I frowned at the blue lion painted on the house number plate. David had only one set of house keys, and if I took them, he wouldn't get back in.

Irises bloomed on the hills, and apple trees were softly rustling their leaves. Pigeons cooed inside the fortress. They all appeared to mock me.

I slowed the car as I meandered down steep roads from Montemassi to Paganico. Trees were not in full bloom, their greens varying between mint and moss. Grapevines on the hills had started to produce new buds, and the first roses of the season were already blooming in sunny spots. I crossed over a small river on a low bridge that looked like it might be in danger of being swept away during a flood. I swerved around two hens and a pregnant dog that were lurching slowly into the road. Each house was home to a small group of animals; the minimum requirement appeared to be a dog and a couple of cats along with hens and a rooster for fresh eggs.

I remembered how Uncle Jari had brought three hens and a rooster to Hevonpersiinsaari, but our chicken coop had not been sturdy enough. First, one of the hens went missing, then the rooster. Our neighbor Matti Hakkarainen had seen a fox lurking around the area. Without their rooster, the hens soon stopped laying eggs, and they ended up in a large cast-iron pot in our campfire kitchen outside, where Uncle cooked most of our summer dishes. He'd been a fervent defender of organic and local foods even before it became trendy. He would have gotten along well with my friend the chef, Monika von Hertzen, but all Uncle Jari enjoyed these days were the clouds in heaven. Come to think of it, I hadn't heard from Monika for a while—connections to Mozambique, where her makeshift kitchen was located, weren't always the best.

I spotted the restaurant I was looking for while driving east past the Paganico village wall. It was a little past seven, slightly too early for dinner for Tuscans, but my growling stomach forced me to play the ignorant tourist. I parked my car and stepped into the empty restaurant. I scouted my surroundings: a couple of dozen tables that could seat about a hundred customers, an easy place to guard because of the clear layout, just one dining area without booths or labyrinthine private areas. I sat at a table where I could see the entire room, as was my habit. A waiter popped up immediately with a menu, and I began scanning for a meal that matched David's receipts. I'd never had truffles before, but I did like mushrooms. The prices looked quite reasonable, even for someone with a small budget. I soon figured out that the expensive appetizer David had ordered was a selection of five different truffle dishes. The waiter luckily knew English and helped me with the menu. I ordered truffle carpaccio and truffle pasta as my appetizer and first course and a Florentine steak as my main course. I needed meat; it would give me strength and possibly a good night's sleep in the bed that David had abandoned. Given that I had to drive back to the house, I only ordered a glass of red wine.

I decided to wait until I'd eaten my appetizer before I grilled the seemingly friendly waiter about David. He looked to be about my age and must've thought of me as an insensitive tourist who didn't understand that meal times were sacred. I knew how pathetic I looked when I placed my cell phone next to my plate. I switched the sound off but kept an eye on the screen just in case. I sipped the house red. Though I didn't know anything about wine, it tasted good. Monika had tried to teach me about wine back at Chez Monique when I still worked as a security guard for her, but she grew frustrated quickly. A six-dollar red wine tasted exactly the same to me as a sixty-dollar one, and for the life of me, I couldn't tell sparkling wine from real champagne.

I could smell the white truffles coming my way, and I instantly forgot about my phone. I took a careful bite of the mushroom and the raw meat. I wanted to gobble down everything in one shot, but Monika's voice in my head instructed me to taste and enjoy the food and made me slow down.

Just as I was finishing my appetizer, the bell above the door rang, announcing new customers. It was a young family with three small children. So long, peaceful dining. Of course they sat near me. If we'd been in Finland, they would have chosen a table as far away from me as possible to ensure the noisy children wouldn't bother me.

I dived into my enormous plate of truffle pasta, relishing the taste, while the kids sang little ditties. The waiter seemed to know the family, which was a good sign; he might remember the strange, towering giant—David—and his companion from a couple of weeks earlier. I tried not to dwell on what sort of beauty his date had been. I'd show David's receipt to the waiter in hopes that he would remember.

Two women came in. They were in their fifties and had a medium-sized dog the color of dark honey. Monika had wanted to allow dogs in Chez Monique, but the food administration officers weren't thrilled about it. These women sat near me, too, the dog curling itself at their feet. They spoke Italian. One of them was short with gray hair, while the taller woman was slim with curious, young eyes.

I devoured my pasta, thinking I'd talk with the waiter when he came to clear my plates. I wasn't sure if the other customers understood English.

The dog stood up to stretch, then walked over to me. I reached out to pet him, and the dog sniffed my shoes as I scratched him between the ears. His fur was silkier than a lynx coat.

"Get back here, Nikuzza," the taller woman said in Finnish.

I drew a surprised breath before I caught myself and turned away. Was it just a coincidence that I'd run into another Finn here, in this godforsaken village in the middle of nowhere? Maybe this woman had been with David. But who was she?

The waiter made a remark about the dog, upsetting the women. Apparently the dog wasn't welcome. The taller woman got up and yelled at the dog, this time in Italian. I may have just imagined it sounded like Finnish. The dog followed her out, bumping into my leg when he passed. The waiter came over to pour more water and smiled, without a hint of flirting. I contemplated whether I should ask him anything now that the women were here and could be Finnish. When I'd studied at the security academy in Queens, New York, for two years, I had shed my thick Savonian Finnish accent from my English during that time, but my accent was still recognizably Finnish. I didn't hear the same accent in the Italian the dog owner had used, but then again, I didn't know Italian that well. I tried to recall the words of Mike Virtue, the founder and head of the academy in Queens: any person of any nationality could have learned an American accent from pop songs or movies.

As soon as the waiter served my steak, I asked him about David's bill and whether he remembered a very tall, dark, bearded man from a couple of weeks ago. His expression was priceless: *not another jealous girlfriend.* He apologized, as he had not worked that night. He said Luigi may have, but he usually didn't remember men—a charming *signora* like me was a different story. I thought of slipping him a twenty for more information, but it might not have been enough, so I just took a bite of my steak. I doubted Luigi even existed; restaurants like these were family owned, with Mom and Pop toiling away in the kitchen and the kids working the floor. I suppose Luigi could have been the waiter's brother.

My phone flickered with a message from my former roommate Riikka, who asked me to save the date for her wedding on the first Saturday of September. A line from an old poem came to mind: "I have funerals to go to, you have weddings." I'd attended one wedding in my life—as a bodyguard. I'd seen far more funerals.

The women at the nearby table ate their pasta. I thought of donating my steak bone for the dog to chew on, but I didn't want to speak to the tall woman in case she recognized me as another Finn, so I just asked for the bill and refused an offer of dessert coffee. My meal had sated my hunger, but I still felt empty inside. I paid and left a small tip before stepping out into the dark. It was now drizzling, and the wind fluttered my coat. As I reached my car, I heard someone calling for me.

"*Signora*, please wait! Luigi just called!" The waiter ran over and met me under an awning that had been built under the cypress trees. "Luigi remembered that man with a black beard. Or rather, he remembered his friend. Not a nice man. Luigi thinks he was Russian because of his accent and the Greek Catholic cross around his neck." The waiter shrugged. "He couldn't speak any other language, not even English. He understood the word for truffle. He just kept saying *tartufo, tartufo*. Didn't know how to eat his appetizer. Just ate it in one bite. You have nothing to worry about. Your man dined with a rude Russian, not a beautiful woman."

I could vaguely see in the fading light that the waiter was smiling. I reached for my wallet, but he shook his head.

"I don't need money." Then he added, "Nor does Luigi. We just wanted to see the *signora* smile."

I forced a smile, although I didn't see much of a reason to rejoice, knowing that David had been dining at Il Tre Canton with a mean Russian.

"Was that Russian also mean to my man? How were they behaving?"

"Well, it was a busy night, and Luigi didn't have much time to focus on them, but he knows they didn't laugh. They just spoke in that hissing language. I remember—I mean, Luigi remembers that your man said *nyet, nyet* many times. Everyone here understands that word."

I thanked the waiter again, and he said I'd always be welcome. Then he went back inside. The dog from the restaurant was now barking at me from inside a dark-blue Ford, and the drizzle was slowly soaking my hair and my canvas sneakers. My car windows were fogged up. What had made the waiter change his mind? Did he come up with this story about Luigi, or did he get the information from someone else? The mean Russian sounded like a villain from a spy movie. Was that the person David had been fleeing from, or did he flee with him?

I was back in a world where no one could be trusted. I'd assumed David was one of the few people who wasn't out to scam me, but I was wrong. Here I was, in a strange land, surrounded by people who spoke a language I hadn't mastered. And what had Mike Virtue told us about the various, far-reaching tentacles of the Italian mafia? Some of them worked closely with the Russian mafia, and it seemed their governments were in on it, seeing how Berlusconi and Putin had been so brotherly toward each other. David claimed he'd come to Tuscany under the guise of a tourist with aspirations of becoming a novelist. It was growing clear that all I had seen was yet another role.

Even as a kid I had been comfortable with darkness, but it was unsettling to drive along an unfamiliar road in the pouring rain. I slowed at the bends because I didn't trust the tread on my old Punto's tires. There was no one else on the road, making it a perfect time for an accident without any witnesses. I was relieved when I made it back to Montemassi.

The rain was coming down so hard that I parked as close to David's apartment as I could. I was surprised to see a light on in the kitchen. Was David back? I could feel the light sparkling within me, too. I opened the door carefully.

"Hello?"

There was no answer. I went into the kitchen, but it was empty. Had David come and gone? There were no dishes in the sink. I peered into the fridge, but it was exactly as I'd left it. I was certain I hadn't turned the lights on when I left. I called out to David again while checking the bathroom, but nobody was there.

Stepping into the living room, I could smell something was wrong before I even turned the lights on. It smelled like sweat, urine, and gunpowder. I flipped the lights on. I didn't see anything out of the ordinary at first. But when I stepped forward, I saw a man's body draped over the sofa by the window, his back to me, his face buried in pillows. His curly black hair had a bloody, gaping hole, and blood had soaked into the sofa and trickled onto the floor. The gunpowder smell indicated that the shooting was recent. The body was still, and I didn't need to get any closer to know the man was dead.

3

The dead man was not David. Whoever was on the sofa was short and slender like a teenager. His hair was long and naturally curly. He wore white cotton pants and a brown leather jacket with no shoes.

I backed out of the living room and into the kitchen. I found three plastic bags under the sink and slipped two of them on my feet. I wrapped the third bag over my right hand and crept quietly into the bedroom and turned on the lights. I checked under the twin bed and found a thin rolled-up rug. I took gloves from my suitcase, put them on, and pinned my hair under a scarf. The apartment would be covered in fingerprints, mine and David's. As far as I knew, my prints were not recorded anywhere else than at the security academy, but I couldn't be absolutely sure. I packed my things quickly. As soon as I was far enough from Montemassi, I'd call in an anonymous tip. Luckily Italy hadn't phased out phone booths yet.

My curiosity forced me to return to the body. It was still warm and limber. I turned the man's head carefully, knowing I could be making the situation worse for myself by tampering with evidence, but I had to see if I knew him. The exit wound had left his face almost entirely intact. His brown eyes were wide open, and his now gray lips and small dark mustache looked like a sketch—lifeless and inhuman. He looked like he could've been twenty-five or forty. A small golden cross hung from his neck. It had failed to protect the man's life, but perhaps it would protect his soul.

I let his head fall back onto the pillows and was glad for the plastic bags on my feet, because there was urine all over the floor. I felt for his wallet but couldn't find it in his pockets. He didn't wear a watch or any rings. His bare feet were covered in curly black hair.

I scanned the room for his shoes and a potential murder weapon. Why were his shoes gone? What sort of shoes could've revealed his identity? Were they custom-made? The way he was lying on the sofa didn't reveal whether one of his legs was shorter than the other, but if that was the case, it could've indicated that he had shoes with special thicker soles.

The room showed no signs of a struggle. What did that mean? Had the room been cleaned right after the man was shot, or had he given in without protest? The way he lay on the sofa was also curious, as if he'd been sleeping and someone had surprised him. The man could have shot himself if his arm had been flexible enough. Then again, hardly anyone who committed suicide would shoot himself in the back of the head, and he couldn't hide the weapon afterward.

There was a commotion outside the kitchen. I tiptoed into the kitchen and looked out the window. A familiar-looking old man was sweeping the street, although it was an odd time for it. A black-and-white cat was following the man closely. Suddenly it turned toward me, narrowed its eyes, and hopped onto the windowsill. I moved away from the window so I wouldn't be seen. Maybe the man was waiting nearby to see how I reacted. I hadn't figured out whether the body had been left there for me to discover or whether someone was trying to frame David. Or maybe David had done it. Daniel Lanotte, the renter, could have disappeared, and only I knew who the real renter was. Maybe David assumed I would never tell on him. Or he could be lying somewhere just as dead as the man on his sofa.

I needed to know what David was hiding in the hutch, but there was no more time for messing around with small knives, so I took a small hatchet and a crowbar from the cleaning closet. I felt bad for breaking such a beautiful piece of furniture, but I had to do it. I hacked away at the hutch and pulled the pieces apart with the crowbar.

The top drawer held a big envelope sealed with red varnish. The paper was thick and white. I removed the top drawer and looked into the drawer underneath it. I assumed I would find a gun, but instead there was a brass kaleidoscope. Why the hell would David have hidden one of these? I was jumping to conclusions—it could have belonged to the owner of the house, too, but if not, it may have been used to hide all sorts of things, from microfilms to drugs.

The village church bells rang at ten thirty. If I left now, I could still find a place to stay in a nearby village. I took a moment to think about what to do with the objects and decided to take them along. Whoever had killed the man had not thought the hutch contained anything important, so I was a step ahead of them. I hid the kaleidoscope and the envelope among my dirty clothes and tried calling David again. A phone rang in the living room.

I hadn't looked for David's phone in the apartment, assuming I couldn't reach him. I walked back into the living room, and once the ringtone went silent, I called David again. The sound was coming from the sofa. I approached the body carefully, realizing I had only attempted to look for his wallet in his pants, but I hadn't checked his jacket. The phone would be there or under him.

I wasn't sure of what to do now—my head was a mess. I had to get out of the house right away. I cleared the call history from my phone and realized anyone looking at the dead man's phone would see my number. I couldn't take the risk of being found out. My heartbeat was probably heard over at the fortress, and my hands were shaking hard as I went through the dead man's pockets. The phone was in his breast pocket, right against his heart. I turned the sound off, then slipped it into my bag. I had to get rid of it as soon as I found out which numbers had been calling.

I bowed at the corpse apologetically, then grabbed a bright-yellow tulip from a vase and placed it on the body, near the head. I had no idea whether the body had been occupied by a friend or foe. I zipped my luggage and carried it outside.

The apartment keys would connect me to this Montemassi apartment and the dead body, so once outside, I locked the door, slid the keys into an envelope, and dropped it through the mail slot. I walked to my Punto and started the engine, then headed straight out of the village.

I drove to Roccastrada, then headed east, looking for the highway leading to Siena and Florence. I remembered David telling me about a restaurant in Civitella Marittima that was inside a bed-and-breakfast. Hopefully, someone was still awake there, but if it came to it, I could always sleep inside the car.

The valley smelled of thyme, and although the stars were aligned just as they were in Finland, the world felt askew. I tried not to think about the dead man. It wasn't the first time I had had to shut out unpleasant thoughts. It was a skill I had to master.

The streets of Civitella Marittima were steep and winding. I had no idea what the bed-and-breakfast was called, and I didn't spot any signs for it. I went to the gas station below the village, but it was closed. I parked my car on the hillside and walked until I found a brightly lit bar that was alive and noisy. There were about ten Middle Eastern men inside, hunched over their coffee, and I could feel them all staring. I asked the bartender if he spoke any English.

"Just a little," he said, looking awkward.

"Bed-and-breakfast?" I pressed my hands together and placed them against my cheek, then cocked my head. The man got it before I had to add a fake snore.

"*Dormire!* Alessandro, Locanda nel Cassero." He grabbed me by the arm and walked me out of the café, gesturing uphill. I had to walk straight and then right. I decided to scout the place and ensure they had a room and a parking spot for the car. I found a building that looked like a restaurant, but the door was locked. The sign indicated that the kitchen closed over an hour earlier.

I knew that restaurant staff didn't just take off after closing. I knocked on the window nearest the door. No reply. I knocked on the next window. Again, nothing. Houses nearby were connected with each other, so if I wanted to get to the other side of the building, I'd have to walk all the way around the block. The sign on the door listed some phone numbers for people looking for a room after hours, so I grabbed my cell phone.

Then the restaurant door opened, and a fluffy black cat sneaked out. I rushed to the door and shoved my foot between the door and the frame. The young lady who'd let the cat out was startled. I asked her in English whether they had any vacancies, and I was in luck. She lifted up two fingers with a nod. I didn't ask what the price was and said I'd take one. A staircase lined with wrought iron handrails took me to the door along the outer wall.

When I managed to drag my luggage to the room, I fell on the twin bed from sheer exhaustion and lay there motionless until I fell asleep. I woke up with a start when the church bells rang at two in the morning. My clothes felt stuffy, and the flavor of truffles in my mouth was too pungent. I opened my luggage to find my tooth-brush, and the kaleidoscope fell onto the floor. I raised it to my eye and looked through it. It was just a regular kaleidoscope, which meant that I had to take it apart before I'd cross any borders; I didn't want to attract drug-sniffing dogs or customs officials.

As soon as I had brushed my teeth and washed my face, I was wide awake. I looked out the window to see the same fluffy cat; he was lying in the plaza in front of the restaurant, as if he owned the entire village. There was nobody else around. The other window opened to the valley and the mountains, and I could see little lights glimmer in the villages below. To cap it off, my room had a painting of Guidoriccio riding a horse, urging me to conquer the village. I just wanted to leave it behind.

I took David's phone out of my bag. There were no new calls or messages, and when I checked the most recent calls, all I saw was my number. David deleted information regularly. The incoming call list was almost empty but revealed an Italian number in addition to mine, so I wrote it down. I'd call it from a phone booth. None of the numbers in the list had been answered. I couldn't help but curse at how smart and careful David had been.

The phone was an unfamiliar Samsung, and on top of that, David had chosen to use it in Italian, so it took me a while to locate the text message folder. Again, the only content was from me. I shut my eyes in embarrassment, seeing my lovey-dovey messages. David had saved them, although they clearly didn't mean anything to him, considering he took off without a word. Maybe he wanted to frame me for the murder. I didn't want to believe that. David must have been going through something he didn't want to let me in on. The voice in my head was doing its best to convince me that David had had no other choice. Maybe someone had wanted to fool the police by switching two bodies, and David was dead in the apartment of the barefoot man.

I located the address book: only four numbers. The first was for Lusis. I tapped on it and saw my own number. It made sense; *lūšis* was Lithuanian for lynx, and we used to call each other by lynx-related names. When David had contacted me from Spain to let me know he had survived the boat explosion, he'd asked me to e-mail him at the address lo.lynx@hotmail.com. The address was no longer in use.

The other three numbers were also named after animals: Hund, Kassi, and Cavallo. Dog in Swedish, cats in Estonian, horse in Italian. I tried to figure out the logic. Maybe they referred to the caller's nationality? Then again, mine didn't. Based on the country codes of the numbers, the dog and the horse were Italian and the cat was Finnish. I wrote down these numbers on two separate pieces of paper and put them in my phone before I tried to sleep again. I tossed and turned until I heard the bells ring at four. After that, it was sweet, dreamless darkness.

I woke up around eight to sounds from the plaza. A man was yelling in a language I didn't recognize, and another man responded in Italian. Car doors slammed. The scent of fresh espresso and bread wafted up to my window. Just the cure for what was ailing me. I got dressed; locked David's phone, papers, and kaleidoscope in my bag; and walked down for breakfast, which was served on the terrace outside. There was only an elderly German couple and that same fluffy black cat from the night before. He was friendly, jumping on my table as soon as I sat down. He purred, and it reminded me of my childhood friend, the lynx named Frida. This cat's purr sounded just as low and powerful as hers. The waiter came over to take my order and didn't shoo the cat away, seeing that I enjoyed his company.

After breakfast I took a walk, wondering whether I should call the police from a phone booth in this small village where people usually remember strangers. It might be a better idea to drive all the way to Siena. I saw a sign for Locanda. I thought I had been careless and not spotted it on the way in, but then I remembered a truck had been parked there as I was driving up.

I sat on a bench and looked to the east at the rolling hills, down the valley, and far off toward Monte Amiata, southeast of the village. I didn't understand how locals were able to pass each other on the narrow roads leading up to their houses or how their hand brakes could hold while parked on such steep inclines. I could hear the soft rumble of traffic on the road leading from Grossetto to Siena. It was warm enough for a T-shirt, but dark clouds were approaching from Amiata. Swallows were making swift swoops in front of me and seemed to enjoy flying just for flying's sake. A large rose bush blossomed in a nearby yard, and the purple sea of plum blossoms shimmered a few hundred yards away. Despite all the beauty, this place may as well have been a desert or a barren moonscape, as it was whipped constantly by hard winds. I had already once thought David had died, and I'd taken one day at a time, turning those days away from me like stones and clumsily climbing to bed in the evenings, thankful like an alcoholic for each sober day. But now he had left me without a word.

I knew my rationalizations by heart. Someone had forced David to go. Someone had told him I'd be killed if he didn't do as he was told. In truth, he knew my profession was dangerous, and I wasn't scared easily. I was used to taking care of myself.

I wandered through the village, checking out the scenery. A few villagers greeted me. It appeared to be laundry day. I straightened an old lady's bedsheet that almost fell on my head. The people of Civitella seemed cautious; any street-level window was barred or had thick wooden storm shutters. They weren't lulled into a false sense of security in their idyllic surroundings.

At eleven I drove toward Siena. About six miles past Civitella, I turned onto a small road and continued until I reached a secluded riverbed snaking among high cliffs. I turned David's phone off and removed the SIM card. I placed them carefully behind my Punto's back tire and reversed over them. I tossed the broken pieces into the river and returned to the main road. After a mile I hit a crossing with signs for Montalcino, Sant'Antimo—wait a minute. David had been looking to hide in that monastery. Maybe his friend Brother Gianni could help.

The steep, meandering roads made my trips to my childhood home in Hevonpersiinsaari, at the border of Savonia and North Karelia, seem like child's play. I'd never been one to obey speed limits, and I'd managed to accumulate a lot of tickets and almost lose my license, but this time I was driving slowly, and a line of cars formed behind me. When I pulled over to let them pass, one of the drivers who'd been stuck behind me honked, irritated. I honked back, but no one cared.

As soon as I got to Montalcino, I found a phone booth in the market square, across from one of the *enoteche*. I had heard this word for a wine store once on television when I was ten, and I thought it was a place for uncles to congregate since *eno* means uncle in Finnish. When I'd told my uncle this, he'd laughed but then admitted that he had no idea what the word meant, either. Uncle usually bought hard liquor or strong wine called Karjala from the state-run liquor store, so the pride of Montalcino, Brunello, would have been an unknown treat for him.

I was able to call the emergency line without buying a phone card. I explained in English that they'd find a man shot dead in Montemassi village, in the apartment facing east in the house that had been on the market for so long. Then I hung up. It was the carabiniere's move now.

When I went back to my car, I was suddenly surrounded by a group of American tourists. Their New York accents sounded familiar and soothing, but spotting a familiar face in the crowd startled me. Wasn't that my former neighbor from Morton Street? No, it couldn't have been. I was trying to rack my brain, and then he noticed me staring and turned away. Had someone gotten this close to me already?

When I began my descent into the Sant'Antimo valley, I kept an eye on the rearview mirror. It wasn't unusual for people to drive right behind one another. One gray Peugeot 208 kept at it all the way to the little village road that led to the monastery.

This world holds places where your mind can rest. My old home in Hevonpersiinsaari was one of them. I could find peace as easily in Bryant Park in the heart of Manhattan or in a bog in the middle of nowhere. It was rare, however, to be made so secure by a building, but as I saw Sant'Antimo's limestone walls, they appeared to glow with an inviting and irresistible light. I parked my car and uncharacteristically fed the parking meter before I began my walk toward the church.

Its tower was accompanied by an ancient cypress, almost as tall as the tower, with Monte Amiata serving as a beautiful backdrop. I inched my way into the dim, high-ceilinged space within. Someone was chanting, and as I searched for the source, I realized it was only a recording. That dropped me back to earth. A white-bearded man wearing a robe was replacing old flowers in a vase at the altar. Although it felt like a crime to break the silence, I went over to greet him and ask if he knew where I could find Brother Gianni.

"*No parla inglese*," he said bluntly.

"Brother Gianni?" I asked again, this time in Italian. He shook his head with a nasty frown, grabbed his flowers, and left, water droplets from the flowers trailing behind him on the stone floor.

I sat down and closed my eyes. The singing had grown louder, the sounds reflected off the ceiling. David was a Christian and believed in God. I had a hard time thinking about religion, so I avoided the subject. How could God allow such evil, like my father murdering my mother when I was only four?

I heard footsteps behind me, and someone touched my shoulder. It was the grumpy bearded fellow. I jumped to my feet.

"Brother Gianni," he said and pointed. When I was small I'd seen a movie about Robin Hood, and I thought all monks looked like Friar Tuck or our own representative at the European parliamentary, Father Mitro: round, red-faced, and jolly. Brother Gianni was nothing like that. He was about my age and height, his thin figure and slender bones reflecting an ascetic lifestyle. His curly blond hair fell to cover his ears, and he wore round John Lennon–inspired glasses. He took my hand and said to me in Finnish, but with a noticeable Estonian accent, "*Tere*, Hilja. I've been expecting you."

4

I wasn't able to hide my confusion, which made Brother Gianni laugh and squeeze my hands harder.

"David never told you that in my former life, I was Jaan Rand, his classmate back in Tartu?"

"No." I tried pulling my hands away, but Brother Gianni held on.

"I'm so glad we have this shared secret language. Forgive me if I forget some words. I studied Finnish at the University of Tartu, but that was twenty years ago, and I haven't had much use for it since. Whenever I was with David, we spoke Estonian. That's spoken by even fewer people than Finnish, and oh, man, how the Russians were annoyed when they couldn't understand us. How's David?"

I shook my head. Brother Gianni was a complete loon. I finally managed to pull my hands away, my palms throbbing. He certainly wasn't a weakling.

"I don't know," I admitted. "He's missing." On my way to the monastery, I had tried to recall everything David had told me about Brother Gianni, but all I could remember was that they went way back. Monasteries offered safe haven for refugees and the oppressed, so I hadn't been surprised about this friendship. Even the Finnish Lutheran church had recently provided a hiding place for deported people.

"Missing?" Brother Gianni's eyes flickered behind his glasses.

Another monk had moved a few steps away from us, realizing he didn't understand our conversation. "*Miserere nostri, domine,*" the invisible monks cried from the church's loudspeakers, with swallows outside rivaling the noise.

"Let's take a walk," Brother Gianni suggested. "Unfortunately, I can't take you to the monastery garden, but follow me along this little path."

Brother Gianni took off toward the door, almost colliding with a group of tourists that had just entered the church. I followed him carefully, not wanting to draw attention. We walked on a wide gravel path surrounded by white and purple lilies. I had a hard time keeping up with his frantic pace. We climbed quickly to the monastery roof level, then past it.

"You can never be too careful, not even when we have a secret language," Brother Gianni said and slowed down enough for me to catch up. Although the road was wide, it was covered in puddles from the rain. We had to walk on the edge of the path so close to each other that our sleeves kept touching. My classmate from the academy had told me stories about a Catholic boarding school he'd attended in New Jersey; relationships between the sexes were prohibited, and sexuality was a taboo that made little boys feel like they were sinners. I doubted Brother Gianni's mental health, too. Why had he become a monk? There weren't a lot of Catholics in Estonia or Finland. And in Sant'Antimo, monks would encounter the forbidden fruit daily: female tourists. As for me, I had been open to taking different lovers in New York and didn't understand why I should pine for a single person or demand loyalty, but David had made me change my mind. When I thought of him, I didn't have room in my head for anyone else, and David hadn't tried pressuring me into monogamy.

"Why have you been waiting for me?" I asked Brother Gianni as soon as we'd walked a few hundred yards from the church and were hidden in the shade of old oaks and laurel trees.

"David told me you were going to visit him. You are his lover."

His *lover*. I was furious at hearing that word. What sort of a lover disappears without a word, leaving the other to deal with a dead man?

"What else has David told you? Do you know who he was hiding from in the monastery?"

Brother Gianni stopped walking and touched my arm.

"Oh, Hilja, you can't ask me that. If someone is in need, we provide shelter. Even when David didn't return to Tartu before Estonia became independent, we both understood that dangers lurked everywhere. When we were young, we got tangled in all sorts of things, and once I even made a grave mistake . . . well, maybe David has already told you. There are other reasons for me being a monk." Brother Gianni hung his head.

"David hasn't told me anything about what the two of you were up to." I was too proud to pry, although I did want to know everything about David. He'd often told me stories about his childhood in Tammisaari and his sailing trips, about his parents, siblings, and the mixed marriages across nationalities in his family, but he'd kept quiet about his years in Tartu. The only reason he had told me about his time at the Swedish police academy was because he found out that Chief Inspector Laitio had already told me most of it. Someone had arranged a place for him at the academy, which otherwise should have been difficult since he wasn't a Swedish citizen, although he had somehow gotten a Swedish passport. Identities and nationalities could be changed easily, just as long as you knew the right people and had money. Brother Gianni had been a Tartu resident, and now he was here, praying in a dead language, and I had no idea where I was going to spend my nights or where to find my next gig. Nothing was permanent in this world. The hymn we sang at my mother's funeral echoed in my head.

"David claims he believes in God. Pretty curious for a killer, isn't it? He's also managed to violate the sixth commandment with me. Who's going to forgive him for all these sins? You?" I asked.

"Man does not provide forgiveness. It comes from God. You seem upset with David. Do you know where he went or what happened?"

I tripped on a loose rock on the path. I wasn't sure if I could trust him. Hadn't the Catholic Church been in cahoots for ages with all sorts of mobsters and evil doers in high places? Whoever donated the most was blessed by God. If Brother Gianni had arranged for David to rent the apartment, he may have lured him into a trap, which would mean he already knew David had been framed.

I told Brother Gianni how David had left early in the morning without a note. I also told him about how I had traced him back to the restaurant in Paganico and how a waiter had spotted him with a mean Russian. I told him about the barefoot body, but I didn't tell him I'd found David's phone in the dead man's pocket. I also kept the contents of the hutch a secret. I just wanted to see Brother Gianni's reaction, to test how reliable he was. He remained silent for a long time. We'd reached an open area where we could see the valley and the village rising above it. The neat rows of vineyards and olive trees were guarded by towering cypress trees. The pastoral view was shattered by the painful bawl of a donkey.

"I think David assumed he had more time. That they wouldn't strike yet," Brother Gianni said. "They certainly didn't wait long."

"Who are they?"

"We don't know. We only have a hunch."

That *we* really hurt, especially because David had not told me anything.

"The Europol operation David was a part of in the Gulf of Finland was extremely controversial. An international police force cannot go around slaughtering people, not even if they're super criminals. Europol is not supposed to be an antiterrorism organization. So now David has no one to protect him, and he's left alone to fend for himself. The Belarusian businessman, Gezolian, the one who sold the dirty bomb, never received his money. Some middleman took it, and Gezolian is vengeful. Although Vasiliev, who bought the bomb, and his trusted men all died in the explosion, someone who knew about all this survived. David. Some people at Europol don't like that he knows so much. Threat is everywhere."

"But even the Finnish government knows about it. The former prime minister, the minister of the interior, and—"

"Do you really think they care about the life of a Europol agent? It wouldn't bring more votes in the next election." All sweetness had drained out of Brother Gianni's voice. "Hilja, David is a killer, but it doesn't mean he wants innocent people to get hurt. If he's taken off, he's done it for a reason. You have to believe me. The monastery has a fresco on its wall depicting Daniel in the lions' den. Maybe David—Daniel Lanotte—had to do just that."

"Do you know who the Russian at the restaurant was?" I asked.

"I have my suspicions. And he's not Russian. He's Belarusian. That man is bad news for everyone." Brother Gianni brought his hand to his throat, as if recalling something.

"What's his name?"

"No use in making guesses," he said and shrugged. "It may not even be the man I'm thinking of. Or at least I hope not."

The monastery bells began ringing down below, and Brother Gianni turned around with a start.

"Is it already that time? I should be at the church. They'll notice I'm gone, and I'll have to come up with excuses again." He took off down the path, lifting his white robe so he could jump over puddles and rocks. I spotted gray sweat pants under his robe before he disappeared around the bend.

I started to walk back as well, listening to the calming sound of the bells that had been echoing in the valley for centuries. People had been born and died, and they'd keep on doing the same thing. Someone, right at this moment, was missing the dead barefoot man. Maybe news of his death had already reached his beloved, and they'd light a candle in his memory at the six o'clock mass.

I saw Brother Gianni rushing into the monastery yard, and he came to a halt right before he ran into a line of monks making their way to the church. At least Brother Gianni had made it to vespers in time. The bells were replaced by singing, and although it came from behind a stone wall, it was oddly powerful, even if I couldn't understand Latin. I wondered whether monks were chosen to join the Sant'Antimo monastery based on their singing chops.

By the time I reached the churchyard, vespers were in full swing. The monastery was closed to the public, so the only cars in the parking lot were my Punto and a rusty gray van. I waited for Brother Gianni, although I had no idea how long the mass would take.

At the Queens security academy, we had taken part in various religious services—large events that could be targets for attacks. I remembered how Mike Virtue looked desperate and shook his head at the nonexistent evacuation exits at an Orthodox Jewish synagogue in Brooklyn. Mike had wanted us to realize there were no safe places, no place so holy or innocent that it couldn't be attacked. Our practice had once included creating a safety plan for a nearby foster home, and unfortunately we'd had to put it to good use when some religious fanatic attacked the home, thinking orphans with HIV were spawns of the devil. The staff had called the academy before reaching out to the police, and one of the students, Rudy from California, had been shot through the hand by a stray bullet from a police gun. The fanatic received a bullet between his eyes. I still remember the little girl I tried to soothe afterward. She cried and drooled on me, and my first thought had been about whether I could get HIV from saliva. I can't believe I thought that; I was still embarrassed to recall it. I'd taken an HIV test twice, and it came back negative both times. Mike Virtue had been right; you're not safe anywhere.

I thought about how everyone would react if I just waltzed into the church. Would the church become impure from my presence? The Catholic way of thinking wasn't familiar to me. Maybe they locked the church door just in case.

I sat on the stones in the churchyard and made myself as comfortable as possible. I could hear the monks singing again. When I closed my eyes, the sounds seemed timeless: singing in a church, the chattering of swallows, the wind rustling in the grass. Then a motorcycle revved above in the village, drowning all other sounds.

I dozed off to a state between awake and dreaming, where David's face and the dead man's bare feet kept changing places. I fell asleep and didn't stir until the church bells started ringing again. As I opened my eyes, I saw a group of monks walking out of the church door as an unorganized horde. A sharp pain shot across my lower back when I got up. It had been a bad idea to lie down on the hard stones.

Either Brother Gianni didn't see me or the monks had a vow of silence to observe after the service. I managed to catch him as he was leaving the monastery yard, and I grabbed the back of his robe. The other monks stopped, curious.

"Brother Gianni, we weren't finished!" I yelled.

Gianni turned around with wide eyes.

"Sister Hilja, we were finished. I told you what I was supposed to. There's no further business for you here. Go back to Finland. That's for the best. That's what David would have wanted."

"How do you know?"

"I know that he wished you all the best." His gaze grew softer, and Brother Gianni lifted his hand to bless me. "Go safely, Hilja. Go back home. It's the best place for you. Believe me." He disappeared through the gate, behind the fence that mere mortals could not pass. Not that a two-foot fence would have held me back, but the stone wall was higher and more uninviting.

On my way to the car, I noticed the church door had been left open, so I walked inside. The church was completely quiet, and my steps echoed. I paid for a small candle, lit it, and bowed while I placed it on a candlestick below an image of a saint. "Please let David be alive," I requested, but I did not know from who. Maybe from the god David believed in.

I found the fresco Brother Gianni had mentioned. It was painted on one of the columns in the large hall. Daniel had a strong nose, and the supposedly ferocious lion did not look all that intimidating to me. The lion of justice. Why did that phrase pop into my head? Then I remembered that Chief Constable Teppo Laitio had once signed a letter to me with those words in it.

I was startled when I felt something brush my leg. It was the largest cat I'd ever seen: a long-legged gray tabby so massive that it must've weighed twenty pounds. Maybe his ancestors were Italian forest cats. I wanted to hold it, but when I reached out, he retreated. The light from the door was suddenly dimmed when an angry monk stood in the doorway. He began to blather at me in a quick, sputtering way. I didn't understand the words, but the gist of his message was very clear: I had better take a hike, or else. Back in Eastern Finland, people used to say that if you don't behave yourself, God will throw a hot rock on you. I wouldn't have been surprised if the monk was saying the same thing.

I'd run out of time on the meter, but the monastery spirits had protected me from a ticket. I made my way toward Montalcino. I saw signs pointing toward Val d'Orcia, with promises of bed-and-breakfasts. I was in luck and got a room at the first one. In addition to breakfast, the house offered dinner, so I had a Margherita pizza and a small pitcher of Brunello. I mustered enough energy to check flights from Florence to Helsinki, and my luck continued: a flight with a layover in Vienna had some seats left, although catching it would mean an early wake-up call. The sooner I was out of Italy, the better. Brother Gianni was right; there was nothing for me here anymore.

I woke up at five in the morning and took stock of everything I'd forgotten to do. I had never checked what was in the envelope, and I'd also not bothered to figure out who Hund, Kassi, and Cavallo were. Leaving the envelope in checked luggage may have been too risky, as luggage could go missing, especially if I had to switch planes. I shoved the envelope and the kaleidoscope in my carry-on bag and left the envelope untouched. I'd deal with them when I could be sure nobody was watching me. Some of my belongings were on Untamo Road in Helsinki with my neighbor, Mrs. Voutilainen, and some of them were in storage in Hevonpersiinsaari. Mrs. Voutilainen probably hadn't received my postcard from Italy, so she wouldn't know to expect me, and I couldn't stay with her forever.

I stopped at a gas station to buy a phone card and make some calls. The clerk gave me a pathetic look: *Jeez, one of these relics from a generation with no cell phones.*

First I called Hund, but all I got was his voice mail in Italian. I called again to listen to it more carefully, in case the recording mentioned a name. Not as far as I could tell. I had more luck with Cavallo; someone picked up.

"*Pronto*," a woman screamed. "*Carlo, dove tu? Con una donna.*"

I interrupted her to ask whether she spoke English. She said yes but continued in Italian, angrily asking who the hell I was and why was I calling Carlo.

I begged her to switch to English, at which point she asked if I was Carlo's American lover. The story began to unfold. Cavallo was some guy named Carlo, and his wife hadn't seen him in two days. She had found his phone in the glove compartment of his car.

"Where would Carlo go without a car? Did you pick him up?"

"No. Have you gotten in touch with the police about his disappearance?" I asked. I had a bad feeling about Carlo's whereabouts.

"No! They'd just laugh at me! The police in this village know nothing! I'd have to drive all the way to Florence!"

"Where do you live?"

"Lago di Scanno. As if you didn't know."

"I have never met your husband, Mrs. . . . ?"

"Dolfini."

"Mrs. Dolfini, does your husband have one leg shorter than the other? Does he use insoles?"

"You've never met him, but you know all this? Who are you? What do you want from me?"

I couldn't bring myself to tell Mrs. Dolfini that her husband had been murdered. The least I should've done was make sure someone was there to comfort her, but she had no reason to believe me. So I made like a real coward and hung up. I didn't know where Lago di Scanno was. All I knew was that there were large lakes in the mountains of northern Italy.

I decided to call Kassi when I got back to Finland—that number was Finnish. I drove off and left my car at the airport in Florence, causing an argument with the rental company, because I was returning the car two weeks too early. I checked in, checked my bags, and rushed toward security. Only there did I remember that I still had the kaleidoscope in my backpack, and I didn't know what was inside it. I saw a drug-sniffing dog on the other side of the gate. It looked calm, but I'd seen these dogs enough to know they could switch from calm to alert in a split second. I did my best to look like an innocent tourist on my way home from a short visit to Tuscany. I hoped the security agents wouldn't look at my neck, where my pulse was visibly beating twice as fast as usual.

I went through security without a hitch only to find out that my plane would be fifteen minutes late. Last chance to buy souvenirs, like aprons adorned with the statue of David. David's parents had been in Florence when his mother was pregnant, and David was named after Michelangelo's statue. The Stahls claimed they didn't choose a naked sex symbol; to them, David was the embodiment of courage against an overpowering enemy. David's dad had seen Michelangelo's David as Estonia and Soviet Russia as Goliath, who had to be defied even if it meant destruction. David occasionally made fun of the whole notion; who was he supposed to attack with a slingshot? I looked at a postcard of the statue's face, and there was nothing erotic about it—just a desperate-looking young man. We were supposed to visit Florence together to see his namesake, but like so many other things, we'd never done it. When we began boarding I decided to buy the postcard, even if it made me feel like an idiot. After all, it wasn't a picture of the man I had thought of as my David a couple of days before.

Air traffic over Vienna was chaos, so we had to circle over the airport for an excruciatingly long time. Once we landed, I had to run like a maniac to make it through security and catch my flight to Finland. My forehead was already beaded with sweat when a security official began to reel items back inside the scanner.

"Is this your backpack?" a man with a walrus mustache asked. He could barely fit in his uniform, and he hadn't bothered to button his jacket.

"Yes, it is," I replied.

"Could you step aside, please, and open it for me?"

"But my plane's about to take off."

I had worked airport security and knew resistance was futile. I just had to make it as quick as possible, so I stepped aside and opened my backpack. The security officer dug around for a while and beamed when he found the kaleidoscope.

"Too dangerous. You could hit someone with this."

I knew he was right. Then again, there was always room for interpretation: kaleidoscopes were not weapons. I tried to think about what would make me give in. This guy seemed like a real by-the-book type.

"All right then. Hit me with it," I urged him. "It's a gift for my niece who collects kaleidoscopes, and she's nine." I flashed a benevolent smile. "Come on. Let me take it—I promised her a kaleidoscope. Her mom will skin me alive if I let this kid down."

I was actually surprised when he waved his hand, urging me to move on with all my things.

Vienna is something else, I thought, striding past a bar gray with smoke. You could smoke at the airport.

I bought a yodeling lemming for Mrs. Voutilainen. She'd once commiserated on how she had passed on a chance to buy one of these kitschy Austrian equivalents of a singing fish on the wall on her trip. "Remember, Hilja, we regret what we don't do more often than things we have done," she'd often told me.

I was still thinking about her words on the plane. Had I not done something I should have? Maybe I should have stayed in Tuscany, talked to the police, and told them about David and Carlo Dolfini. I was innocent, so what did I have to worry about? That was hard to believe. My connection to David was worrisome enough, and sharing secrets with Finnish government leaders didn't make matters easier. Whoever was after David could not have known what David confided to me.

Unfortunately, he'd told me nothing.

Returning to Helsinki-Vantaa Airport made me feel trapped. I'd left the country with such high hopes, and here I was again. Finland was still gray, and there were no leaves on the trees. Spring was standing still, with sooty piles of snow lining the roads. My brain felt the same. I had to wait for my bag for over half an hour— there was a strike again.

The following morning I thanked my lucky stars for leaving Italy when I did; the ash cloud created by the volcano Eyjafjallajökull in Iceland had messed up all the flights within Europe, and if someone was after me, they wouldn't be able to follow me to Finland anytime soon.

5

I went for the simplest accommodation and hopped on bus 615 at the airport and got off at the intersection of Mäkelä Street and Koskela Road. I didn't have keys to Mrs. Voutilainen's apartment, nor had I told her I was coming. She had a cell phone for emergencies but preferred her landline. Nobody answered when I rang her doorbell, so I called the cell, only to get her voice mail. I left a message on her cell and then on her landline answering machine. I decided to go to Käpygrilli for a beer to clear my head, which rarely worked. When I finished my second beer, I was in such good shape that I decided to book a night at Hotel Torni. Whenever David was in Finland, he stayed there, so I'd get close to him by doing the same. Torni might prove to be the most secure place to finally open the secret envelope.

I got a room with a panoramic view on the tenth floor. It was a single, and David would have fit perfectly next to me. The sea surrounded Helsinki from all sides, and I could see the Old Church Park and the tower of St. John's Church to the south. After all the small villages in Tuscany, the city felt like a metropolis.

I looked in the minibar and pondered whether I should have another beer, but then I realized I should open David's envelope before I got tipsy. I looked toward the railway station, and the rides of Linnanmäki, the amusement park, loomed behind it. I lifted the kaleidoscope to my eye and watched the city view change into a swirl of colorful pieces. Our neighbors the Hakkarainens, back in Hevonpersiinsaari, had a kaleidoscope when I was a kid, and I'd admired it often.

There was space between the protective glass and the rotating section in the kaleidoscope, but because the shards of glass were moving freely and completely visible, it seemed like nothing was hidden between them. I was avoiding the inevitability of breaking the kaleidoscope to make sure, and I decided to avoid it a bit longer and focused on the envelope. The red seal had to be broken, so I got my nail clippers. Just as I started cutting, my phone rang; it was Mrs. Voutilainen.

"Hilja, dear child, you're back," she exclaimed.

"I just got back today."

"Is everything all right? Weren't you supposed to stay there longer?"

"A change of plans. Where are you now?"

"I've been in Tuuri and the Ähtäri Zoo, on a trip for retirees. They even have lynx at the zoo—you liked them, right?"

"Tell them hi for me. Do you think I could stay with you for a couple of nights when you're back?"

"You can let yourself in now if you want. Oona Nykänen from downstairs has the key, and she's usually home with her baby. I'll call her to let her know."

I told her I wouldn't get there until the next day, when Mrs. Voutilainen would be home. If she thought I was being uncharacteristically curt, she didn't say anything. I'd have to come up with a story about Italy. I couldn't allow her to be in danger if someone came asking questions.

I went back to opening the envelope, and the red wax fell in crumbling flakes to the table. I realized I had not used gloves when handling the envelope and kaleidoscope. My fingerprints had only been taken at the security academy in Queens for the school's purposes, and although I trusted Mike Virtue, the rest of the staff could be bribed. Both the CIA and the FBI may have had information on me, but I doubted they were coming after David or me.

The envelope contained another envelope, small and brown, nothing unusual. "David" had been scribbled on it, and it was glued closed. I opened it only to find another, smaller envelope softened by Bubble Wrap, and I had a feeling I was playing with a nesting doll that would disappear before my eyes.

There was a hard rectangle under the Bubble Wrap. I furiously tore the envelope open. The package had two small silk paper rolls. I opened the larger of them first to find a white-and-purple USB stick.

I'd left my computer behind in the Untamo Road apartment because I had wanted to leave everything behind. There was probably a computer downstairs in the hotel lobby, but checking the contents of this stick in a public area seemed like a bad idea. I unwrapped the smaller package. It contained a ring, a thin golden band with three red stones embedded in it. They looked like rubies. The ring was small and meant for a woman. I slipped it on my ring finger, and it almost got stuck on the second joint. There was no engraving.

Had David bought this for me? Was he planning on proposing? In Finnish tradition men didn't go around getting engagement rings by themselves; independent Finnish women wanted to select the jewelry they'd be wearing. I didn't even like rubies; they looked too much like drops of blood. But how would David have known? We had never talked about it. We could never make our relationship official because the less documentation there was about David, the better, and if I married Daniel Lanotte, it would not be seen as a valid marriage, as David had never officially changed his name.

The USB stick could have clues about the ring, and I evaluated my options. The hotel lobby was out of the question, and I was suspicious about Internet cafés. It was best to just pay for the room and get the keys for Mrs. Voutilainen's place.

I gargled with mouthwash to get the flavor of beer out of my mouth and changed into a fresh shirt. I put the USB stick and the ring into my wallet among the coins. David had joked that my wallet looked manly, but it made sense. I could use it when I was dressed up as my alter ego, Reiska Räsänen. I just needed to remember to switch out my real driver's license with Reiska's fake. Carrying it was always a risk because if it were spotted as a fake, I'd be charged with document forgery and lose my bodyguard license. Right now Reiska's driver's license was in the same locked safe as my licensed gun, back in the Hevonpersiinsaari cabin. The safe was fireproof and burglarproof. I hadn't needed to use Reiska since I'd gone to see David in Spain a little over a year ago. Sometimes I missed my rude male persona.

Just as I was leaving the room, my phone vibrated. The call was from a Finnish number, but I didn't recognize it, so I didn't pick up—although it could have been David. I closed the door and waited. Soon there was a voice mail.

"Hey, Hilja, it's Monika. Call me when you can. I'm back in Finland and not doing too well."

Monika had left the message in Finnish. Her voice was higher and more strained than in her native Swedish. I called her back right away.

"Monika, hi! I didn't recognize the number. How are you?" I asked.

"It's a new provider. Are you still in Italy?"

"I just got back to Finland today." I'd sent her an e-mail before I'd left for Tuscany, thinking she was still in Mozambique. We hadn't met in a long time because Monika had been staying in the remotest, poorest areas of Mozambique for almost four years. She ran a restaurant that fed those in need for free. This radical change in a celebrity chef's life had caused quite an uproar, and Finns called her a foolish idealist and a Finnish-Swedish millionaire who could afford to throw money into a bottomless pit of third world aid.

"So you're in Helsinki?" asked Monika. "Would you have time to meet me today? I'm staying on Yrjö Street in my cousin's place while he's in India."

"You've got to be kidding me. I'm in Hotel Torni right next to you! I can come right now. Do you have a computer there?"

Monika was one of the few people in the world I trusted. Or perhaps the only one these days, seeing how David had betrayed me.

"I do. Don't pay for another night at the hotel. There's plenty of room here. The code for the door is 6664."

"I'll think about it. See you soon!"

It dawned on me in the elevator what Monika had tried to tell me: she was "not doing too well." I walked across the street and punched in the code. I felt foolish. She had tried to get me to visit her in Mozambique, but instead I'd used my money to run after David.

The woman who opened the door looked familiar but not. When Monika left for Africa, she had cut her blond hair even shorter, cropped like a little boy. She tanned easily and looked like she'd just gotten back from a couple of weeks of sailing. Monika was about five foot three, and the delicious food she prepared never impacted her slender, muscular body.

This Monika looked worn-out. Her crow's feet and dimples ran deeper than ever, and not from smiling. Her hair was blinding white from the sun, and she'd pulled it into two thin pigtails. She was frail. As she hugged me I could feel her bones poking out under her skin.

"Hilja! I'm so glad to see you. Come in." Monika spoke in Finnish.

I didn't learn Swedish until I worked for her. I'd considered Swedish as Monika's language, but it had become David's language in such force that single words could make me recall joyful and painful memories. It was good that Monika was sticking to Finnish.

The apartment inside the old art nouveau–style house was furnished in a variety of colors. Monika's cousin collected string instruments and images of Buddha, and I was afraid I'd break something. I sat on a low, silky sofa, and Monika lowered herself gently onto a sofa across from me.

"You want something to drink? I assume you still prefer tea over coffee?"

What I would have preferred was a stiff drink. It was hard to watch Monika's slow movements as she carefully put her feet on the sofa.

"I thought you'd stick around Tuscany for a while by what you said in your e-mail."

"Well, things don't always go the way you plan. David performed one of his disappearing acts again."

"What do you mean?" Monika drew a sharp breath, then shuddered as if her lungs were in pain.

I wasn't sure how much I should tell her. Any outsider would have thought I was reckless and insane, and I needed to get help from the inside. I couldn't let David disappear like that.

"He just took off. He can't stand still for a moment, it seems. He won't tell me who's after him." I hadn't dared to tell Monika the truth about what David had been up to; e-mail and phone messages could easily be hacked. Last Christmas I had sent her a package with a hidden letter inside, which contained pretty much every-thing about David, although I kept him anonymous. "We don't need to talk about David. Nothing we say will change the situation. What made you come back to Finland?"

Monika stood up awkwardly, as if she had no sense of balance.

"I'll make you some tea," she said. "Give me a minute." Monika wore sandals, and she shuffled toward the kitchen. Once she reached the parquet, the sound was eerie, as if she were slowly skating across the floor. I thought about rushing over to help her. I could hear clanging in the kitchen, and something fell but didn't break. Soon she was back with a tray, tea bags, two cups with saucers, a pot of honey, and a plate of cookies. She held the tray as if it weighed twenty pounds, and her arms shook from the strain. I stood up and grabbed the tray from her and set it down on the coffee table.

"Spit it out. What's up with you?" I demanded.

"Nobody seems to know. Doctors back in Maputo first said it was an intestinal disease, which would have explained why I can't keep any food down. But then my muscles began to get weaker, so I came back to Finland for more thorough testing. I didn't want to leave my kitchen, but Joau promised he'd take over."

"Joau?" I remembered Monika mentioning a man over the phone and in some e-mails. I'd assumed he was her lover.

"Joau." A sad smile came over her face. "My lover. He's Catholic, in his forties, and has a wife and five children in Maputo. Obviously that didn't prevent us from getting involved. Maybe he was my ill-ness. I knew it wouldn't go far. My heart and mind wouldn't let me give him up, so my body broke and forced me to leave. Maybe I'll heal now that I'm hundreds of miles away."

Monika's arms stopped shaking, and she turned to fill the cups. The rooibos tea had a deliciously ruby glow, its scent promising comfort.

"Sounds like we both have rotten luck with men," I said. "Have the doctors given you a prognosis?"

"My first appointment is tomorrow. I've always avoided private practices. I think it's unfair for people to get different service based on how rich they are. But when push comes to shove, my idealism apparently means nothing." Monika lifted the teacup to her colorless lips. "I wasn't going to just sit around waiting for horrible news from the doctors. I had to come up with something, so while I was still in Mozambique, I looked for restaurants for sale. I want to bring Chez Monique back. Organic and locally produced foods became super trendy while I was gone, so there'll be plenty of customers. I'm just trying to think of how to combine an African kitchen organized for the poor with Finnish cuisine."

"Watered-down buttermilk and manioc?" I was glad my clumsy joke made her laugh.

"You've told me about what your uncle Jari fed you as a child. You fished and picked berries, and only that lynx got meat from the store," said Monika.

"Frida." Saying her name out loud felt like a religious rite, even after all these years. I'd never get over losing her. Mother, Uncle Jari, Frida, and now David, gone without a trace. I wouldn't let Monika leave me, too.

"Chez Monique or perhaps Uncle Jari's Corner Café? I'm open to new names." Now Monika's eyes were sparkling with excitement. "Are you working for anyone right now? I'm looking for a strong and efficient person to work security and crowd control."

That's exactly what I wanted. Working for Monika had been the best time of my life. There had been meaning to my existence, which was mostly filled with drifting from job to job since Uncle Jari died. I nodded, and she talked about ideas for the new restaurant, obviously trying to block thoughts of her illness, which could prevent the whole thing. I didn't want to think about that, either. She'd offered for me to stay with her; her cousin would be back from India at the end of May, but by then Monika would have a place of her own. We tried to hold on to each other because we had no one else.

I remembered that I needed to use her computer, so I asked to borrow her laptop for the night. I told her I'd spend the night at Hotel Torni, having paid for it already and wanting to pamper myself. I needed some time to think. Once I found out what David's USB stick held, I'd know what was safe to tell her.

She knew I was up to something but let me have the laptop. I promised to be back early the next evening with my belongings from Mrs. Voutilainen's apartment, and Monika would be done with her appointment by then. I offered to go with her, but she said she wanted to go alone. I told her to go to bed. Once the excitement was gone from her eyes, she turned pale again, like a raw piece of dough.

A group of Japanese tourists was waiting for the elevator to access the upper floors at the hotel. I began to climb the stairs, but after a couple of floors, I was blocked by a gate, so I snuck back down and squeezed myself into the elevator with the Japanese ladies. They were shorter than me by a good fifteen inches and had such small bones that I could have easily snapped their wrists or necks.

I resisted a drink at the bar and got off on my floor. Dusk had shrouded Helsinki. Lights twinkled in the streets and parks, and in the distance a sailboat glimmered with festive lanterns, probably having a party. David had loved sailing. Goddamned David! It was time I figured out what he was hiding.

I turned the computer on, and it whirred. The desktop image was a plate of fruit salad. Oranges, mangos, cantaloupes, and kumquats glowed in shades of orange. The yellow of a lemon and pineapple competed with red cherries and strawberries. It was Monika's power picture from years before, and apparently she hadn't felt the need to change it. My computers never had desktop images or personalized screensavers revealing anything about me. Besides, I didn't even have a digital copy of the picture I would have used. I had a couple of faded pictures of Frida that Uncle Jari had gotten developed all the way in Kuopio, in case pictures of a lynx in Outokumpu or Kaavi would have raised some unwelcome questions. I carried the pictures in my journal, inside a small plastic pocket, and hardly anyone got to see them. When I was in Spain with David, we'd had one of the pictures on our wall, the one where Frida is lying down with her head in my lap and I'm scratching her neck. Looking at the picture I could still hear Frida's purring and feel the warm, soft fur rising under my palm as she breathed.

I inserted the USB stick, and there was only one folder, created a week before I traveled to Tuscany. The title was weird: "copper/ *mednoi*." I opened the folder and cursed. It was all in Russian. I clicked through the files and found a map, where most of the place names were in Swedish, although a few had been translated into Finnish. At first glance the topological features of the map looked familiar, and when I looked closer I realized it was the Kopparnäs camping grounds, its archipelago, and Pickala's golf course near a large villa. All of these were mere miles away from my cabin in Torbacka.

The next map appeared to be an architectural sketch, and the area looked completely different. Fake islands appeared between actual islands, and the pristine shores of Kopparnäs were packed with new houses. Some were private residences, others large housing complexes. The area was surrounded by fences, and the sea had been marked with borders. The map didn't reach the golf course or villa.

I knew the Cyrillic alphabet and some basic expressions but had not used Russian for over a year, and I was rusty as I tried to understand the writing over the maps. I understood *domi* and *kvartiri*, houses and apartments. The large building in the center looked like a concert hall.

I scrolled down below the maps. It looked like the file had been scanned from a paper document, because there was Finnish writing underneath. The handwriting was barely legible.

"Environmental permits. Decide who? Next minister? Russians are no threat. Return to Porkkala. Ask about election funding. Cur partner better than ex? Risk analysis better than Vasiliev's."

There was a familiar logo at the bottom of the file. I associated the logo with multipronged business ventures and had seen it in news coverage of election funding scandals. The logo belonged to Uskon Asia Inc. and portrayed a building resembling a temple, sketched with three lines. The owner, Usko Syrjänen, had been Boris Vasiliev's business partner. Vasiliev had died aboard Syrjänen's boat when David had blown it and its crew into smithereens. Syrjänen had denied involvement or knowledge of Vasiliev's activities to sabotage the oil pipe in the Baltic Sea; he claimed their only connection was planning to build an international recreation center into Kotka's Hiidenniemi. So what was Syrjänen planning to do to the campgrounds in Kopparnäs, and why did David have these papers?

6

I woke up around four in the morning and looked outside. I felt David near me, and it seemed like he had something to say. I checked my phone and e-mail, but there was nothing. I kept watching the sleeping, quiet city. Only a couple of cars buzzed on the street, and a lone pedestrian took unsteady steps near the Old Church Park. Although I didn't believe in anything that couldn't be logically explained, such as telepathy, I tried opening myself up to David and his messages. The only message I felt coming through was a clear command: "Call Laitio and tell him about Carlo Dolfini's body."

Bummer. I was planning on doing it anyway, although I knew it would cause problems. Chief Constable Teppo Laitio and I had a strange love-hate relationship. I think he liked me more than I liked him, and he had been visibly annoyed when he'd guessed my feelings for David. I couldn't stand people who could see through me like that.

Unable to fall asleep again, I turned on the computer. I hadn't requested a password for the hotel network, but there were plenty of unprotected Wi-Fi connections. Using them was risky, but searching for information about a businessman named Usko Syrjänen should be harmless; his face was constantly plastered on the covers of tabloid magazines and newspapers.

Syrjänen had made his fortune by selling cars in the 1980s and expanded his business to real estate during the recession of the early 1990s. He'd taken huge risks buying a bankrupt estate, empty office spaces, and small-town schools that had been closed. Somehow he lucked out. As soon as the recession was over, he was able to sell some of his property and turn a large profit. He used some of the land to build holiday rental villas, nursing homes, and karaoke bars. He'd successfully snatched the villa in Hiidenniemi from my former employer Anita Nuutinen, and he was planning to build more structures on the land of a heavily guarded private club. Unfortunately for him, neighbors didn't want to sell any of their land. In an interview for a local newspaper, Syrjänen complained about a lack of an all-inclusive holiday resort where international superstars and Finnish celebrities could spend their free time without running into curious "regular people." Syrjänen claimed that wealthy people would prefer vacations in Provence or the Caribbean over staying in Finland if they could leave behind the everyday annoyance of being recognized. He knew what he was talking about.

The decks of his swimming pool were frequented by a variety of beautiful women, intent on getting money out of him. It looked like Syrjänen had learned from his mistakes and was now seeking privacy after his divorce the previous fall. Websites time stamped a couple of weeks ago indicated that there was a new love in his life: a twenty-eight-year-old Russian model named Julia.

Syrjänen hadn't uttered a word about the events that had led to the destruction of his boat, the *I Believe*, and the death of his Russian business partner and his minions. He was buddies with a number of leading politicians, such as the Finnish prime minister, and had provided funding for multiple campaigns. They may have convinced Syrjänen to keep quiet in the name of the country's security—ordinary folks didn't need to know what was going on behind the scenes. They'd never understand that sometimes people in power had no choice.

I wondered when Syrjänen had made his Kopparnäs notes. The document was last saved this spring, but that didn't mean he created it then. David had worked in Hiidenniemi as Boris Vasiliev's bodyguard and drove his boat, so the document could be over two years old. When I'd run into him in Kopparnäs, I had assumed he was after me, but now it seemed he had other reasons for scouting the area. I checked whether Syrjänen's logo had changed recently, but that three-lined column drawing had been in use since 1986.

Syrjänen had known David. Did he think David survived the explosion? Only a handful of people in Finland knew about his mission. I knew the top politicians were mostly trustworthy, but it wouldn't be the first time one of them let a secret slip while sitting in a sauna with a friend. Mike Virtue had been flabbergasted when I told him about the sauna traditions of Finnish politicians. They really went naked into a sauna with the leader of another country? Didn't they realize the potential of taking secret footage and using it as blackmail? And was it really smart to reveal to other leaders what you looked like naked? You could be considered weak in a negotiation that way. In his usual forward style, Edgardo had asked Mike if he meant that men with smaller dicks wouldn't be respected when confronted by a man with a larger one. Mike had nodded, and I swear he also blushed. I described to the class how business in Finland was often conducted in saunas, and Mike made us map out the potential risks.

Nudity wasn't the only cause for Mike's disapproval. In the saunas, a live fire roared in a fireplace or a wood-burning stove, boiling the water and causing temperature changes of 212 degrees when people left the sauna to frolic outside in the snow. When I added that negotiations often included drunkenness in addition to rolling naked in snow banks and diving into the lake or the sea through a hole cut into the ice, Mike exclaimed that he'd tell his clients to never take part in this crazy ritual. But I had earned the respect of my classmates: Finns sure had balls! Afterward, some of the men in my class tried to convince me to go to a Finnish sauna with them, and I declined.

I did another search for a recent picture of Usko Syrjänen and took a few more moments to memorize what he looked like. There was nothing special about him. He was in his fifties and medium height, and he kept himself in shape by golfing and skiing. His shoulders were wide like a swimmer's, and he had a slight paunch. His legs seemed a bit short compared with the rest of him. Syrjänen loved wearing cowboy boots and referred to himself as a self-made man. He stopped wearing glasses after his laser eye surgery, but in most of the pictures, he was squinting under his heavy lids, with large bags under his eyes. His mouth was small, his lips narrow, his chin covered in whiskers.

The sky to the east began to gather light, and purple streaks were spreading over Käpylä. I turned the lights off and shut the computer down, but it took a while to stop my mind from running. I kept thinking about the Kopparnäs map, mixed with memories of how I'd run into David while picking mushrooms on the shores of Kvarnträsket and how hard it had been not to feed him the poisonous ones. I was still carrying the dried milk-cap mushroom pieces with me in a small vial. They wouldn't have as quick an effect as cyanide, so I couldn't rely on them for myself. They were reserved for my enemies. You never knew who'd turn out to be one. I drifted into restless sleep.

When I finally woke up, I had to get dressed in record speed to make it down for breakfast. The staff was already clearing some of the food when I shoved my way through to slap frozen berries, scrambled eggs, bacon, salted herring, and a helping of rye bread onto my plate. The frozen berries tasted pretty good on an empty stomach. I'd been too preoccupied to eat the day before. I ignored the annoyed waiters who made sure I heard them clearing dishes and took my time eating and drinking my three cups of coffee. Only then did I feel nourished enough to call Teppo Laitio, but not until I'd brushed my teeth. I realized I should have brought him a cigar or two; most of the time he worked from his apartment on Urheilu Street, smoking was not allowed at the Bureau, and Laitio's mind was at its sharpest when shrouded in a thick cloud of smoke.

"Ilveskero! I'll be damned. Where are you?" he said.

"Hotel Torni."

"Ha! A maiden in a tower, huh? Aren't you being Sibelian?" Laitio laughed at his joke. It went completely over my head. "To what do I owe the pleasure of this call?"

"A dead body."

"What? Where?"

"I can't tell you over the phone. You're tapped for sure. Can we meet?"

"Bullshit. My phones aren't tapped. Maybe you should see a shrink for your paranoia."

"Can we just meet at your place?"

I heard the lighter click. Laitio needed a smoke. "Come over around one thirty. Rytkönen should be gone by then."

I didn't ask who this Rytkönen was; I wasn't interested. Laitio drew a deep breath, and I could almost smell the cigar smoke. His employer had offered to pay for a class and hypnotist to help him quit smoking, but Laitio declined; he wasn't the one with a smoking problem—society had a problem with it. I could imagine what Mike Virtue would've said about Laitio's attitude. "Remember that those who protect others must set their own needs aside while on a mission. Sleepiness, thirst, and full bladders do not exist. And the only way you can forget about them is to practice your concentration skills." The academy in Queens had offered classes in meditation and sitting in complete silence, which had seemed weird to most of us. These classes on emptying your mind were easy for me; meditation seemed to be a distant relative to the ice fishing trips with Uncle Jari, where we'd sit in silence for hours.

I was supposed to be checking out of the hotel, but I wanted to try reaching the mysterious Kassi first. I didn't want to wait to get a phone card, so I'd call from another room in the hotel. I pulled on a pair of gloves, slipped into the hallway, and checked for any maids with their carts. There were none on my floor. I walked down the stairs to the floor below. No carts there, either, but the door to one of the rooms was open. I went inside, closed the door, picked up the phone, and dialed Kassi—an immediate answer: "The number you have dialed cannot be reached. Please try again later." I called the national number service and was informed that there was no information attached to Kassi's number. I should've guessed that.

My annoyance was quickly interrupted by the jangling of keys at the door. It must have been the maid. I went into the bathroom and closed the door. If she came into the bathroom, I could always try to act like an idiot who had wandered in, wanting to know what the other rooms looked like.

I heard a door open, then some glass clinking. To my relief the room door was opened again and closed, but I didn't leave right away; the maid might have still been in the hallway. I counted to five hundred and left. I went back to my room to get my stuff and left it with the front desk. I'd forgotten to get a key from Monika, so I couldn't move in yet.

I needed to get out and do something besides sit at the computer, so I took a stroll to Töölö. Along the way, I read tabloid headlines about the ash cloud and travel in chaos. As I passed the parliament building, a politician was being interviewed about the event. I thought I'd met him when I worked for Representative Helena Lehmusvuo as a bodyguard and temporary assistant. That short stint made me realize that the parliament was not meant for sane people.

Although crocuses were already in bloom in Töölönlahti Park, the weather was still nippy, and I picked up my pace. I could have used the warm clothes I'd left in the Untamo Road apartment, as the thin parka I wore was no good against this wind. Because I had plenty of time on my hands, I walked around the ice rink and the soccer stadium. A women's team was practicing, and a couple of full-time drunks were shouting and cheering, fueled by several beers from the looks of the empty bottles around them. I stepped into Reiska's shoes for a moment and imagined how he watched women: the breasts on that blond were bouncing nicely, the tight pants on the brunette showed her round butt. When I became Reiska, I wanted to be a man all the way, thoughts included. Suddenly, Reiska seemed to want to take over. Maybe I could use him for reaching out to Kassi; Reiska was such a clumsy guy that he could easily fat-finger a wrong number, especially if he was a couple of beers in.

The sky was shrouded in thick, dark clouds that were sending down drizzle, so I rang Laitio's buzzer early to get out of the cold rain.

"Is that Ilveskero?" he said through the speaker. "Come on in, although Rytkönen is still here."

I walked up the stairs to the top floor, avoiding elevators; I didn't trust them, and the elevator in Laitio's apartment looked ancient. Once I'd spent a great deal of time in an elevator with five other people in a forty-story skyscraper in New York; one of them had worn a gallon of perfume and another pissed himself from sheer terror. I managed not to panic, thanks to Mike Virtue's teachings.

It was smoky upstairs. Laitio, his wife, and a grumpy cat named Kokki occupied the larger apartment, and Laitio had turned the adjacent one-bedroom apartment into a work and smoking office, and he'd left the door open. The average Finnish neighbor would have barged in to complain about the cigar smell in the hallway, so I had to wonder what sort of threats Laitio used to keep his neighbors at bay. I walked in and slammed the door to announce my arrival. A man I had not seen before walked out of Laitio's office. He couldn't have been much taller than five foot two, but he adequately compensated for his height with his muscles; his shoulders were as wide as David's, and his thighs were about to burst out of his white cotton pants.

"Teppo is in the bathroom," he said. Just what I wanted to hear. "How are ya? I'm Mara Rytkönen, inspector from the foreign unit of the National Bureau of Investigation." He extended his hand.

I didn't shake it right away because I thought he was lying. He had no business in the police academy looking like that, but I realized there were other routes to reach an inspector position. His handshake was just as I'd expected; if I'd been any other woman, I would have shrieked in pain. I squeezed back hard. Although we were about the same weight, I was taller and could take him down with a judo throw, unless he was equally skilled in martial arts and could put me in a choke or an armlock.

"Ilveskero," I told Rytkönen when he finally released his grip.

"Us folks over at the old En Bee Aye have a real fat folder about you." Rytkönen flashed a wide smile. His facial muscles were tight, his cheekbones stood high, and his Adam's apple was ridiculously large, as if he'd made it lift weights, too. "I've been hearin' you're a gal from Savonia, from Kaavi, to be exact. I'm from close by. Iisalmi."

I wasn't enthusiastic to have a friendly chat about my background, especially with a cop who appeared to know more about me than I found appropriate. Had Laitio fallen in the toilet? Why wasn't he back yet?

There was a cough behind a closed door followed by a flush, soon accompanied by running water. Laitio was in no hurry. He strolled back with a grin, adjusting his pants. I'd seen him very briefly before Christmas. We'd had some *glögi*, similar to mulled wine, and smoked a cigar. His bushy mustache had collected gray hairs during the winter, and his face was pale.

"Rytkönen, I thought you had to be somewhere," Laitio said. Rytkönen must have been his boss. Laitio was only a chief constable.

"Heck, I had to keep this young lady company," Rytkönen said, "but I'll be off now. See you at the meeting tomorrow." He closed the door behind him.

Only after Rytkönen's steps stopped echoing in the hallway did Laitio make a move toward me. Neither of us was the hugging kind, and shaking hands seemed forced, so we greeted each other with a nod.

"Damned nosy man. You better not mention any bodies while he's around. Want some coffee or a smoke?" Laitio walked to his room and closed the window. He reached for a partially smoked cigar in the ashtray and stuck it between his lips.

"The answer to both of your questions is no," I said. "Let's get to business." I sat down, but Laitio remained standing at the window. "Greetings from Tuscany," I said.

"A romantic little getaway, huh? With Stahl I suppose?"

"Also known as Daniel Lanotte these days. I don't know how many alter egos David has, but he appears to be in real deep shit, because he took off suddenly." I tried to keep my voice steady, although Laitio's humiliating comment had made it tremble. I filled him in on David's disappearance, how I'd visited the restaurant, how I found the body and David's phone. I didn't tell him how I'd broken into the hutch and kept the items inside. I told him I'd found Dolfini's number in David's cell phone and that I was pretty sure I'd identified the body.

"And where's this famous phone now?" Laitio quickly lit the cigar.

"I threw it in a river."

Laitio walked in front of me and blew smoke in my face. It felt like a slap. "How does a woman as smart as you do something so stupid? You left the body behind?"

"I had no idea who he was. And what if David had killed him?"

"So you're saying he first ditched you, then he waited until you were gone and dragged this man to the apartment to off him there? Certainly not a man's logic, but fit for a woman, I suppose. How do you even dare come to me with this nonsense? I wish I'd never heard any of it."

Laitio was pacing. His brown walking shoes were worn-out, and the right toe was almost poking through. The legs on his dull brown pants were slightly too short, revealing blue-and-mustard-yellow striped socks. Laitio's stretched-out cardigan was a matching mustard color, and while he was walking around the room, small hairs fell out of it, probably from the cat.

"I want to find out who Dolfini is and why he was killed. You're a policeman and should be able to contact your Italian colleagues."

"And what sort of a reason should I give them? How would I even know about this body?"

"You'll make something up. You can lie as well as I can."

"But you won't get into serious trouble with your foreman who wants everything done by the book. I mean, look at Rytkönen. There's an old saying about Savonians that once they begin speaking, all responsibility is handed over to the listener, but not with him. He's not a storyteller or a con artist, and he doesn't understand that sometimes rules have to be bent. He's getting his law degree and writing a dissertation on some nonsense that has nothing to do with police work. That man hasn't spent a single day in the field—he's never arrested a wino, and I doubt he's ever seen a stiff. And that's the type of guy we get as our boss these days, goddamn it."

"So rebel and bend some policies." I knew I was taking a risk, especially since I forced a smile when my heart was about to beat out of my chest. I could always travel to Lago di Scanno in Italy to have a chat with Mrs. Dolfini, but with what money? I'd drained most of my savings coming back to Finland, and besides, Monika needed me here.

"I don't know anybody in Italy, and our snitch fund gets cut more every year," Laitio said. He sat down in a leather armchair behind his desk and pulled out a thick, leather-covered journal.

"Florence . . . is it part of Tuscany?" he asked.

"Yeah, a capital."

"I wonder if Caruso has already retired. I once saved him from . . . Well, that story's not really relevant. But let's just say he owes me one."

I grinned at Laitio's attempt to protect me. I'd probably seen worse cases of cops sweeping crimes under the rug. I'd let him keep his secrets. I had mine, too.

"Give me Dolfini's number. And what was that stuff you said about his legs being different lengths?" Laitio wrote furiously in his journal. I repeated all the details I could remember about Dolfini.

"Now get out of here before I regret this," Laitio said when I was done. His labored breath sounded like an onset of pulmonary disease. "I'll get in touch with you when I know something. Only contact me if you hear something about Stahl."

"Got it," I said and left. Walking down the stairs, I wondered if I should've crossed my fingers behind my back when I made that promise. If David contacted me, I would decide who got to know about it. But he better have a good explanation, one worth protecting a murderer.

7

I didn't hear from Laitio for days. The entire country had gone crazy because of the ash cloud. People had to cancel their travel plans and come up with ingenious ways to get back home. Mike Virtue had constantly reminded us to never underestimate the power of nature. In the United States, floods and earthquakes were nothing out of the ordinary, and snowfall caused traffic problems in towns not used to it. When I traveled around Finland in my youth, I never saw trains stuck on icy tracks, and if a car slid off the road into a snowbank in the remotest of countrysides, someone with a tractor always showed up to pull the poor sap back onto the road. Planes occasionally crashed, but was anyone forced to get into one? People had gotten so used to changing scenery quickly that long bus rides and overnight trains were now fodder for heroic tales. I swore, these ninnies wouldn't have survived a summer night in a tent in the middle of a forest. I remembered the wimps we'd had in the army who weren't able to poop in the forest, even though most of the world doesn't have access to toilet paper.

Monika returned confused after her visit to the doctor. There was something wrong with her intestines, but the three doctors who had examined her couldn't say what it was. They'd drawn vial after vial of blood for tests, and now she was scheduled for an x-ray. One of the doctors was concerned about Monika's years in Mozambique.

I ended up spending my first night at Monika's cousin's place searching online for intestinal diseases, southwestern African viral diseases, and worms. Parasites seemed the most plausible explanation, but I didn't dare mention that to Monika. Who'd want to know they were carrying worms?

Monika spent a lot of her time looking for a good space for the restaurant, and she also had to set aside time to rest, so we hadn't agreed on a contract for my services. Monika insisted on cooking for us, so I promised to take care of all the physical work. I brought my stuff over from Mrs. Voutilainen's apartment, but I wasn't in a hurry to get to Hevonpersiinsaari for my gun. I felt like the ash cloud was still protecting me from Italian hit men.

On one of Monika's resting days, I went to see what was up with Kopparnäs. I printed the maps from David's USB stick. I hadn't figured out when the original text was created, but with a computer translator and a dictionary, I'd gotten the gist of the Russian text. The maps showed a similar luxury resort to the one Syrjänen had originally planned on building in Kotka. It was zoned for a recreational area, but it wouldn't have been the first time such decisions were overturned. I doubted all the uproar about politicians accepting money for elections would change the way things happened in this country. I'd never been interested in politics, but based on the most recent articles, it appeared politicians were for sale to the highest bidder. I knew I could always get in touch with my former employer and Monika's friend Representative Helena Lehmusvuo. Helena was one of those people who would do her research and then get busy, so I couldn't really tell her how I got the maps; I could just hypothetically ask her about changing a recreational area's zoning. Now that national parks were going to start charging entrance fees, why would valuable plots of land be reserved for the general public?

When I got on the bus at the Kamppi station, I looked around for signs of anyone tailing me, but I didn't detect anything. It was just me and three Swedish-speaking elderly ladies.

Once we passed Espoo the road looked unfamiliar. Many of the trees had been cut down in anticipation of a new freeway, maybe so the wealthy could take a leisurely drive to Syrjänen's resort.

I hadn't been to Degerby in a year and a half. I'd parked my rusty bike in front of a bank before I'd left. On the off chance that the bike was still there, I'd packed a pump and a tire repair kit, and believe it or not, my bike was still there. The back tire was flat and had a gaping hole, but at least the front tire still had some air. I carried the bike to a nearby playground and flipped it on its seat and got to work. The chains were dry but not broken. Surely the bike could handle another ten miles.

Fields along Kopparnäs Road were still brown and too wet for farmers to bring out their plows. Only the miniature suns of dandelions growing along the ditches gave off some color. Storks were making a commotion in the reeds as I approached the bay. Ice had already melted, and wherever the sun hadn't reached on the north side of the bay, piles of snow were left, covered in gray soot and dirt. Compared to this, Tuscany's summer had been in full swing, but the gray suited my mood better. The sun tried to peer through the clouds but quickly retreated from the bone-chilling winds of spring.

As I drove deeper into Kopparnäs, memories flooded my mind; that road would take me to the inn where David and I made love for the first time. I needed to erase the thought and focus only on the moment.

I drove to the tall cliffs where a wind energy station had been. According to Syrjänen's maps it would be the future location of a restaurant with a sea view and a ballroom, with some of the building hovering over the water so customers could dance on the deck as if they were on a cruise ship.

I walked from the cliffs to the beach, where I found a camping shelter. It protected me from the chilly wind, and I had just managed to pour a cup of tea from my thermos when my phone rang. The number was from the National Bureau of Investigation. It was Teppo Laitio.

"How often do you see ghosts, Ilveskero?"

"What are you talking about?"

"Shoeless corpses, for one. I thought the days when you tried to pull a fast one on me were over. My friend Guido Caruso has been investigating the body found in Montemassi. The police in Siena had received an anonymous tip about it last week, but they weren't able to check in on the apartment because the owner was stuck in London because of the damned ash cloud, and it took a while for him to get a seat on the train through the Chunnel. The police got the keys this past weekend, and they didn't find a body or anything else. It seems Stahl had gone back to get his stuff. The owner claimed everything in the apartment was his."

My throat was dry. I took a sip of tea.

Laitio continued. "Rent was paid until the end of May. Daniel Lanotte has not been seen since, and no laws have been broken."

"But how about Carlo Dolfini, the man who went missing? Did the police check on him?"

"Caruso went through the missing persons reports. None was made about Dolfini. He also gave Mrs. Dolfini a call, but she said Carlo was visiting relatives in New York. His cousin has a pizza place in Little Italy, it turns out." Laitio pronounced all the English words as if they were Finnish. I would've laughed at him under other circumstances.

"But I saw his body," I insisted.

"Did you take any photos of it?"

"No. I remember perfectly well how he looked without photos."

"You know how these things go. No matter how the lion of justice roars in Finland, his roars will not be heard all the way in Italy."

"But isn't Italy part of the EU? Surely they have some laws about this."

"What sort of law would believe you over two competent police officers and a landlord?"

David's landlord had claimed that nothing was amiss in the apartment. But what about the hutch I had broken? I couldn't understand why the landlord, Brother Gianni's friend, hadn't mentioned it, unless he, too, was in on some conspiracy. I couldn't fight Laitio further without revealing that I hadn't told him everything. I had dug myself into a hole.

"I'll ask around about Stahl," Laitio continued. "But I doubt they'll tell me anything. The big boys were already pissed off about how much I knew about the boat explosion. They're still reminding me to never talk about it. And Rytkönen has no clue." Laitio's laugh had an odd, hissing quality to it.

"Ilveskero, are you planning on sticking around for a while, or are you going to wander all over Europe chasing after Stahl?" he asked.

"I'm certainly not going to follow him. I'm changing careers," I told him.

"And what are you going to do?"

"Work at a restaurant."

"As a bouncer, I hope. In that job you're allowed to be mean. I couldn't imagine you as a waitress. A shitty customer would have a face full of beer or pasta in no time. And I doubt you can cook."

I let out a sigh. I didn't feel like bullshitting with Laitio. I did end up telling him about Monika and her restaurant plans.

"I see," he said. "I bet a box of cigars that as soon as you hear from Stahl, you'll go after him, all the way to the deepest parts of Africa if necessary. Speaking of traveling, my summer vacation is in July, and Caruso was hoping I'd visit Florence to enjoy its treasures. He says Lago di Scanno is beautiful, too. So we thought we'd drop by there. Maybe Carlo Dolfini will be back from New York by then."

"I doubt it," I said. "But maybe you'll locate Mrs. Dolfini."

"Caruso is on it. He's looking into Dolfini's background. I believe you, you know."

In the background, his cat's impatient meows had grown loud and distracting.

"Kokki demands shrimp. I need to go before he pees in my shoes. Take care." Laitio hung up.

I sipped my sweet black tea. Brits thought it was the cure for everything from shock to heartaches. It didn't seem to work on me, though. I may have needed to try the Finnish version of a national cure, Koskenkorva vodka, although since my time in New York, tequila had been my poison.

I was wondering whether David had really murdered Dolfini, if the body had even been Dolfini's, and if David had left the body for me to worry about. I tried to think of what he had wanted me to do with it. And who had come back for David's belongings? Brother Gianni had arranged the apartment for David, so he knew the landlord. I contemplated getting in touch with him, but a monk may not have been the most talkative informant. I supposed all men of the cloth were very disciplined, abstaining from sex and whipping themselves to tolerate pain better, or so I had read. Brother Gianni wouldn't have been swayed by verbal or physical threats. What's more, he was a former cop. Why had he quit his job?

The Syrjänen documents I pulled out flapped in the wind. Maybe my next move should be to contact him. It was no secret that Syrjänen was a ladies' man. His pretty Russian girlfriend may have slowed things down, but Syrjänen was known to wander, and it was good to know someone's secrets could be bought with sexual persuasion. Mike Virtue had warned us about two types of clients: addicts and nymphomaniacs. Anyone whose life was dictated by desires was a slave to those vices, and they could be convinced to do almost anything for a fix. Mike had been above addictions, although he occasionally joked about how obsessed he was with exercising, but that was more of a virtue. Sound mind in a sound body.

I strolled toward Kvarnträsket. Spring was taking its time to arrive, so I didn't have my hopes up about finding morels in the forest. I happened upon the clearing where I'd met David, and I could almost see him standing in the grass in his camo gear. Back then I hadn't known whose side he was on, and for the next year and a half, I had convinced myself it was mine.

Walking toward the shore I spotted familiar animal tracks. There were about ten sets of paw prints that were well-defined, a message left for me to read. A lynx had passed here. I swallowed and tried not to think about it. Of course there would be lynx in Kopparnäs, but they had nothing to do with me. Syrjänen would probably catch them and display them in his vacation paradise.

According to the newspaper and web articles, Syrjänen was the type of man who had visions no one had even dreamed of, and he had the money and drive to make them come true. This area was over a thousand acres and could easily fit a luxury resort for millionaires, but surely Syrjänen didn't really think such an endeavor could pop up overnight. There had to be someone else who would benefit from turning the public lands of Kopparnäs into private property.

Between 1944 and 1956 the bay had been included in areas that were leased to the Soviet Union as a result of the Continuation War, and if the original plan had gone through, it would have been returned to Finland in the late 1900s. The Gulf of Finland was at its narrowest in Porkkala, making it easy to survey. When the Soviets left Finland, they tried to destroy everything that could have imparted information about their military strategies, or so I had learned at the small museum back in Degerby village. Kopparnäs had been used as shooting grounds. Maybe something was left behind that Syrjänen and his new business associates were interested in. Had David left me the map on purpose so I'd go after Syrjänen? I went from peaceful to livid. Here I was, trying to make a flimsy connection to David when I was supposed to just forget about him. I'd once grieved for him, thinking I'd left shards of my heart on the snowy banks of Hevonpersiinsaari, but all that crying had been in vain, and I wouldn't let it happen again.

I picked gypsy mushrooms in the forest. Monika could make delicious dishes out of them. There were no mushrooms next to the inn. Instead it looked like armored vehicles were growing there, indicating a potential warehouse for the armed forces. A chain-link fence and signs made sure outsiders wouldn't walk in. What would happen to the warehouse if Syrjänen bought the area?

The mushrooms gave off an intoxicating smell on the bus. I'd occasionally nod off and dreamed of picking black trumpets with David. Back at the apartment, Monika was gravely ill. She hadn't made it to the bathroom and had thrown up on the foyer floor.

I took Monika to a private hospital's ER, and for the next couple of weeks, I thought only of her. I sat by Monika and held her hand, sometimes reading her sad Swedish books, where people felt disconnected and ended up in hopeless lives. It felt comforting at that time. I also took care of her errands and scouted potential properties for her restaurant. Monika's lawyer helped me negotiate restaurant licenses, and I looked for a new apartment for us.

Then, at the end of May, we found out that Monika's condition was nothing more than a persistent intestinal worm she'd most likely gotten from drinking dirty water in Mozambique. She was put on antibiotics and told to rest.

"I'm lucky," Monika said and sighed. "I got to return to Finland and have the best treatment. Ordinary folks in Mozambique die of this. Little kids have no hope," she said as we slowly walked through the Old Church Park, known as Plague Park by the locals.

"You can't save the entire world," I told her. "First you must heal yourself. Don't try to be Florence Nightingale when you barely have the energy to walk up to the third floor."

It was futile to try to change her. We were too similar. Working was our answer to sorrow. June turned from chilling winds to a heat wave as we went around Helsinki, looking for restaurant spaces. Monika didn't want her restaurant in some fancy neighborhood. She wanted to be within walking distance of common folks and had to be realistic about locations that made sense. We finally found a spot on the bottom floor of a cubistic-looking office building in Salmisaari. A large IT company had taken over a small business venture and outsourced their services to India and Taiwan. Although we had quite a renovation ahead of us, the property was close to the subway station and bus stops in Ruoholahti.

In July, Laitio sent me a postcard from Italy of a lake surrounded by high mountains called Lago di Scanno. The text was blunt: "Wine is good and food is passable, but you can't smoke anywhere. Old Lady Dolfini has taken a trip to the US. Cunning folk, these locals. You can't get anything out of them. Greetings, T.

Laitio." He must've been pissed off for having followed my shitty lead.

Monika's cousin was going to stay in India until the end of the fall, so finding an apartment became less of a priority. Monika had hired me as an assistant, but I was really a general handyman. Uncle Jari had been a competent carpenter and had a good command of other building-related work. He'd taught me a thing or two about the business and was often in my thoughts when I was tiling a floor, painting walls, or hammering kitchen cabinets into place. I'd been in Queens when Uncle had gone out on the lake in the late, chilly fall, checked his nets, and gotten tangled in them. He drowned. When I heard the news, I went into shock, and only later did it occur to me how odd it was that a seasoned fisherman could be so clumsy.

I waited until I had returned from the security academy in Queens to read the autopsy report. Uncle's cause of death was hypothermia. There had been no reason to suspect foul play, so the investigation was vague and closed quickly. It wasn't the first time a middle-aged fisherman had drowned. Uncle was never a big drinker, but the investigation found alcohol in his blood. Uncle Jari's neighbor Matti Hakkarainen told me he'd seen Uncle suddenly grow pale and complain about nausea while they'd been chopping wood in the forest. Matti had assumed Uncle had heart problems. I'd left Uncle by himself because I ran from my problems to Vantaa and then all the way to New York. I neglected taking care of the one person who'd loved me and raised me. Had I been in Finland, I would've told Uncle to see a doctor immediately.

I wasn't going to make the same mistake twice, so I put all my energy into taking care of Monika and making her restaurant dreams come true. She was still thinking about fusing cuisines from Hevonpersiinsaari and Mozambique, and I did my best to remember the cooks Uncle Jari used to like. Toward the end of August, Monika and I traveled together to Hevonpersiinsaari, where our old neighbor Maija Hakkarainen showed Monika the secrets of making traditional Karelian pastries and *kalakukko*, fish and fat baked inside a loaf of bread. This was the first time I'd brought a guest to my old haunts. I wasn't ashamed of the simple rural house I grew up in. I was more worried about sharing my past with another person. I had hoped to one day swim with David in Rikkavesi, the lake, although David had told me he was done with swimming after freestyling for miles in the cold Baltic Sea after he blew up the boat.

Monika and I spent many warm and illuminated evenings outside in the gazebo, huddling in front of a fire pit, swatting mosquitoes, and cooking rutabaga stews and cubed turnips in the embers. Monika was going to build an old-timey baking oven in the restaurant, where the traditional Finnish dishes could be cooked to perfection. She got along with Maija, although Maija had felt awkward about Monika's Swedish accent and tried to speak in a less regional dialect. While they cooked I helped Matti fix the pasture fence where a large animal had forced itself through. Matti wasn't sure whether it had been a wolf or a lynx. Men in the village had suggested a neighborhood watch.

"Your uncle was never really into hunting," Matti said. "He'd always come along, but I could tell he didn't enjoy killing animals. Last winter there were lynx tracks in our yard multiple times, and I thought about bringing it up to the village boys. We'd get permits to hunt the big cat and stop it from scaring our cattle. And you may laugh, but the next night I had a dream about your uncle. He told me to leave the tuft-eared felines alone and just mend my fence."

Matti made a cut in the wooden latch with his knife, looking embarrassed. Someone else would have taken that as a cue to hug him, but I just smiled and pulled the electric fence wire tighter.

On our last day in Hevonpersiinsaari, I watered the rose bush I had planted on Frida's grave, and suddenly I felt David near me. I tried to drive him out of my mind. I planned to end this stupid celibacy as soon as I got back to Helsinki. I had nobody to be faithful to, and random sex would do my body good—maybe even my mind. I'd go for a man in a bar who had the signs of a hastily removed wedding ring. That kind of man wouldn't cause any trouble.

The sun was disappearing behind the lake, and my thoughts turned to Uncle Jari again. He had been buried in the Kaavi churchyard because I hadn't thought of cremating him. He belonged here, not under a rock. Then again, it didn't really matter where the body's final resting place was. Uncle Jari would always be in Hevonpersiinsaari, just like Frida.

I'd occasionally tried to reach Kassi for months. In July I stopped, thinking the number was no longer in use, but now I decided to give it one more try. If nobody answered, I'd let that one last connection to David disappear. I walked along the dock and called.

"This is Rytkönen."

8

I hung up on him as quickly as I could and turned the phone off. Although I was using a burner phone, it could still be traced. What was Rytkönen's game? Laitio considered him a pencil pusher, but Laitio wasn't always right.

I walked back into the house where Monika was working on her laptop. I hadn't brought mine with me and asked Monika if I could use hers after she was done. I was going to run some searches on Rytkönen. Laitio had called him Mara, so his full name was most likely Martti or Mauri or Markku. He had a connection to David, and Laitio didn't know about it. I could feel sweat on my lower back, and my breathing become labored, like it always did when I began to panic. Monika noticed my attempts at calming my breathing.

"Is something wrong?" she asked.

"No." I grabbed a beer from the fridge, and the Olvi bottle made a familiar hissing sound when I opened it against the edge of the counter. Uncle Jari had taught me this nifty trick well before I'd reached legal drinking age.

Monika knew I was lying, but she didn't ask any questions. It was one of the reasons I liked her. She listened to me and didn't assume she had to know everything about me.

"Maija's *sultsinas* will definitely be on the menu," Monika said as she got up. "I've rarely had such a treat. I just thought they came from farther east, from Russian Karelia."

"Didn't Maija tell you that her mother was evacuated from Salmi? That's where her sultsinas, Karelian pastries, and mushroom dishes come from," I said before turning to her computer. "Let me check something before we go to bed."

Monika had bought a company van, but she didn't like driving it, so I was often her chauffeur. I was glad we had only one beer in case we needed to leave in a hurry. Monika went to Uncle Jari's old bedroom to read, and I began searching for information. First I tried Mauri Rytkönen, but there were no relevant results. Martti Rytkönen, however, brought up something interesting: "'Although we should be mindful of escalating security threats, it bears repeating that it's now easier than ever for international criminals to become active in Finland,' comments Officer Martti Rytkönen from the National Bureau of Investigation's foreign department."

A couple of clicks more and there he was, winning a bodybuilding competition for the police department. A link took me to his bio. Rytkönen, Martti Kullervo, licentiate of law, born 1975 in Iisalmi. Currently employed by the National Bureau of Investigation's foreign department, previously worked under Europol in Brussels between 2003 and 2009. Likes bodybuilding and karate. No mention of a family or an address, which was understandable. I called the white pages for his personal number, but all they could give me was his work number.

Obviously I couldn't start stalking Rytkönen, but Reiska might be able to do it. I'd try the old-fashioned approach once I got to Helsinki. But why was Rytkönen called Kassi in David's contact list? All the other code names had been animals, so I was sure the Estonian word for *cat* would have been used for someone from

David's home country, maybe Brother Gianni. Once again I was proved wrong. And why did Kassi Rytkönen pick up the phone now, after months of silence?

Before bed I put my small gun case into my equipment bag. Monika didn't need to see the gun, and once I got to Yrjö Street, I'd get a lock for the closet where I was going to keep the locker. When I had some free time, I'd set up a fake wall in the closet and practice at the shooting range. I was a real liability with my rusty skills.

Back in Helsinki we were greeted by an uptight building inspector who claimed our blueprints weren't up to code. Monika filled me in on his reputation among restaurateurs; he was known to accept payoffs from larger chains who wanted to keep out competition. The next few days we had to clarify our blueprints and do our best to convince the inspector that our restaurant would serve traditional food, not an ethnically confused lunch buffet. There were a few times I thought of bringing Reiska out to school the stickler, but Monika would never have approved.

I did end up using Reiska when I needed to call Kassi. I'd practice speaking in Reiska's unintelligible, raspy, stuttering voice. So far nobody had questioned the speaker's sex, but I was treading on more dangerous ground now that I used Reiska to create a voice that sounded like David.

Whenever I was alone in Helsinki, I tried out his voice, but there weren't many opportunities. The safest places were the jogging tracks in Hietaniemi Park and Kaivopuisto Park. My next three calls to Kassi came up empty; the number could not be reached. Most likely Rytkönen only picked up when he was in a safe place.

We'd been in Helsinki for ten days when I finally got through. I was walking along the seashore, just about to pass the rock club Nosturi. As soon as I switched my voice to a muddled tenor, I began to swagger like Reiska, too.

"This is Rytkönen. And don't hang up this time, goddamn it."
The Savonian dialect was completely absent from his voice. Perhaps
he thought a foreigner like David wouldn't understand it. "Are you
back in Finland?" he asked.

"No," I replied, although this lie would be very short-lived.
I could just imagine him grinding his teeth. Was he surprised or
fearful to hear from David? The other guy in David's contact list,
Cavallo, had been snuffed. Was Rytkönen aware that a phone call
from David might mean danger?

"You're only supposed to call this number when you're in
Finland. Where are you?"

"I followed Cavallo."

"Cavallo? Am I supposed to know who that is?"

"You don't know Cavallo? Who is this?" I demanded.

"Seriously, what are you on? Did you forget our agreement?
If you have nothing to say, then let's hang up. Or is your burden
becoming too heavy?"

I hoped Rytkönen would address me by name. He had already
revealed who he was, but anonymity for the other caller didn't give
me any clues, so I had to risk it.

"Who do you think you're talking to?" I began to cough, and I
wasn't faking it. Making my voice this raspy was beginning to take
its toll.

"Stop messing with me, Stahl," Rytkönen said.

"Phones can be stolen, you know. And isn't it strange that I'm
speaking fluent Finnish, with no Estonian accent?"

The other end went quiet. My mind was racing. Maybe
Rytkönen wasn't Kassi. Phones could indeed be stolen. People could
find out unlisted numbers, and then use them for new phones. I
needed to quickly come up with a plan that would confuse Rytkönen
even more.

"I have Stahl's phone," I continued. "Unfortunately, he's unable to talk right now. You better find him before he loses something more valuable."

Rytkönen hung up. I turned the phone off and removed the phone card with my gloved hands. I crushed the card under my heel and tossed it into the nearest trash can and buried it under some empty beer cases. I kept listening for police cars. Rytkönen wouldn't take long to trace the call. I wore a baseball cap, large sunglasses, teal-colored yoga pants down to my knees, a tank top, and a fanny pack where I kept my keys, phone, money, and gloves. I didn't look like a man who had just called Rytkönen.

I spotted the first police car as I turned on Tehdas Street to head back downtown. A coincidence, or were they after me? Had there been CCTVs around, recording me making the call? I was hoping Rytkönen wasn't that smart and was looking for David, or at least a man. My cap and sunglasses had hidden my face pretty well, and I'd maintained Reiska-like body language the whole time. If Laitio saw the CCTV images, I wouldn't be fooling him.

The police car passed me near the corner of St. John's Church. I hopped on the tram, feeling bad about destroying David's phone; it was my last trace of him. Still I expected to find a message from him every time I received a new text or when I checked my e-mail. I gave Mrs. Voutilainen a hopeful call every now and then to check if I'd gotten any mail. Her voice grew more pitiful each time she said no.

When I hadn't heard anything from Laitio, I called to see how he was doing. He didn't say anything about Rytkönen getting calls from someone pretending to be David Stahl. Information didn't seem to travel well within the Bureau, or at least not between Rytkönen and Laitio. I hadn't yet come up with a good plan to talk to Rytkönen without revealing my identity. I wrote to Brother Gianni, but all I got back was a postcard of Sant'Antimo's monastery in the mist, with a deflating note: "Dear Hilja, I have nothing new to tell you. You just need to accept it."

When Monika was out one evening visiting family, I took the kaleidoscope and broke the bottom. First, all I saw were shards of glass spread on the table in bits of white, purple, pink, and violet. The next layer contained yellow, green, and black. The spy novels I'd read as a girl came to mind, thinking of enormously valuable jewels within pieces of glass, so I started scrutinizing each piece. Although I had planned on buying a microscope after I'd graduated from Queens, I never followed through. A magnifying glass would suffice, and I could also use it for the classic glass-scratching test to find valuable pieces.

There were a few hundred pieces, and nothing stood out. When I brought the kaleidoscope to my eye, all I saw was a reflection from the mirror inside. There was some room between the mirror and the brass casing, but I didn't know how to get to it. I could try melting it, but that would destroy the contents. I had to find someone who knew how the thing was constructed. I didn't believe in seven years of bad luck from breaking a mirror, but I still didn't feel comfortable breaking it. The object was so masterfully made that breaking it seemed wrong. Still, I needed answers, so it had to be done.

The broken mirror revealed a rolled-up piece of paper, and I opened it. The message was short and in Swedish, and it made me curse out loud: "Dear Hilja, I know you too well. I hope you've figured out the meaning behind the map and the ring. David."

If I hadn't already broken the kaleidoscope, I'd have thrown it out the window. What was this childish treasure hunt? As if David were laughing at me from afar, maybe even beyond the grave. For a moment I hated him.

I didn't want to look at the ring, but I couldn't bring myself to throw it away. There was something familiar about it. Was it a ring we'd both looked at in a shop window? I couldn't recall that happening, especially because I'd only worn jewelry as a front. I'd never dreamed of an engagement ring like some other girls who had plans of how many diamonds they wanted. The image of my mother's severed hand with gleaming rings on her fingers had destroyed any notion I had of a safe marriage.

At Riikka's wedding I got wasted and almost had sex with the groom's barely legal cousin. Luckily I had had my wits about me and backed out. I would have only hurt the young man, and he would have become a nuisance. I had a moral hangover for two days afterward.

Luckily starting a restaurant didn't allow me time to dwell on things. Our staff was almost ready. The chef who prepped cold foods and two of the waiters who'd originally worked at Chez Monique had been planning on leaving their current jobs, and Monika had been clear about the new restaurant being quite different from Chez Monique.

We were trying to come up with a name for the restaurant one evening while screwing handles onto the cupboards.

"We can't have a nameless restaurant forever," I said after we'd come up with one ridiculous suggestion after another.

Monika stopped. "Nameless . . . that's actually a pretty good name! Just think about it. We're serving dishes that have no names—there's no beef Wellington or Sacher cake. We have foods developed by regular people over hundreds of years, treats for unknown, everyday people. Chez Monique had always been about my personality, a stupid brand. This should be the opposite. The person who cooks doesn't matter. It's the taste and the origin of the food that's important."

"You do know what *nameless* means in Finnish, right? Panties," I reminded her. She laughed.

"It's a bonus if the name is slightly playful. Besides, nobody uses euphemisms to talk about underwear when most clothing stores display it in their windows," Monika said.

"But Nameless doesn't sound convincing. What would it be in French?" I asked.

"*Sans Nom*," Monika said, pondering. "Kind of in the same vein as Chez Monique. Its opposite."

That's how the restaurant became Nameless in French. Monika demanded that the grand opening had to be on October 8, the date for Hilja's name day in the Finnish calendar. Before that we'd go to a food convention in Turku to advertise our concept. I tried to convince Monika not to, because conventions were terrible from a security standpoint, but she wouldn't budge. At first she had refused to set up CTTVs and burglar alarms in Sans Nom, but she changed her mind in early September.

When we arrived at the restaurant on a rainy Wednesday morning, we saw that the large window next to the entrance was broken. I couldn't tell what the burglars had been looking for; the restaurant was barely furnished, and none of the alcohol had been brought in from storage. There were muddy footprints and broken glass. The prints were everywhere, even in the untiled restrooms and the break room. The lock for the back door had some scratches on it that weren't there the day before. These burglars weren't very experienced.

"Should we call the police?" Monika asked.

I didn't know what to tell them. Maybe whoever broke in was just looking for a place to stay the night, something to eat. The back patio often hosted a group of drunks, and I knew some of them had been living out of the Dumpster. They may have been looking for warmth on a damp night. I told Monika I'd go talk to them, but I couldn't find them. So I called the police, but they didn't care. They didn't even check for fingerprints, just told us to fix the window and get security cameras. They said there had been similar break-ins recently, and they'd get in touch with us if they found anything.

There was a knock on the door that afternoon. It was one of the regulars from the back patio, Veikko. He seemed harmless and was never aggressive when he was drunk. He spent most of his time sitting on a folding chair and looking out to sea.

"Come on in," I told him in a friendly tone, but Veikko stood at the door and pointed at the window that I'd temporarily covered in cardboard.

"They really did a number on the place, those rascals," he said.

"Did you see who broke the window?" I asked.

"They were them bald-headed men—what do you call strong boys like that—the size of tanks? I was too afraid to intervene. Did they make a huge mess?" Veikko asked.

Veikko had woken up around two in the morning to steps and clinking sounds. The baldies had first tried to break the back door but failed. Then they moved to the front of the building, and Veikko had followed to see what they were up to.

"They were looking for someone. They left shouting cuss words. I didn't go near the window, thinking I'd be blamed for it. The cops love to toss us in jail even if we haven't done anything."

"So you think they were looking for someone? Was it Monika?" I asked, although I was pretty sure that wasn't the case. "Were they Finnish?"

"Yes, they spoke in Finnish. And if I heard correctly, they were talking about some dude. Saying that the dude wasn't in," said Veikko.

"Dude? What dude?" asked Monika, but I already had an idea.

A break-in at Sans Nom could have meant that Rytkönen or one of his allies thought David Stahl was in Finland and staying with me.

I bought and installed the CCTV at the restaurant that evening, and I didn't hear anything from the police. Instead, David began to appear in my dreams. In them, a creature with David's body and the head of a lynx appeared and made love to me. Once I woke up to the feeling of a rough tongue on my cheek. I kept on calling for David, then Frida, and once I realized they were both gone, I almost burst into tears.

"Leave me alone, Stahl," I yelled into my pillow. I still wanted to keep Frida close to me.

At the end of September, I went to the Tapiola neighborhood with Monika. She hadn't found fitting flared black waiter's slacks from the Stockmann department store in Helsinki, so she was sent off to a store in Tapiola to try on possible options. The pants mostly fit, but they'd need to be shortened an inch, and neither one of us had time for sewing despite our van being full of cotton tablecloths and towels we'd salvaged from secondhand stores, all in need of mending. Monika's plan was to use lots of recycled items in Sans Nom. Even the van was used. Monika had it painted by a student at the vocational school. The restaurant sign looked like it was created by the best local graffiti artist, and it was surrounded by artistic renditions of vegetables: carrots, potatoes, beets, and artichokes. I thought the van was too flashy. We should have invested in a more anonymous-looking van to match Sans Nom so nobody would pay attention to us.

It was early afternoon as I left to pick up Monika's tailor-made slacks. On my way she called me and asked me to get two pairs of medium beige pantyhose while I was at it. For the first time in her employment, I had to wonder whether I was a bodyguard, an assistant, or an errand girl. When I left Stockmann with my purchase, I pulled next to an SUV at the traffic light and glanced over. The man riding shotgun looked familiar, and it took me a moment to recognize him. It was Usko Syrjänen. Apparently I ogled long enough, because he rolled his window down.

"You want an autograph or what?" Syrjänen sounded shocked. "This is certainly not the place for it."

Syrjänen's car got the green light, and although mine was still red, I swerved quickly to his lane and disregarded the angry honking of cars behind me as I began to follow the SUV onto Länsiväylä. I wanted to see who was working for Syrjänen as a driver.

I almost crashed into the median when I finally caught up with the SUV again and saw who it was. He'd shaved the goatee off his pale face and was wearing aviators, but I knew it was him. He'd once kidnapped my employer and gone after me, too. The SUV was driven by Yuri Trankov.

9

I barely got the van under control. I'd sped past the SUV and couldn't slow down because the car behind me was riding my bumper. What was Trankov's business in Finland, and what was he doing with Syrjänen? Trankov had kidnapped a Finnish politician a couple of years earlier, which got him banned from the country. Had the ban been lifted? Had Helena Lehmusvuo, the politician, known about it? Although Helena had claimed she'd survived the incident without a scratch and very little emotional damage, seeing her kidnapper would rip all the old wounds open again.

I didn't know what to do. Follow Syrjänen and Trankov? I didn't know if Trankov had seen me. I was a nobody to Syrjänen, who hadn't recognized me. I didn't know how far they were going and if following them would give me any answers, so following them seemed insane.

At Suomenoja I took the exit and turned back toward Helsinki. Monika was waiting for me at the restaurant, but I needed to see Laitio first, and I trusted he was at his place on Urheilu Road instead of the main offices. I could also ask him about Rytkönen.

Traffic was at a standstill in Ruoholahti. Why weren't people using public transportation instead of driving? Most of the cars had only one person in them. To the left of me, a woman was applying lipstick and talking into a Bluetooth earpiece. She was probably one of those people who watched TV on an elliptical machine while frying phyllo dough dumplings.

When I finally got to Urheilu Street, there was no parking. I didn't want to get a ticket with the company van—bad publicity—so I parked behind the nearby hockey arena, then jogged back to Laitio's place. The jog did me good, my only recent exercise.

I rang Laitio's buzzer.

"We're not buying anything," a curt reply came, the voice I had hoped to hear.

"This is Ilveskero. All hell's broken loose. Trankov is back in Finland. I just saw him, and you won't believe this. He was driving Usko Syrjänen around."

"Yuri Trankov? Paskevich's bastard son? He wasn't supposed to ever come. I'll let you in, but wait a minute. I'm not decent yet."

I took my time climbing the stairs, trying not to think about what Laitio meant by *decent*. I was pissed at myself for not getting Syrjänen's license plate number. What was that thing Mike Virtue had said? Even if we were knocking on death's door, we couldn't let our concentration waver. And that's exactly what I'd done when I was stunned at seeing Trankov.

I waited behind the door a while before it opened. Laitio was wearing mustard yellow again, but he was not wearing a tie and had on a cardigan. Maybe ties were reserved for visits from the boss. The apartment smelled like French fries. My stomach growled.

Laitio invited me in with a nod. The usual wall of cigar smoke was gone, and the place felt like it was just cleaned and aired out. Laitio opened an enormous leather briefcase and pulled out a laptop.

"Proper archives, all gone. Now everything is here, behind a password. What if I forget the passwords or someone else gets ahold of them? It was different back in the day. Multiple padlocks and a damn angry lady, Eini Rantanen, made sure no outsider would have access to the Bureau's classified information. Whether it was the president or the police chief, you still had to explain what you were looking for. Even President Koivisto had to wait for almost half an hour before Eini brought him the information he needed. Not so these days. And where did that damned mouse go again?" Laitio was poking the laptop's touch pad and cursed.

"I'd get an external mouse," I said.

"Cats have a damn external mouse," he said. "There we go. Let's see. Trankov, Yuri Valentin. There. What the hell? His ban was overturned in June."

Helena Lehmusvuo had never pressed charges for the kidnapping, and instead there'd been an agreement to keep quiet about it. I had no desire to protect the ministers and members of the Finnish Security Intelligence Service who had made the decision, but I did as Helena told me and didn't leak any information to journalists. Mike Virtue had made sure we'd remember how important being loyal to the client was, and I kept that in mind even when I got nothing out of it.

"Who made this decision? Who has authorization?" I demanded.

"Goddamned bosses at the Bureau or Intelligence Service have run some sort of a secretive preliminary investigation and decided not to press charges. Or Trankov was let in the country because he could be used to catch a bigger fish. Maybe they were after Trankov's dad. Paskevich may have an ax to grind with Syrjänen, as he was a business partner to Paskevich's now-dead enemy Vasiliev. Remember how Syrjänen claimed to know nothing about Vasiliev's criminal activities? It was an easy part to play—all the witnesses were dead," Laitio said.

"And nobody thought of asking Stahl what Syrjänen's role had been?" I asked.

Laitio gave me a sideways glance. "You didn't ask, either, did you?"

"I tried, but he doesn't reveal much, not even in bed." The thought of this was really painful. Besides, Stahl wasn't interested in Syrjänen. He was tracking Vasiliev and his business plans. "What does your database say about Stahl or Usko Syrjänen?" I asked.

"Why would I tell you?"

"Do you know if Syrjänen was aware of what was going down a couple of years ago?"

"I have no idea what the bosses know," yelled Laitio. "All right, Syrjänen, let's search for him." Laitio's one-finger typing method was painfully slow. "Here we go. Syrjänen has had so many speeding tickets that they could pay for months of my salary. Looks like his license was taken away because of the tickets, so no wonder he needs a chauffeur. The plate number for the SUV is USK-O3. He has four other cars, too, and the license plates all have the letters USK and numbers from two to six. The first seems to have been demolished already."

"Man wants his name everywhere in some form. His boat was called *I Believe*, *believe* being the English translation of his name, Usko," I explained to Laitio.

"His current boat is *I Believe 2*, three feet longer than the previous one. Syrjänen doesn't place small bets when he's in the game, but I can't find anything else about him besides the usual. I guess I don't have the right passwords. I'll look into why Trankov's ban was overturned. I still have it in me to blackmail my bosses. They don't want their messes in the newspapers."

My stomach rumbled even louder now, and Laitio heard it.

"Are you on some sort of diet?" he asked.

"No. I just didn't have time to eat today."

"Women. Always trying to lose weight. My daughter isn't eating carbs these days, and my old lady is on some bizarre soup diet. With the money we've spent on those soup mixes, I could've gotten a freezer full of good steaks. Anyway, I'll make one more search for Stahl."

There was commotion in the apartment next door, and something heavy fell onto the ground. Then there was a familiar-sounding yelp. Frida had made the same sound when she was annoyed.

"Damned Kokki destroying the house again. I just hope he knocked down that damn ugly vase my wife inherited from her aunt. If that hideous pot broke, I'll give the cat extra shrimp in his dish tonight. Wait a minute while I check on him. My wife wants to get rid of him because he pees on the rugs. Honestly, Kokki has better taste in interior design than she does."

I couldn't believe my eyes when Laitio got up and started walking toward the other apartment without locking his computer. He had to know I was going to snoop around. This man was a walking intelligence risk to the Bureau. He'd also saved his login name and password on the home page. I put them in my cell phone. When Laitio returned I was back in my chair, stomach still growling.

"He knocked over a chair playing with a ball of yarn. The old tom still has energy. I told the wife that if the cat goes, so do I. So far that's been effective," Laitio said.

I'd never seen any of Laitio's family, and he wasn't in the habit of talking about them. He understood that someone could use them to hurt him, although it seemed like the best way to torture him would be to snag his cat.

He settled at the computer and began poking at the keys with his right index finger. Didn't they teach typing in his days at the academy?

"Well, I'll be damned. Stahl's information seems to have been wiped ever since Rytkönen got on board this summer. Nothing's like it used to be. I have copies of those old papers, but there's nothing in them you don't already know. Caruso has tried to track down Dolfini, but he's been having a hard time without resources to bribe people. Those Italian informants are damned greedy. And as long as there's no body, there's no murder. The Italian boys know what they're doing. Listen, Ilveskero, it's best if we mind our own business. When the big shots decide to stay quiet, the lion of justice becomes a petulant kitten whose neck can be broken at any moment."

"Why did you become a cop?" I asked, my stomach growling.

"Oh, I almost forgot." Laitio dug into the pockets of his stretched-out cardigan and produced a banana. "Eat that. I don't want to listen to your stomach anymore. My wife says one banana is enough for a woman's lunch."

Laitio was still full of surprises. The banana would have satisfied me as well as a skinny squirrel would've filled a lynx's empty stomach, so I tried not to eat it too fast.

"Why did I become a cop? Because it's fun to bust criminals. Or just for the feeling of being in power, you know? You get to insult people legally." Laitio opened the top drawer of his writing desk and pulled out a cigar. The cutter made a sharp snap, and he put a Cohiba in his mouth. He got the match to light on his third try.

"And the reason you became a bodyguard was to make up for your mother's inability to protect herself from your father," Laitio said. His eyes lit up when the first puff of smoke escaped his lips.

"Armchair psychology. I was four when it happened—how would a kid prevent a murder?"

"Kids often think everything is their fault. Have you heard anything from Keijo Kurkimäki?"

My back stiffened as it always did when I heard my father's name, though he was no father to me. He'd sired me and left me with the genes of a murderer. I shook my head. As a teenager I'd imagined the most gruesome ways to kill my father. Uncle Jari had been worried about me when I'd placed a hold at the library for books on torture methods.

"Books really should come with age limits," he had said when I was reading an English book on the Inquisition. Uncle didn't understand much of the text, but the pictures of Catherine wheels and testicle-crushing devices were illustrative enough. "Why are you reading this? No wonder you scream in your sleep with all these nightmares. Maybe you should go and talk to one of those—"

"I don't need a shrink! I just need to know what I should look out for," I'd told him.

My phone rang. It was Monika asking what was taking so long. She thought I'd been in an accident. This gave me an excuse to take off. Laitio told me to keep him updated if I saw Trankov again, and he'd ask around about Syrjänen.

I stopped at a nearby deli for a bacon sandwich and ate it while I walked to the van. I appreciated Monika's ideology on ethical foods, and I liked working for her, but I had my vices.

It was almost midnight by the time we got home. The grand opening was on the following Friday, and we had to spend some of the weekend in Turku at the convention. Monika took a shower and hit the hay—she had to wake up at seven. I broke into the Bureau's database. I was worried that Laitio was computer savvy enough to check the last time his username was used to log in, but I had to take that chance. I made random searches for ministers, business owners, and trashy celebrities, and I could find something on almost anyone. There were not just criminal records; this database also included information that should never have been saved about some people's private lives. Hardly anyone had anything interesting in their records. This told me more about Laitio's status in the Bureau than anything else: secrets were kept from him.

Of course I couldn't avoid checking what was listed under my name. I had no criminal record, so there shouldn't have been anything. It looked like the Bureau thought of me as a security risk, because my folder was larger than the current prime minister's. In addition to my current and former name (Hilja Kanerva Suurluoto), there was a description of how I'd witnessed my mom getting stabbed to death by my father when I was a kid, information on my time at the security academy in Queens, copies of my security guard and weapon license (no record of misuse), and a list of my work history. Anita Nuutinen's murder and my role in it were described briefly. I'd quit the gig a day before she was shot to death near Moscow's Frunzenskaya subway station. The culprit was a homeless alcoholic who had tried to rob her.

I looked for Helena Lehmusvuo next. There was no mention of her kidnapping two years earlier. I felt sorry for Laitio. Maybe Rytkönen and his cronies were just happy to keep him from asking difficult questions. The smoking rule had been a convenient excuse for Laitio to work from home, where he didn't bother the *important* people. Before I turned the computer off, I checked my e-mail. Nothing.

Turku hosted a book and music convention at the same time the food convention was going on. I'd always hated places that were teeming with people but where nobody performed security checks. You never knew when a frustrated young author whose work had been rejected by every publishing house would decide to take revenge, though people from the fine arts realm were a naïve bunch—the first to condemn acts of violence, although they made those acts possible by not preparing for them.

Monika was supposed to cook everyday food from Mozambique for an hour in a studio kitchen that introduced people to foods from various cultures. I'd demanded the blueprints for the space beforehand, and I saw that the nearest exit could only be reached through narrow hallways—death traps to people stuck in them if there was a panic. The organizers had offered to provide ingredients, but I'd told Monika not to use them. I wanted to double-check each package. Sans Nom had raised some interest and hubbub in Finland's restaurant scene, and it wouldn't have been the first time Monika had enemies. A public kitchen at a convention was a great place to prove how incompetent she was.

"Hilja, I know you're looking out for me, but aren't you being a bit too paranoid?" Monika asked as we drove past Muurla on the Turku highway. Cars were whizzing past us while the van was going at its maximum speed of fifty-five. Monika thought our van was ecological, and if we hadn't brought a bunch of ingredients with us, she'd demand we take the train.

I didn't reply. Monika knew my background. I'd made mistakes before. Anita Nuutinen had been killed, and although I had technically quit before it happened, I still felt responsible. Helena Lehmusvuo was kidnapped after I'd left her alone one afternoon. I wouldn't make these mistakes with Monika.

A Brazilian chef had taken over the convention center kitchen, preparing steaks so thick they'd feed an entire village. Monika shook her head. The meat counter had a banner: "Conventionsale." It was written in enormous letters, and Monika asked me if those words were really supposed to be written together. I laughed at her pickiness.

After the steaks, people wouldn't be interested in cassava or chicken marinated in piri-piri. We might as well have been showing French people how to cook mac and cheese. I was, however, happy that the crowd was at a controllable size. A couple of excited older ladies in colorful caftans talked with Monika after her show, and the hostess responsible for the kitchen tried to shoo us off the stage. These ladies worked for a small publishing house specializing in alternative books, and they were trying to convince Monika to write a cookbook.

"Let's get Sans Nom's name out there first," Monika said, and the ladies giggled at her pun. Working at Chez Monique had shown me how some people treated Monika like a guru. I'd never understood people who put someone on a pedestal and followed every word and suggestion. Weren't we supposed to think for ourselves? That's what Mike Virtue had always told us: the security academy would provide us with tools to protect others, but the way we used those tools was up to us.

After her gig Monika wanted to look around the book convention. I reluctantly let her go. Someone played an alto violin in the lobby. I was afraid of a certain type of classical music, although I didn't know who the composers were; I didn't care for some symphonies and operas, but then there were tunes that forced me to look deep into myself. The blond-ponytailed violinist was playing exactly that type of tune, and of course it made Monika stop in her tracks. I breathed as deeply as I could and tried to think about something else, but the music forced its way into me, forced tears down my cheeks, made me uncomfortable yet immensely peaceful. To make matters worse, he played directly to us, looking from Monika to me, back and forth. His music saw through me. When the tune was over and Monika went to chat with the man, I had to walk away.

I pushed through the crowds to the book convention. Luckily the corner café wasn't very crowded. I could've had a beer right then, but I had to drive home. I was walking back to Monika and the violin man when I noticed a familiar face at a café table. Apparently Martti Rytkönen was the literary type. He had a pile of thin poetry books, and he was drinking something bubbly.

The music had made me careless, so I snuck closer until I was only a few feet away from Rytkönen. The different sections in the convention center were separated with large curtains, and I slipped behind one and pretended to be interested in the young adult novels. Then I pulled out my phone, called Kassi, and watched Rytkönen. He furiously patted his pockets. First he pulled out an iPhone, then another phone, then a third phone, an ancient bright-red Nokia.

"Rytkönen."

"I hear you," I whispered in Swedish.

"Lanotte, is that you?" Rytkönen's Swedish had as bad a Savonian lilt as mine. "Are you all right? Some scam artist called me a few weeks ago, speaking in Finnish and saying your phone was stolen. Nobody has heard from you since April, not even Jaan. What on earth is going on?"

10

Damn. So Rytkönen knew as much about David's whereabouts as I did, and he knew about David's fake identity. Was I supposed to swallow my pride and walk over to beg for information? Rytkönen had no reason to tell me anything. If David Stahl had a lady friend, what was the big deal? David didn't seem to think it was important. It had been almost six months since he'd taken off.

"Are you still there?" I saw Rytkönen furrow his brow. "Who had your phone?"

I was really tempted to mess with Rytkönen, and I was startled when I felt a hand on my shoulder. It was Monika. I had to hang up. I could hear Rytkönen cursing in Swedish.

"I tried to reach an old friend, thinking she might be here." I didn't like lying to Monika, but it had become habit. I saw Rytkönen shoving his phones back into his pockets. The women at the table next to him were amused. Then he got up. He didn't have a ring on his left hand, but that didn't mean anything these days. Rytkönen was storming toward me, so I quickly turned to peruse the books. I could feel him walk past me. I suggested to Monika that we head back to Helsinki because we had a lot to do before the grand opening.

It was so typical of Monika to organize an opening that embraced everyone. It was such a risk in a myriad of ways. Some of the people who were used to VIP treatment would get huffy and not show up—they didn't want to be lumped together with commoners—and an open house attracted questionable members of society. Monika was planning on serving a two-euro lunch soup every Monday, and everyone was welcome. Those who could afford it could pay a bit more if they wanted.

A couple of staff members were skeptical before the opening. They were worried about the business model. I calmed them down, convincing them that with Monika's savings from before, they'd always get their paycheck and that the restaurant's concept would catch on.

Wealth was a weird thing. I had always been a penny pincher, and when the euro came, I switched to pinching cents. The reason I'd been able to go to school in Queens was because of an inheritance from my grandmother on my father's side, but all that money and any other savings I'd scraped together before that was spent in New York. Uncle Jari had left me the cabin in Hevonpersiinsaari. He'd used all of his money to make sure I had food and shelter. I'd watched some of my wealthier employers blow ten thousand euros on furs and luxury vacations and not bat an eye. That money would've lasted us a year in Hevonpersiinsaari. Monika's wealth was also the worst kind: inherited money. I strongly believed she was trying to buy herself freedom from the sins of wealth.

David claimed he worked for the highest bidder. Where had Europol gotten the money to hire him as a hit man, and who had given his orders? Why did they have the right to kill terrorists? My American classmates accused Europeans of being morally prudish and not realizing that sometimes the only option would be vigilante justice and the death sentence. Mike Virtue silenced those voices quickly.

Oh, Mike, what advice would you give me now? I considered writing him an old-fashioned letter asking for help. I just couldn't find the right words. Mike would've told me off for the risks I had taken.

Mrs. Voutilainen used to be my source of good advice, but she had no idea about my problems, and I had no energy to make up stories. A couple of days before the grand opening, I saw her for tea, and the lynx painting Yuri Trankov made for her was still hanging in the living room. She'd thought Trankov was a nice young man who was artistically gifted. Mrs. Voutilainen thought of herself as a good judge of character, but even the best were sometimes mistaken.

The night before the opening, I dreamed about David. We were sitting on the Montemassi ruins, watching swallows. Suddenly David took flight with them and glided down into the valley. As he flew he grew wings on his back. I woke up sobbing. I got up for tissues and tried to forget the dream. It meant nothing. It was just a dream.

Monika wanted the restaurant to be spacious and bright. The walls were painted sunny yellow. The tables, chairs, and shelves were all ecologically selected domestic pine, and the upholstery was made of bright-red and black fabric. Soft elements had been added to the space to minimize echoing. Monika said it was hard to taste food if there was a lot of noise. The outside of the building looked fairly uninviting, its dark brick reminding me of a prison. Monika tried improving the look with potted cypress trees on both sides of the front door—you couldn't plant trees in cement.

Because people didn't need to RSVP to get in, we couldn't predict how much food and drink we would need. Monika had prepared for a crowd of hundreds. We were supposed to open the doors at six, so at five thirty, the staff came together in the dining room to make sure everything was in order. I was supposed to keep an eye on the room; the assistant became a bodyguard tonight.

Chaos broke a little before six. Monika received hugs, kisses, congratulations, and flowers. The youngest hostess and I did our best to rush the gifts out of the way. Monika was dressed in the slacks I'd picked up for her from Tapiola and a sunshine-orange blouse, but her face was as pale as ever.

Helena Lehmusvuo was among the first guests. She and Monika had met through a climate-change association as teenagers. Thanks to Monika, Helena had hired me and trusted me. In my own way I had screwed up that gig, too, so I wasn't particularly happy to see Helena. She looked frailer than I remembered, and her black hair and red lips made her look like a doll. Looks could deceive; Helena wasn't afraid of even the most powerful men in the world. Russian Prime Minister Vladimir Putin was one of her rivals because Helena felt Putin was restricting freedom of speech in Russia and abroad.

Helena gave Monika a Swedish cookbook. Just what she needed. I supposed she could use it for researching the genre if she was going to write a book about Sans Nom's recipes. Uncle Jari had owned one cookbook: a red waxy-covered *Home Cooking* from 1961. We'd done just fine with it, especially as Uncle rarely needed to check recipes for the foods he liked to make. I remembered the pictures. As a ten-year-old, to me the decorative tower cake covered in almonds looked fascinating, and I'd asked Uncle if we could bake one.

"That's beyond my skills, but go ahead, make one. Maija can probably help you," he suggested.

But even Maija from next door had been in over her head. She'd never made anything that fancy, and it was in a different category than sweet buns and sugar cookies. I remained stubborn like I always did when I really wanted something. I cut the patterns out of wax paper and shredded the almonds, then mixed the almonds with eggs and powdered sugar. The mixture behaved like it was supposed to in the oven, but building the tower was impossible. I managed to create a ten-inch-tall lump that looked nothing like the picture in the book and showed it to my uncle, slightly embarrassed. He stared at it a while, then did his best to sound encouraging: "My girl, you've baked the Leaning Tower of Pisa!"

The almond dough was so overly sweet that neither one of us could finish the cake. We left it in the yard for the birds, and it was soon gone. It became a funny memory. If Uncle or I said "Leaning Tower of Pisa," we'd laugh and almost taste the overly sweet cake. Once, in New York, I had bought a cake like the one from the book, and it didn't taste any better than the one I made. I told Uncle Jari about it in my last letter to him. The two of us would have preferred glazeless cinnamon rolls and *kalakukko* over those oddities from around the world.

Helena greeted me. A photographer for a magazine wanted her to pose with Monika, and they were pulled away from the crowds. People were congregating at the punch bowl; it looked like Monika's brother, who was in the visual arts, had parked himself next to the drinks. One of my missions for the evening was to make sure Petter didn't get too wasted, and if he did, I had to make sure he got home in a taxi. I liked Petter; even when he was completely plastered, he was never mean. He just got too emotional. Once, he was so drunk that he proposed to me. I'd given him at least fifty-three refusals.

Monika had set the food on a long table in the middle of the room, and the guests ate at smaller tables. I tried to eavesdrop, but I could only hear words without context.

"Bold."

"Very personal."

"Won't be around, come summer." This last snippet came from a mean-looking woman whose nose was shaved really small, and she had heavy eyelashes. I wanted to play clumsy and bump into her, spilling her glass of red wine all over her white satin shirt, but that would only hurt Monika.

Suddenly, Helena grabbed my wrist. She was upset and doing her best to remain calm.

"The man who drugged me is here," she said.

"Where?"

"At the large window next to the door."

I turned sixty degrees. Trankov was looking pleased with himself while he surveyed the crowd, as if he were the one netting the profits. He wore a perfectly fitting black three-piece suit, a black shirt, and a white silk tie. His hair was slicked back. He looked like a cheap mobster.

"Don't worry. I'll take care of this. Trankov won't attack you again," I assured her.

"But he's not even supposed to be in Finland."

"I know. I don't want to call the cops to the opening—it'll cause a ruckus. Just calm down."

Trankov had kidnapped Helena and drugged her enough that she barely remembered the incident, but she was able to recognize Trankov. I slowly moved toward the door because people I hardly knew wanted to greet me, and Petter gave me a hug on his way out to have a smoke. Trankov stood at the window like the king of the world and didn't seem the least bit surprised to see me.

"Good evening, Hilja Ilveskero," he said in English, pronouncing my name poorly. "It's been a while."

"You better leave. You're not welcome here. Or do you want me to call the cops?" I asked.

"But this event is open for everybody," he said innocently.

"Not for you. Get out."

Trankov remained calm. His smile annoyed me.

"I'm a free man in a free country. I'm not interested in Representative Lehmusvuo now that the decision to build the gas pipe has gone through. She's just a small fry. But you and me, we have some unfinished business. Women don't get uppity with me." Trankov said these last words tenderly, as if admitting his undying love for me. The old man next to us glared at Trankov.

"You put on quite a show for Valentin that one time. I'm pretty interested in all the sides you still haven't shown me," Trankov said. "Although, it looks like you've lost your touch since you're this easy to find. Do you still dress up as a man and look for me at railway stations? Did you miss me?"

"Don't flatter yourself." It was pretty impressive that he had figured Reiska out when I had tried to find Trankov before he found me. Of course I wouldn't tell him about this newfound respect.

I rested my hand on his shoulder. It was time for action. I could see in his eyes that he was ready to fight, but I didn't want Sans Nom in the papers because of a scuffle.

"You fooled Valentin, but you've never been a Vasiliev woman. Just a fuck for his apprentice, David Stahl."

Hearing David's name got to me. I couldn't hit Trankov out in the open, but I had a hard time controlling myself. I squeezed his shoulder harder.

"What do you know about Stahl?"

"A lot. Probably things you have no idea about, and Stahl's so-called employers are just as ignorant. But this is not the place for that conversation. Don't worry, Ilveskero. I'll find you again. We'll have a nice chat, *dorogaya maya.*" Trankov took my hand off his shoulder and kissed it.

I had to will myself not to slap him.

"Hilja, is this your new boyfriend?" Petter had smoked his cigarette pretty quickly. He saw that I wasn't enjoying Trankov's company.

"You'll always be my number one," I said to Petter and put my arm in his. I thought of how hard it would be to get in touch with the minister of the interior or the national police commissioner. Helena would know. Trankov had to be thrown out of the country, preferably in handcuffs. I followed Petter without taking another look at Trankov. When I glanced at the door a few minutes later, he was gone. Petter poured me some punch, but I refused. I had to stay alert.

I didn't have a chance to chat with Helena until later. Usually she didn't drink more than a glass of wine every now and then, but tonight she had more than usual. Her face was flushed, and her eyes were glazed. She seemed to be having such a good time. I hated to bring up Trankov.

"I'll get my police friends to find out why Trankov was allowed into Finland. Or do you want to take it up with the minister of the interior?" I asked her.

Helena waved in a way that showed she was tipsier than I thought.

"If he doesn't bother anyone, let's not get into it. I can't imagine anything worse than gossip magazines finding out about my kidnapping. I'm all for transparency, but everyone doesn't need to know about what happened." Even the wine couldn't hide the fear in her eyes.

"I'll have a word with Chief Constable Laitio nevertheless. You remember him—he was in that meeting at the Government Palace."

"I think I do. The cigar smoker with the bushy mustache."

"That's the one. And I have a question," I continued, although Helena probably wasn't in the mood for politics. "What would it take for a public recreation property to become private?"

"Who owns the land?"

"Some foundation or an association. Or the government. I don't know," I said.

"Whoever owns the land has to be willing to sell. If there are plans to change the purpose of the area, then the change has to be put into the regional assembly plans," Helena explained.

"And what does that take?"

"The plans are usually prepared by the regional council, then decided on by the regional board and finalized by the Ministry of the Environment."

"How easily can these people be bribed?"

Someone ran into me from behind, and I bumped into Helena, spilling wine on her dress. Helena went to the break room with Monika to try to get the stain out. I memorized what she'd told me. Syrjänen's note had contemplated who the next minister would be, probably referring to the minister of environmental affairs. If Syrjänen was funding the person in charge, he'd have someone on his side.

Jouni appeared, screaming at me to help out in the kitchen—someone had to fill the dishwasher. Except for a couple of broken plates, toppled glasses of wine, and guests who had had a bit too much punch, the opening had gone well. Later on the crowd thinned, and Veikko dared to show himself with some of his buddies.

"Apologies for the stench," one of them said. "At least Veikko has a clean shirt on. He bought it for a euro from a secondhand store. Nice, huh?" The man shakily poured punch into his glass. Petter, who now drunkenly loved the entire world, began to praise the man's deeply wrinkled face. He wanted to paint him. He'd asked me to model for him, too, wearing as little as possible. I'd always declined. Petter was more eager than Monika to please everyone, like a golden retriever. Monika was more of a shepherd, herding others onto the right path.

I put on my jacket and stepped outside. The seashore was only a few steps away. I could hear the hum of traffic from Länsiväylä and Lauttasaari Road, and the evening was getting nippy. Hints of stars were in the sky; they were so pale I wouldn't have seen them if I hadn't known where to look. I thought of my dream about David from the night before, him growing wings high above Montemassi. I could feel his presence. Someone snuck up beside me, but it wasn't David. He never smelled of cigars.

"Thanks for the invite, and sorry I'm a bit late." Laitio stood there, holding a small envelope. "My sister-in-law had a bridge party, and you can't miss those if you want to keep a roof over your head. Happy Name Day, Hilja." Laitio handed the envelope to me. "Open it when you're alone. I'm not sure if it's a proper gift, and you didn't get these papers from me, understand?"

"Thank you."

"Don't thank me yet. Is there any food left? And I could use a shot of something strong. My sister-in-law is such an Anglophile that all she serves is tea and biscuits."

Judging by the smell, Laitio had some drinks already—he'd known how to prepare for bridge night. I realized I'd never heard him call me by my first name.

"Trankov was here," I told him as he handed me a cigar. I needed it.

"That's what you told me yesterday," Laitio said.

"No, I meant here in Sans Nom. Helena Lehmusvuo saw him and almost had a panic attack."

"What a damned nuisance. Trankov, not Lehmusvuo." Laitio's cigar went out, and he had a hard time lighting it again with the gusts of wind. I stepped in front of Laitio to protect his cigar from the wind and lit his Cohiba with my lighter.

"I got all the way to the national police commissioner's secretary. I couldn't get any further. Why would they tell a regular police officer why someone's warrant and entry ban had been revoked?"

"How about you ask Rytkönen," I said.

"And you think he'd tell me? Was Trankov threatening you?"

"Sort of."

"I still have authorization to arrest anyone guilty of unlawful threats, you know. Tell me if you need my services. I'll put that guy behind bars," Laitio promised.

A long gray hair stood out from Laitio's left eyebrow, and the bags under his eyes were heavy. His bald head was covered in a brown-checked wool cap. We walked toward the front door. Neither of us felt like staying outside to finish our cigars, so we stubbed them out. Laitio placed what was left of his into a tiny box he carried around. There were about thirty guests and fifteen staff members left in the restaurant. Helena had gone home. I went to the kitchen to find food for Laitio. I was sure Chef Jouni would have a hidden stash of bacon somewhere, and the shelves were overflowing with organic eggs from Monika's friend's chicken farm in Fiskars.

"Could I get you to fix bacon and eggs for a hungry bridge player?" I asked Jouni. He was a year older than me and had tattoos from head to toe. Even I would've switched sides of the street if I'd seen him approaching.

"Is garlic all right?" he asked.

"All the usual spices please." I took a peek into the restaurant and was surprised to see Petter serving Laitio a beer while they chatted. Sans Nom didn't have beer on tap, and even the bottled selection was small; Monika had focused on a couple of domestic microbreweries. Petter had guessed Laitio was a fan of darker beers, just like himself. "I take my women blond and beer dark." I'd heard this tired joke a million times.

Looking around I realized this was a good life—a group of people with common goals and great friends. There was no room for unnecessary feelings, no David Stahl–like characters to mess things up. My life would be perfect if I could stop breaking down. If there wasn't so much to lose. I would no longer look back and only push forward. Even if I never found out what happened to David, I wouldn't care. I had never let anyone mess up my heart the way David did, and I couldn't afford any more mistakes.

I brought Laitio's plate to him and went to lock the front door. The security camera was right above it. Another camera was at the back door, and the other two were in the dining area. Monika hadn't allowed me to install one in the kitchen; she was worried her staff would think she didn't trust them. I'd already run a background check on a couple of the oddballs, but nothing came up.

Laitio looked satisfied, bacon grease dripping from his mustache. His breath reeked of garlic. My shift was over, so I had a beer. Monika looked happy but exhausted. The opening had been like a wedding: not a resolution or a happily-ever-after ending, but a beginning to an uncertain future.

I told Petter to take Monika home in a cab—I'd take care of closing. By two in the morning, the last of the dishwashers had gone home. The cleaners wouldn't arrive until later. I sat in the dark restaurant and enjoyed the smells of garlic, thyme, tarragon, and rose. According to Monika one of the toughest problems in running a restaurant was keeping the place smelling fresh and inviting, which was why I hid my cigar smoking from her.

When I left I took the shortest path to Yrjö Street. Hardly anyone was out, and the walk got my adrenalin pumping. I suddenly remembered the envelope Laitio had given me, and as I read it everything became uncertain again.

11

The first of the reports—or rather, copies of the reports—were in English. The recipient and the names of the senders had been blacked out, but it was clear the sender was a big shot at Europol, probably the one who had hired David to infiltrate Vasiliev's crew and given the order to kill. The report mentioned how David Stahl had fulfilled his mission, received severe frostbite at sea, and retreated to an unknown hiding place. Probably the mountain hut in southern Spain where I had visited him. The report also described how Stahl had delivered the SR-90 isotope to the "headquarters," whatever that meant. The report was dated March of the previous year, when I had been with David in Spain. It also noted how Stahl's whereabouts were only known to his closest colleagues and a female friend whose reliability was vouched for by the Finnish National Bureau of Investigation. She'd sworn confidentiality. I was aware that Europol knew about me. All agents were under observation, and I was a potential liability.

The next report was from March of this year, detailing how Spain had become too hot for Stahl. An anonymous entity had found his location, and he'd received numerous death threats that he'd reported to his bosses. A decision was made to move Stahl, and during the winter he'd reported from Kiel and Tartu. Europol had arranged a passport for him under the name Daniel Lanotte. After Lanotte left his family, he'd gotten an apartment with the help of personal connections.

I knew about all of this. Then the more mysterious section began. After Lanotte arrived in Italy he'd stopped reporting to his contact in Europol. David was never officially on Europol's payroll, because his mission and true identity were supposed to be known to a select few to ensure his safety and protect an extremely delicate mission. Because he'd been in touch with an international mega-criminal, Ivan Gezolian, when he purchased the isotope, it was determined that he needed a secret identity. However, it turned out that during an investigation of some other business Gezolian was conducting, Stahl-Lanotte was found to have been in communication with Gezolian's Italian contact without an order from Europol. I thought of the mean Russian at the truffle restaurant. Was he Gezolian's contact?

"Gezolian has not been arrested, as there is an ongoing investigation about where he received the SR-90 isotope. Reconnaissance missions to Belarus have produced no results. It is possible that the location is one of the decommissioned nuclear power plants from the Soviet era. The situation in Belarus is unstable, and intelligence recovery missions are problematic. It is also unclear whether Gezolian was paid to deliver the isotope. Inquiries have given rise to suspicions that Stahl had somehow fooled him.

"This is not the first time Stahl has gone rogue. He is excellent in infiltrating. Another confusing aspect is an anonymous tip the Italian police received in April about Stahl's apartment and a dead body contained within. The police found that the tip was false. When"—the unit name was blacked out in the document—"from Europol received this delayed information, it ran a separate investigation. Traces of human blood were found in the apartment, but it did not match Stahl. The hutch in the bedroom had been broken, a fact that went unnoticed in the initial investigation because it had been covered in a tablecloth. No signs of homicide were found. Multiple other unrecognized fingerprints were found in the apartment in addition to those of the apartment owner, Stahl, and Stahl's Finnish female friend, Hilja Kanerva Ilveskero.

"There have been no further signs of Stahl/Lanotte since April. His bank accounts have not been touched, and the credit cards under either name have not been used. It is highly likely that Stahl is deceased or has established a role in the enemy's camp. The investigation continues, and if Stahl is found, this must be reported to"—name blacked out—"who will decide a course of action."

The letter had been dated October 1, a week earlier. David had performed an impressive disappearing act—not even an efficient international police search could find him. It wasn't hard to get a forged passport and credit cards and driver's licenses under a new identity, but where was David getting money? Had Carlo Dolfini been Gezolian's Italian contact that had to be silenced? I went back to the evening when I found the body. I'd searched through the apartment thoroughly and alone, but anyone could have been outside in the darkness, watching. Whoever it was could have rushed in to get the body as soon as I left. I felt sick thinking it may have been David. Maybe I'd carried out his plan perfectly. He knew Europol was watching him closely, and hanging around with a lady friend would have looked innocent enough; he could have used the distraction to plan and execute Dolfini's murder. David could have grown tired of me but realized how useful I could be.

It was a little past three in the morning when I finally gave up and took a sleeping pill. My last thought was about where Laitio had gotten these papers and why he'd given them to me. Out of pity? I also wondered why the Bureau had never pressured me into revealing where David was. Someone in the Bureau had to have more information than me. The thought lingered in my mind until I fell asleep.

The weekend turned out to be sunny and freezing. I helped out in the kitchen by chopping vegetables while waiting for an appropriate time to call Laitio. The opportunity didn't rise until three thirty, when the last of the lunch crowd was gone and there was still time before we had to prep for dinner. Monika kept the restaurant open twelve hours a day and didn't want to cut her staff's day into two shifts, very unlike other restaurateurs and typical idealism from Monika. My shift was always scheduled for eight hours, but I worked when needed.

Laitio answered on the second ring.

"Yes?" He didn't sound particularly happy.

"Thank you."

"For what?"

"The papers."

"Don't bullshit me, girl. And, Rytkönen, wait up! We aren't finished with this!" Laitio yelled.

It sounded like he set the phone aside. Although the sounds were muffled, I could still tell what they were saying.

"I cannot allow such exceptions to the policy. There are no legal grounds for doing this. Even the Ministry of the Interior is wondering what's going on." Rytkönen had dropped his dialect, and his voice was even tenser than when I'd called him pretending to be David.

"There's no harm in it. I do my job better than those who hide behind their desks at the Bureau," I heard Laitio say.

"That's not the issue. Police have to follow rules," Rytkönen explained.

"I knew the police law by heart before you were born, god-damn it!"

"And put that cigar away. You'll set off the smoke alarm."

"Are you afraid of your suit getting wet? Get the hell out of here, you piece of shit."

This was followed by the sound of a chair falling over.

"My, aren't you riled up." Laitio's voice revealed a smile.

"Don't you call your foreman names," yelled Rytkönen.

"And don't you talk about yourself in the third person. You're a little boy drunk with power. Go ahead and cry to the chief. He gave me his blessing to smoke cigars. You see, I work the weekends, too. I'm a full-time Bureau man, and I don't fill in useless overtime papers like some people," Laitio said.

There were more clanking sounds, and a door slammed. Then I heard Laitio's husky, evil laugh. I could just imagine his mustache shaking and the unlit cigar wobbling between his lips.

"You still there, Ilveskero? Did you hear that?" he asked.

"Yes and yes."

"That bastard is threatening to get me fired if I don't start working full time at the headquarters instead of from home. We'll see who wins this game."

"Has Rytkönen ever met David?"

"Not that I know of, but then again, nobody tells me anything these days. Forget about Stahl already. If he's not worm food, he's playing a game we shouldn't mess in. Or are you interested in—"

"Stop!" I yelled. Once again Laitio had almost said too much. His office at the Bureau certainly had a camera, and if the reports he'd sent me were supposed to be hidden from him, he'd be in big trouble if his higher-ups found out that he knew about Stahl's connection to the isotope. "You're right," I told Laitio. "I better forget Stahl."

Laitio said he'd go smoke a cigar at the river, work hours or not. I went back to the dining area to pack up flowers. Monika and I had agreed that we'd send them to nursing homes and assisted-living centers, and I was the delivery girl. I'd had all sorts of jobs in my life, but I'd never delivered flowers. On my route I wondered whether I should reveal Rytkönen's identity as Kassi to Laitio, although it would mean I'd have to confess to hiding some details about Dolfini's murder. I would decide later what to do.

I spent the sunny weekend working indoors, so when the restaurant closed on Tuesday after lunch, I went out for a long run. I ran to Länsisatama harbor, then past Hietalahti market square, following the shore to Kaivopuisto Park. Trees were still covered in colorful leaves, but the sea was cool blue and did not look inviting. Short-haired dogs wore jackets, and the finches swarmed the park looking for winter nesting materials. Uncle Jari had always made sure we only fed the birds occasional bread crumbs until the frost settled. "They'll get used to finding food easily and won't know how to find it themselves. Humans shouldn't meddle with nature," said the man who had kept an orphaned lynx cub as a pet. Sure, Frida would have perished if Uncle had left her alone in the woods, but the lessons he imparted to me weren't always logical. I suppose their underlying motivation was love.

I'd often thought about whether my parents had loved each other. They'd gotten married because my mom was pregnant. Maybe the condom broke or she had been too shy to ask her doctor for the pill. Maybe my father, the bastard, had raped her. Still, he married her. First married, then killed.

I had very little information about my parents. The only relative I knew from my mom's side had been my uncle; my grandmother had been an only child, and Grandpa's brothers had died in the war. I hadn't bothered to look up any of my second cousins. I knew there were more relatives on my father's side, but they didn't want to hear from me. The murder had been a terrible shame on the family, and in one version I'd heard, my grandfather had speculated whether I was even my father's child. Father had killed Mom for having an affair, after all. Seppo Holopainen had once boasted to my uncle about knowing this tidbit while they'd sat outside on the sauna porch, and I'd eavesdropped on them. Believe me, I would have rather been someone else's child, but this one photograph I owned showed no mercy: year after year I looked more like my father. His mother had believed blood was thicker than water and left me a small inheritance, although we hadn't seen each other for decades.

Seagulls were screeching over the water, making it feel like summer again. It would have been back in Italy where it was over sixty degrees. I could've run in a T-shirt. But no, I had to trudge on to make sure the sweat didn't dry in the chilly winds of October. I tried to recall people who would have known my mom. The photo album of her funeral pictures, showing the guests, was in Hevonpersiinsaari. I should ask the Hakkarainens to send it to me. Uncle Jari had always written the names of people on the back of the pictures. They were held in see-through plastic sleeves, so I could easily remove them. I'd only wanted to look at them once or twice before. I already had enough memories of the funeral.

Monika took the evening off and went to see a French art house movie with Petter. I wasn't interested. I thought about seeing an action film, but I ended up wandering around the city, window shopping. I'm usually not interested in jewelry, but a glance at a ring display gave me a start. There was a thin band with three blood-red rubies, reminding me of the one David had left. But why would David have bought the ring in Finland? All intelligence pointed to him not even setting foot in Finland since he'd left on *I Believe* almost two years ago.

A part of me wanted to believe that David had intended to propose, but my cynical side reminded me how ridiculous that seemed. And what was with all the riddles? Why was he interested in Kopparnäs and Syrjänen's plans for the area? Or was the map just a sappy reminder of the place we'd made love for the first time? Again my cynical side pulled me back—there had to be something else. David wanted me to visit Kopparnäs to see what was going on. It was humiliating to be his little puppet. "Dear Hilja, I know you too well." I didn't want anyone to predict how I'd react or how I could be manipulated. I was the master of my own fate.

I began to feel chilly, so I stopped by Hotel Torni's bar Ateljée for a hot chocolate with rum. The chill turned inward when I remembered sitting there with David. God, how many places had he managed to ruin for me? I sat next to a window at a table for two, facing the spiral staircase near the restrooms, and watched how darkness fell over Helsinki. One of my favorite pastimes in New York had been riding to the top of the Empire State Building right before it closed and looking over the sea of lights. Helsinki was no Manhattan, but in the evening, it was a beautifully wistful sight.

A hand on my shoulder startled me. How could someone surprise me so easily? I was even more confused when I saw Yuri Trankov standing there. He could have stabbed me in the back or injected me with a tranquilizer. He'd done it quickly with Helena Lehmusvuo, and now Trankov was smirking at me as if he'd seen an old friend.

"Good evening, Hilja. May I buy you a drink?" Trankov asked in Finnish.

"No. Please leave." I wanted to add that I was about to leave, but I wasn't going to let this thug scare me away.

Trankov sat across from me.

"I told you I don't need company," I said.

"Wait." Trankov set his hand over mine. His touch felt disgusting. I had to remind myself that we were in a public place and I had nothing to worry about. My home was only a stone's throw away. Of course Trankov would know where I was staying.

"They don't serve tables here. Order at the bar," I managed to tell him just as the waitress appeared to take his order.

"A Bloody Mary, please." I had never seen a friendlier smile on Trankov's face, and his eyes were glowing. When Trankov sold the lynx painting to Mrs. Voutilainen, he'd managed to charm her by pretending to be a good person. I knew what he was really about.

"And how about you, miss?" the waitress asked.

"Another hot chocolate. No rum this time. Add on some whipped cream please. This gentleman said he's paying." I smiled at Trankov.

Trankov had a quizzical look on his face; his Finnish skills probably weren't up to this sort of conversation. A group of Japanese tourists were shuffling chairs around, pointing excitedly at a cruise ship slowly making its way on the sea. Ships were prisons where you couldn't escape from your tormentors, and they could be easily blown to smithereens.

The waitress brought our drinks, and Trankov paid with his credit card. For a second I thought he could have arranged it all in advance, bribed a waitress to spike my hot chocolate with something unpleasant. He was capable of anything, and in this maze-like restaurant, it would have been easy to move about without me noticing. I had been staring out the window, thinking about David, not paying attention. I took a sip of my hot chocolate. I didn't have to drink it, although the taste was the same, minus the bitterness of rum.

"What was that you taught me about Finnish traffic rules?" Trankov switched to English. Finnish sounded more natural for him. English consonants became thick and muddled in his mouth.

"It's your turn to tell me why you're in Finland. Who revoked your ban to enter the country?"

"How should I know?" Trankov shrugged. "I'm not accused of anything. I have a clean record and a permanent job at Usko Syrjänen's company."

"Which one of them?"

"The construction company. I'm an architect. Well, almost graduated."

"An artistic man. I see. On your last Finland tour, you pretended to be a painter," I reminded him.

"I didn't pretend anything. I still paint. I've always painted. I just can't make a living at it, and my dad . . . not everyone thinks it's a real job," Trankov said.

"How much does Paskevich's opinion mean to you?"

Mentioning Paskevich made Trankov jump, and suddenly he looked like a little boy. I had never thought of asking how old he was, although the Bureau probably had it in their records.

"He means nothing to me. Paskevich is just a small-time crook, and if you hang out with him, you'll end up in jail." Trankov spread his arms and shook his head. "Syrjänen is totally different. I can do great things with him, and he's in need of good Russian relations now that all his former business partners are kaput."

"And you can provide such relations?" I gulped down half of my cocoa.

"I know the right people. Syrjänen trusts me," Trankov said with pride in his voice. It sounded like no one had bothered to fill Syrjänen in on Trankov's background. A businessman of that caliber didn't research his business partners? First Vasiliev, now Trankov. Or perhaps Syrjänen cared about the source of his money as much as the politicians he bribed.

"It's important to know the people you're dealing with in Russia. Syrjänen has a lot to learn in that aspect. Why do you work at a restaurant? Nobody wants to give you a job in your field?"

"And what do you suppose my field is?"

"You're a bodyguard—ready for other jobs, too, if the situation calls for it. And you're not all that bad at it. Syrjänen could use you once Julia comes to Finland."

I chuckled. I was not clamoring to work for Syrjänen, although I was interested in his operations: the papers I'd found in David's drawers; the Hiidenniemi project Anita Nuutinen had been after, too; and Trankov, who claimed he knew things David had been hiding from me. Was that what this was leading to? David, David, and David? I wouldn't find peace until I found out what had happened to him.

I'd accepted my fate after *I Believe* blew up, especially when I didn't hear from David for months. The most likely scenario had been that David had died, and with tears in my eyes, I had accepted that David had trusted me enough to share what he was going to do. Now I was hurt, disappointed, and hungry for more information. Trankov wanted revenge because of how I'd humiliated him at Bromarf, and he better prepare for an encore.

"I'm fine with my current job, thank you. What sort of plans does Syrjänen's construction company have? The papers haven't been writing about his recent projects," I said.

Trankov lifted his glass to his pursed lips and sucked in a seductive way, and it looked ridiculous.

"He trusts me. I'm not telling you. You know how construction is. First you need permits."

"So you're planning buildings for him?" I asked.

"More like . . ." Trankov was searching for the right word, then found it in Finnish. "A city plan. The way houses are built in relation to others. And interiors. I paint directly onto walls. I illustrate entire rooms." Trankov seemed less dangerous by the word, and I knew I could manipulate him again. "Syrjänen holds a grudge against Stahl about that boat explosion," Trankov said.

I tried to keep my hand steady as I set my mug down. Syrjänen wasn't supposed to know that. He and the media had been presented with a story about *I Believe* exploding as an unfortunate accident. Or was Trankov just testing me? Even if he was, how did he know about Stahl? This was information meant only for the inner circles. All of us had vowed confidentiality. Maybe Syrjänen was such good buddies with the ministers that vows and Europol agent lives didn't matter.

"First Stahl slithered his way to Paskevich's camp, then moved over to work for Vasiliev. I suppose he's alone now."

"Who says he's alive?" I tried to sound nonchalant, but I knew I was failing. I had to find out how recent Trankov's information was and how I could make him talk. Would the same methods that worked on his dad work on him? Was he a slave to his desires, too? And would the same bag of tricks work, or was he prepared for them? I had to make myself sound dumber than I was. I'd been really good at it since childhood. Showing your hand didn't always play to your advantage. Trankov wanted to look down on me, humiliate me. If that was the price I had to pay for finding out the truth, then so be it.

I got up and put my jacket on. Trankov grabbed my wrist extremely tightly.

"You know what I want from you, Hilja? I want to paint you. I have a studio over at Syrjänen's house in Långvik. Be my model. I already know what I'll paint," Trankov said.

Mike Virtue was shouting in my head, joined by Uncle Jari. *Don't be foolish! Say no!* I ignored the voices as I set my free hand on Trankov's hand and said, "Sounds good to me. Give me your number, and we'll be in touch."

12

Trankov's business card was impressive. It had Syrjänen's logo and an official-sounding title: "architectural project manager and painter."

"I'm an honest man these days. I have no reason to hide anything," he tried to convince me as we departed. He kissed me on both cheeks, and I washed my face as soon as I was in the apartment.

Petter had come over after the movie for a nightcap; the siblings were having red wine. I settled for a glass of water. I felt like an outsider as they talked. I had nobody to share my childhood memories with, nobody who would get what I meant from hearing part of a sentence. Monika thought the movie was intense, and Petter had enjoyed the colors. It sounded like I would have slept through it. Petter nagged me again about modeling for him, and I didn't have the heart to tell him I had promised to model for someone else.

I arranged a meeting with Laitio for Friday because he was spending the first half of the week at some completely useless training event at the police academy in Hervanta. I wanted to chat with him before I met Trankov. I would go to Urheilu Street on an afternoon when Sans Nom was usually slower. We didn't take reservations during lunch, and there was always a line of customers; dinners were usually fully booked. A couple of restaurant critics had already reviewed Sans Nom in their respective magazines.

They considered it a four-star restaurant, but the concept was still baffling to them. Nobody dared criticize the soup kitchen concept, though. The first run had been a success; in addition to the homeless and poor people from the nearby areas, all sorts of hippies and businesswomen had come to show how tolerant they were by breaking bread with the unfortunate citizens, although the groups never mingled during lunch.

I rang Laitio's buzzer on Friday, but nobody came to the door, so I called him.

"Laitio." He sounded out of breath.

"It's Ilveskero. We were supposed to meet."

"I know, but damned Kokki slipped into the hallway, and I don't know if he went up or down."

"Open the door, and I'll help you find him," I offered.

"Just keep an eye on the door so that damned tom doesn't run into the street. Catch him even if he tries to scratch your eyes out."

I told Laitio I had no experience with cats. He knew nothing about Frida. I didn't see anything behind the door. I looked into the baby stroller that had been left in the hallway—that would be a prime spot for a cat to hide—but the stroller was empty. I slowly walked upstairs. Frida had loved surprising us by jumping off a tree branch and wrestling with us upon landing. I got up to the third floor and saw Laitio's cat crouched in the corner, puffed up, his tail raised. When he saw me he gave a vicious hiss.

"He's here," I yelled down the hallway. I could hear Laitio stomping around a couple of floors above. The cat didn't look like he'd let a stranger hold him, so I moved toward him slowly while avoiding eye contact. He made a nasty growling sound when I was close enough to touch him, his tail now thick as a fur collar. Laitio circled him on the other side.

"Come on, Kokki." I'd never heard Laitio speak in such a gentle tone. It was much higher than his usual voice. "Come now." Laitio crouched down and attempted to pick Kokki up. The cat hissed.

"Here. Wrap the cat in it." I took off my jacket and threw it to Laitio. When Frida was a cub and had a splinter in her paw, it was hard to hold her down. Uncle Jari had wrapped her in a thick quilt and held her down while I removed the splinter with tweezers.

"He'll destroy this." He took off his familiar mustard-yellow cardigan. His shirt underneath was missing two lower buttons, and the gap showed his round, hairy belly. When Laitio crouched down again, the cat hissed and swiped at him. Laitio barely avoided the claws.

It looked like he was afraid of the cat. I yanked the cardigan from Laitio and moved as quickly as I could. I wrapped the cat in the jacket, and he hissed and struggled. He was large for a cat, though much smaller than Frida had ever been. I still had to use all my strength to hold the cat tightly for the two floors I had to climb. Laitio ran ahead of me to open the door. I threw the cat into the apartment, and Laitio closed the door at lightning speed. Laitio wiped sweat from his face. It had trickled all the way down to his mustache.

"The mailman delivered a registered letter, and I was careless when I was signing it. That's how Kokki managed to sneak out. And guess who the letter was from?" Laitio asked. "A written reprimand from the assistant police chief at the Bureau. If I'm not back at the headquarters full time by the beginning of next month, they'll fire me."

I knew it was futile to suggest that Laitio just enjoy his cigars during coffee and lunch breaks. This was obviously about much more than cigar smoke. We walked into Laitio's office, and I accepted the cigar he offered. I let him cut the end off. The snap made a cruel smile spread across his face. The commotion next door indicated that Kokki was up to no good again. Laitio tried to cover his hairy belly with his shirt, then he sat down behind his desk to hide his midriff.

"How would you like some information to torment Rytkönen?" I asked after my first puff. "Like what?"

"It's a long story, and you won't like some of it, but try not to interrupt, okay?" As I began my story from the real beginning—when I had found David's phone in Carlo Dolfini's pocket—I had to look away from Laitio's reddening face and stare at the table. He listened, huffed, puffed, lit his cigar again, and took long drags. I told him about the hutch, the Kopparnäs papers, and the kaleidoscope. I finished with Rytkönen answering the phone as Kassi. When I was done, I didn't look at Laitio; I just gazed out the window and hid myself in a cloud of smoke. I wished I had long, thick hair like my middle school friend Taru. In a sticky situation she'd hide herself behind her hair. Laitio didn't speak for a while, just snorted. When I finally dared to look at him, I was surprised to see that he was pitying me.

"Don't make yourself a fool, Ilveskero. I've seen enough possessive people like you. They don't know how to give up even when they know there's no hope, even when ten doors have been slammed in their faces and they've been issued a restraining order. The type of possessiveness you carry around is the worst kind. You better knock it off. Or did you think, like your mother thought, that love will cure a killer? Didn't you read those reports I gave you, or are you just too stupid to understand what they mean? Forget about Stahl," Laitio said.

"But why are David and Rytkönen connected? Or is Rytkönen overseeing Stahl in some way? Do they know each other?"

"I can find out, but not because of you. I'll do it because Rytkönen and I are at war, and I welcome anything I can use against him. What did Stahl tell you about the night he blew up the ship?"

"Nothing, really. He never wanted to go back to it, saying the memory of killing four people was too much for him. They were crooks, but they were still human."

"And you of course believed Stahl was a gentle killer?"

I didn't respond. I'd only seen what I'd wanted to, a man in love with me who had risen from the dead and called me to him. Now I remembered how he'd evaded my questions in Spain, Germany, and Tuscany. I was curious to know what killing felt like. Maybe David could have told me what my father was thinking, but he wouldn't talk. His face had gone cold, and he'd looked away. I always thought he was just ashamed of what he'd done, and I'd loved him even more. Now it looked like he hadn't told me because he didn't want to reveal what he really was. He was just following orders. David the rogue, *Finnjävel*, the Finnish devil. The man who didn't trust anyone. And I'd assumed we were soul mates.

Laitio got up to open the window. He shivered. I could see leaves being ripped off branches in the cold breeze, and I heard the distant screeching of an ambulance siren.

"You could show me those treasures you found among Stahl's stash sometime," Laitio said. "I have to say I'm amazed you're not in jail. You're screwing around with this stuff so carelessly. And you're not going to see Trankov. I've told you he's dangerous. Do you know anything about him? His mother, Olga Trankova, was a whore for the KGB. Sorry, there's no nice way to put it, although I doubt she voluntarily chose that line of work. In the early eighties, she was Paskevich's main woman. Olga became pregnant and didn't get an abortion, although she was told to, so Paskevich sent her to Siberia to give birth. Obviously he was married at the time, like all proper communists were. When the joys of capitalism reached the Soviets, it was easy to get rid of his wife. She was run over by a car in Moscow, clearly a calculated hit."

I remembered Anita mentioning that Paskevich was a widower.

"Since he was a little kid, Yuri proved to be very talented, mostly in painting, cheating, and stealing. A couple of years in a Siberian foster home made him even more ambitious. He looked up the man his mother had claimed was his father and tried hard to become his favorite boy. I guess he was successful when he ended up staying with Paskevich in Moscow and went to architecture school. He probably believed his father's construction business needed architects and quit school when his father was called away to handle other types of business. You showed Yuri's father that the kid amounted to nothing. Do you think he won't take it out on you?" Laitio closed the window, and another button on his shirt fell off, revealing even more of his belly.

I picked up the button and gave it to Laitio. "It's not hard to sew these back on. I can do it," I told him. He just humphed at me and shoved the button into his pocket.

"I'm a goner, Ilveskero," he said, "and I mean my career. But maybe it's for the best. I can run my own investigation without worrying about getting fired. I'll get in touch with a couple of the tamer journalists. My bosses are afraid of publicity. Once you're considered a crook in this country, it's hard to make people believe otherwise. You stay put in that restaurant and let me take care of this. And forget about Stahl and Trankov. That Swede was a nice man—what was his name again?"

"Petter?"

"Yes, that's right. I hear he likes you a lot."

"Laitio, stay out of my love life. I can take care of it myself."

"By the looks of it, all you do is make a bigger mess of it."

I walked out. I didn't need to stick around for insults. I went to Yrjö Street to get rid of the cigar smell with a change of clothes. At the apartment I found a notice from the post office that I had a package to pick up. I grabbed Trankov's business card and my towel. I'm not a big fan of swimming, but the Yrjö Street swimming pool was one of the best I'd ever been to. I'd arranged to meet Mrs. Voutilainen there. She was a regular. She'd been going there since the 1940s. We reserved a relaxation room on the second floor and ordered some nonalcoholic mead. Mrs. Voutilainen brought apple pie. We didn't wear swimsuits; I had always hated them.

"The wrong sort of nudity is constantly pushed on us. The young and beautiful flashing a bit of skin. We were all born without clothes, but nowadays you're supposed to hide all the wrinkles and fat rolls. As if people are covered by some sort of a spiritual burka, and only perfectly beautiful people are allowed to show themselves. This pool has been one of the few remaining sanctuaries for us women with saggy tits. Here we are equally beautiful or equally ugly," Mrs. Voutilainen ranted when she'd taken me to the pool for the first time.

I wondered what ten-year-old Hilja who'd grown up in the countryside of Hevonpersiinsaari would have thought of the place. The atmosphere was straight out of an ancient Greek story. The columns, vaulted ceilings, and delicious treats would have left me speechless. Heck, even now I was in awe. Mike Virtue would have been terrified to see this place; rumor had it that he didn't take his Kevlar vest off even when he went swimming.

Mrs. Voutilainen's breasts were small, empty bags lined with stretch marks, as were her inner thighs and calves. Her legs had multiple scars from surgeries attempting to fix her varicose veins, and her belly displayed a deep scar from a cesarean in the 1950s. As we sat in the sauna, a woman in her twenties covered in tattoos sat next to Mrs. Voutilainen, and she began grilling the girl about her tattoos. Most of them were different kinds of cats, and her right shoulder displayed a familiar tuft-eared sight.

When we were done swimming, we ate our refreshments, and I told Mrs. Voutilainen how I'd met the man who'd sold her the lynx painting and that Trankov had made an appearance at Sans Nom's grand opening. I said I recognized him by his name and from a sketch Mrs. Voutilainen had made.

"He's doing well. He's moved on from being a garbage collector. His background is actually in architecture, and now he's working for Usko Syrjänen's construction company. Look at his fancy business card." I showed Mrs. Voutilainen.

I knew I needed someone to rely on if I had plans of seeing Trankov. Mrs. Voutilainen would be perfect, as soon as I figured out how to use her. She'd recognize the man and could sketch him for the police if needed, and a man who vowed to have gone straight wouldn't hurt a woman in her seventies, even if he wanted to hurt me.

"Well, that's nice to hear. How about you? Any men in your life? When you took off to Italy in the spring, I was expecting to hear wedding bells."

I forced a smile. I had hoped the same.

"Things didn't really go as planned, and that man is a bit . . . well, not the marrying type. And I'm in no hurry to get married. My life is great as it is."

"Are you sure you're not into women after all?" Mrs. Voutilainen asked nonchalantly. Occasionally Mrs. Voutilainen showed her true colors by making snide remarks about conservatives who were afraid of anything that deviated from their values. I heard she'd caused plenty of fights on the trips she took with other retirees.

"Maybe I just haven't found the woman of my dreams." I kept my tone light. "I've tried that approach, too, but I loved David." I watched the tattooed girl swimming in the pool with confident strokes. "Right now I don't want anyone, and I'm not unhappy," I lied and took a bite of apple pie.

I barely made it to the post office before it closed. I'd asked the Hakkarainens to send my mom's funeral photo album, but the package was so large there had to be more. When I opened it I didn't know whether to laugh or cry. Maija had baked a ton of potato pasties and bread rolls. The Hakkarainens had also sent small bags of dried porcini, black trumpets, black currant leaf tea, and dried dill. Maija had written me a card, reminding me how the currant leaves were from the bushes in front of our cabin in Hevonpersiinsaari. I'd planted them with Uncle Jari. I boiled some water and let the tea seep while I took out the album. The cover had an image of a sunset over an ocean, and the colors looked unnaturally bright. The photos within had lost their color after thirty years. There was a photo on the first page, and it showed my mom's cheap, plain coffin, with a floral arrangement of pink carnations. My head began to hum. I wasn't sure if I could go through with this. The next page had a photo of the priest. He looked sad. He'd patted me on the head and told me my mommy was now happy in heaven and one day I'd join her, if I behaved like a good girl. I'd asked him when that would be, and he told me at least seventy years and that I shouldn't hurry.

In the next picture I was walking down the church aisle between my grandmother and Uncle Jari toward the coffin. Grandmother's mourning veil covered her face entirely. Uncle wore a black suit with wide pant legs. He'd worn a more modern suit to my high school graduation, something in light gray. My short hair had been tied into pointy, stiff pigtails with black ribbons. I walked on my tiptoes in my patent leather shoes. Uncle Jari's hand was in mine, and his other hand held on to an arrangement of flowers made out of pink and white roses. He'd given me a single rose to set on the coffin. I remembered hearing a strange whimper from behind me as I lowered the flower onto the coffin and waved good-bye to my mother.

What was I doing? I was supposed to be locating my mother's friends, not reminiscing. I flipped onward. The Hakkarainen couple had also been at the funeral, and their teenaged children looked miserable. There was a young man, standing alone, and I didn't recall seeing him before. I took the photo out and flipped it. "Kari Suurluoto, Keijo's cousin" was written on the back. His face was scarred with acne, and his blond hair was permed. The suit hung off him awkwardly, obviously a loaner. Based on his name, he had to be my father's relative from his father's side. He looked a few years younger than my father, but they might have been close. Or what if Kari Suurluoto had fallen in love with his cousin's pretty wife?

All of my mother's friends were on the next page. Tarja Kinnunen, Päivi Väänänen, and Tiina Turpeinen. Their faces were red from crying. Tiina's hairdo was straight out of the TV show *Dallas*. Did my mom know these women from middle school? They appeared together in all of the pictures. If I found one of them, I might track them all down. With my crummy luck they'd probably changed their last names at least once since the pictures were taken.

I thought about setting up a Facebook page in my mother's memory. Although she'd been dead for decades, the page might bring about some good contacts. There was of course the risk that Keijo Kurkimäki would decide to get in touch with me. He was locked up in the prison's psychiatric ward, and his contacts to the outside world were very limited. He'd tried to call me a couple of times, but I hadn't heard from him since I made all my numbers unlisted.

A Facebook page would also attract true-crime aficionados—there were plenty of those freaks. I wouldn't publish my contact information there. Once again, I could hear Mike Virtue's sermon about being careful with the information we put on the web, and back in those days social media wasn't as big as it is now. There was no Facebook or Twitter, and only the most technologically advanced people had websites. The security academy in Queens had a website, but there was no information about its students or the staff, and it was no use trying to track down Mike through Facebook.

I flipped to the last page in the album and saw two photos. One had been taken at the memorial service: pink roses and a burning candle surrounded a framed photo on a table. The picture below was the photo from that frame. Uncle Jari had taken it on my third birthday. The blond, smiling woman's bangs were teased into waves, and her skin was smooth like a porcelain doll. She wore a necklace with three charms: a heart, a cross, and an anchor. She was wearing an engagement ring: a thin band with three red stones, most likely rubies. It took me a moment to recognize it.

I stormed back into my room. I'd hidden David's USB stick, the ring, and the kaleidoscope in my gun safe. I fumbled with the lock, forgetting how to breathe. David had never been to Hevonpersiinsaari, so he'd never seen this picture—he couldn't have!

I pulled out the ring, and it was the same as the one my mother wore in the picture. How was this possible?

13

I'd never thought about what had happened to my mother's jewels. Dad had cut her left ring finger off with a knife, removing her engagement and wedding rings. But the ring with three rubies was neither of those. I had a memory of a ring with a rock in it shining in the pool of blood. I did my best to wipe the memory and that other ring from my mind and focus on the ring in the picture. Where had Mom gotten it, and was I now holding the very same ring? It didn't have any engravings, but a jeweler would be able to tell whether an engraving had been sanded off, maybe even where the ring had come from. It couldn't be just a coincidence that David had this ring. Who'd know more about my mom's jewels? The only person I could think of was Maija Hakkarainen. I looked at the clock. Nine thirty may have been too late to call. She and her husband were farmers, so they went to bed early to get up at five and milk the cows. I would wait until tomorrow.

I called a service to find information on my mother's friends. The names Päivi Väänänen and Tiina Turpeinen came up in the Helsinki area, but I didn't want to call them this late—with common names like that, they might not even be the people I was looking for. And what would I say? "Hello, did you go to high school in Tuusniemi at the end of the seventies? Do you remember Anneli

Karttunen? I'm her daughter. We met at her funeral when I was four."

Lying had never been hard for me, and being honest was difficult. The service gave me both home and cell phone numbers for Kari Suurluoto and an address in Espoo's Tuomarila. So at least he wasn't a cop or so secretive that he needed to hide his address. I turned my computer on and searched for him on the web. The only results were for the Finlandia skiing competition. He was in good shape and had skied the thirty-one-mile route in three and a half hours. He was in his late forties by now.

I heard the door slam. Monika was back. There were only a few dinner reservations, and everything seemed to be going smoothly at Sans Nom, so the two of us weren't needed there all the time. I hid the ring in my pocket and took the photo album to my room. Maybe I would show it to Monika later, when I was less upset about the images.

"Want some black currant leaf tea and potato pasties? Maija Hakkarainen sent me a care package," I said to Monika. We'd invited the Hakkarainens to the grand opening, but they couldn't leave their cattle behind that easily. Maija had promised they'd come and visit the next time they secured someone to look after their farm. Uncle Jari and I had occasionally milked their cows when the Hakkarainens had funerals or graduations to attend. However, dealing with modern milking equipment wasn't learned overnight.

"Ah, great!" Monika said and quickly bit into a pasty. A restaurateur who didn't have time to eat was such a cliché. I drank three cups of tea, listened to Monika talk about her evening, and did my best to calm down. Still, as soon as I'd fallen asleep, I had dreams of being stuck inside a coffin that was shot into space. I knew I'd suffocate if the coffin left the atmosphere. I woke up in pitch-black to see a faint glow from my cell phone. A text message. From an unknown number. There was no message, just a question mark. Maybe it was an accident. Still, I couldn't forget it, and it took me a while to get to sleep.

On Saturday I planned on working the night shift, so I slept until noon. Sans Nom would be packed by six. I called the Hakkarainens' landline, but nobody answered.

I finally got a hold of them on Sunday after they'd returned from milking the cows. Matti answered and asked how I was before handing Maija the phone. I praised her tea and baked goods and marveled at the mushroom loot she'd secured this fall. With the niceties out of the way, I asked about the jewels.

"Your mother's jewels? I'm sorry to say I don't have a clue. Your parents lived in Lappeenranta then. I have no idea where her belongings went," said Maija.

"But you were at the funeral. I saw the pictures."

"Matti is your dead grandfather's cousin on your mother's side. We were there to support your grandmother, and I helped out with baking. I used to be quite a caterer back then. We didn't really know your mother, and we knew your father even less, but when Jari looked for a house for you two, Matti suggested he buy Hevonpersiinsaari. I suppose such a remote place wasn't all that fun for a child."

"It was perfect for me," I said. I asked about Maija's animals. She said they'd seen lynx tracks every now and then, but nothing had been bothering the cows.

"Where did you keep the funeral album?" I asked.

"On your uncle's bookshelf, among the other photo albums. Your childhood pictures are still there—do you want them?"

"I'll get them when I have a chance." I knew it would be no use to ask Maija about potential signs of break-ins or odd characters hanging around Hevonpersiinsaari. I'd taken down all the security equipment I'd temporarily set up there, because they'd only be tripped by wild animals and cause unnecessary attention. I'd often told David about Hevonpersiinsaari and my childhood, and I'd shown him the island on the map. It would have been so easy for David to find the cabin and break in. But why would he have done it, and when? There had to be another explanation for the ring.

As I biked toward Sans Nom, I thought of the jewels. They should have gone to my grandmother, but maybe she had sold them. Or maybe Mom's friends had taken them. I only wore jewelry as a cover, and anything I had I was willing to give away—my will included a clause that my friends could take any item as a memento. I doubted my mom had a will. She was twenty-six when she died. Uncle Jari had made remarks that sounded like my father's murderous rampage hadn't been his first act of violence. Uncle Jari had seen black eyes and swollen wrists, but Mom had claimed they were from slipping or bumping into things. Classic. I'd never believe such excuses. Mike Virtue had told us to never turn away from violence: "If we don't intervene, we become accomplices. You have to be smart and think about what you can actually resolve and what should be left for the police, but ignoring violence is a crime."

On Sunday afternoon, I decided to try my luck with all the Tarja Kinnunens I had located in and around Helsinki. None of them had lived in Tuusniemi, and most of them hadn't even heard of it. It was frustrating to have to use a paid service to find locations for the rest of them. One Päivi Väänänen-Huttunen lived in Kuopio, which seemed promising, but she didn't pick up when I called. My number was unlisted, so a lot of them probably chose not to answer. I didn't want to send a text explaining who I was. I was more interested in Kari Suurluoto than the women anyway. I thought of the few times I'd heard my father's low drone, as if he'd been pumped with drugs. Would Kari sound the same? There was only one way to find out, but I hesitated. I looked outside; the theater in the corner of Yrjö and Eerikki Streets must've had a matinee, because lots of people were pouring in. Monika had season tickets, and she tried to drag me along a few times. Then I thought about hanging the laundry to dry in the living room before I left for work. I was coming up with things to do instead of calling Kari Suurluoto. Maybe he was some other Kari, or maybe he'd cut my father out of his life the same way I had.

I forced myself to dial, and he answered immediately, as if he had been waiting for the call.

"Hello, this is Suurluoto."

"Hi, this is Hilja . . . formerly Suurluoto. Keijo's daughter," I said.

There was a long pause. I could tell he was in a car and using a hands-free device, which would explain how he'd answered so fast.

"Hilja?" he finally said. "I thought you lived abroad. I was told you were in the US."

"I'm in Finland now," I said.

"This is actually a bad time. I'm driving a car full of people. What were you calling about?"

"I wanted to talk about my father. You were his only relative to come to my mother's funeral."

There was a long silence. Girls were giggling in the background.

"Like I said, this is a bad time. Can you call me in a half hour?"

But then I'd be on my way to work. We agreed to talk on Monday morning. Suurluoto would be at his office filling out reports, so he was available to chat.

Now that I'd finally gotten a hold of him, I had a hard time letting him go. Even such a short time felt like an excruciating wait. Monika had taken the van to pick up some newly harvested potatoes, and I made it to Sans Nom in time to help her unpack.

Veikko and his buddies were hanging around the back door, hoping to get some leftover bread and mashed potatoes from the previous evening.

"Did they catch those burglars?" asked Veikko.

"We haven't heard back from the police," I told him.

He looked disappointed. "Want a swig?" he asked, offering me a bottle of table wine. I told him no thanks and offered him some coffee to keep him warm. Nights were already chilly, so I was sure it was getting cold in the recycling bin he slept in.

"This building is a good place for me. Nobody ever chases me away. Apartment buildings call the cops right away. We don't mean any harm, and these newspapers and magazines were abandoned here. We're not stealing," Veikko said while chewing on a piece of bread with his four remaining teeth.

"But what are we supposed to do when they stop printing papers and put all the news on the web? Kilobytes don't make for warm blankets," his friend said.

"That won't happen anytime soon. We'll be gone by then." Veikko smiled. "How many winters did they promise you? Last time in rehab they told me the Grim Reaper would come any day, unless I quit drinking. Every day could be your last, so let's drink to that!"

It could be the last day for anyone, I thought while I fed potatoes into the peeling machine. People can't handle thinking about this, so they refuse to. There have been times when the Grim Reaper was on my heels and I barely avoided looking into his eyes. I had told myself I wasn't afraid of death, but I couldn't possibly know how I'd react until the moment arrived. At least I'd fight until the bitter end. I wouldn't be an easy catch.

It was nine o'clock when the last people with reservations arrived. One of the waitresses, a cute brunette, Helinä, told me someone had asked for me in the dining room. I checked the CCTV to see who it was, and sitting in the waiting area near the door was Yuri Trankov with a drink in his hand.

"Did you tell him I was in the kitchen?" I asked Helinä.

"Was I not supposed to? He's so cute."

Helinä was closer to Trankov's age than I was.

"You can have him. What's he drinking?"

"A Bloody Mary." An alcohol license was granted to Sans Nom immediately, mostly due to Monika's good reputation. Still, most customers came to eat, not drink.

The room was full of people, but the murmur of voices and the background music were still low. Sans Nom's playlist included mostly classical music and old jazz, except during lunchtime, when we played folk music from Mozambique. I had thought about switching the music to the Finnish oompah cover band Eläkeläiset as a joke, but that would have to wait until Monika wasn't there or when our customers were being exceptionally annoying.

Trankov looked casual. He wore light-blue jeans, a white shirt, and light-brown hiking shoes. He'd taken the matching suede jacket off and draped it over a chair. He got up and greeted me by grabbing my shoulders and kissing my cheeks. His eyes were deep blue. It looked like he wore contacts. His eyelashes were dark and unnaturally thick.

"Hilja! I had to come see you when I never heard back from you. I'm so excited about the painting—when are you coming?" Trankov asked.

He smelled good. I remembered Laitio's warning, but I wasn't going to heed it. Was Trankov running errands for the Grim Reaper? I could only find out by finding out.

"I'm off on Thursday. Would that work? And how do I get to Långvik?" I asked. I wasn't sure if I could borrow the company van.

"I'll pick you up," Trankov said.

"In the ostentatious SUV?"

"That's Syrjänen's. I have my own car. What time should I get you?"

There was no *safe* time of day, so I agreed to meet him in front of Hotel Torni at 11:00 a.m. Laitio was screaming in my head, and I wouldn't dare tell Monika. I'd use Mrs. Voutilainen as my safety.

"Are you going to have dinner?" I asked Trankov. "The perch fillets from Kaavi are excellent."

Trankov shook his head. He'd remained standing, acting like a true gentleman, but quickly snatched his cocktail from the side table and lapped it up so the tomato juice beaded on his lips. He looked like a supporting actor in a low-budget vampire movie, and I had a hard time taking him seriously. I told him I had to get back to work. Unfortunately, I wasn't quick enough, and Trankov grabbed my hand and kissed it. It didn't feel completely disgusting. I hadn't had sex for six months—far too long. I was probably better off finding a random man in a bar so I wouldn't end up in Trankov's arms. If I messed around with Petter, could we still be friends? I needed a cold shower. I spent the rest of my evening thinking about acne-riddled boys in my middle school.

On Monday I woke up at six. It was still dark outside, and streetlights dotted the roads. I couldn't see the horizon from my window, but the arch of the sky looked promising; it would be a sunny day. I skipped breakfast and had a cup of coffee with milk before I went on my morning jog. Once again I roamed the Helsinki shores and observed how the city was slowly cranking itself up. The lines of cars grew slowly longer. Lights turned on in apartments and then went off as the sun climbed higher. Old ladies chatted on street corners and dads took their screaming kids to daycare. I wondered whether any of them had a murderer in their family or had found a dead body in their boyfriend's apartment. These experiences hadn't made me a better person.

Once I got back I fried eggs and beans as if I needed all that energy to speak with Kari Suurluoto. Again, he picked up immediately; this time he was waiting for it.

"Hi, Hilja. Sorry about yesterday. I had just picked up my daughter and three of her friends from the stables. I didn't want to talk with them around—too tough a subject for a thirteen-year-old."

"Were you and my father close?"

"We were the only boy cousins. I have two sisters, just like your dad. Still, we were six years apart, and that was a lot for young men. I think I admired Cousin Keijo, but I was afraid of him, too."

"Afraid? Why?"

"I was afraid whenever Keijo wanted me to be afraid. What did you want to know about him?"

"Stuff like that. Did you think he'd be a killer one day?"

A long silence. I heard clicking noises. A tree in the courtyard cast a shadow over the window in our living room. I could see individual leaves in the shadow. Some of them had already fallen.

"How old are you now?" Suurluoto asked. "You're over thirty, right?"

"Right. And I'm a bodyguard. You don't need to protect me from the cruel world," I told him.

Suurluoto sighed. "We can't protect each other, but we can do our best. I don't talk about your dad to my daughter, but of course she's searched for him on the web and found out about the murder. She knows all the details. I've told her not to go to those sites, and I've set strict parental controls, but not all of her friends' parents care. They just say kids these days are more mature than we think."

I let Suurluoto talk. Eventually he began to talk about my father. Keijo Suurluoto had always had a short fuse and a mean streak, but he was also nice. Keijo looked like an average kid, and he wasn't bullied in school. Kari's older sisters had never liked Keijo, but Kari had admired his self-confidence. Sometimes it turned into cruelty.

"Once he twisted my arm, and it dislocated. We were supposedly just wrestling. I told him to let me go, but he just laughed. I had to be taken to the hospital, and he kept saying how sorry he was and how he'd forgotten how much younger I was than him. I was ten, and he was sixteen. I think he enjoyed his time in the army, and that's when he met your mother. He'd bragged to his mom how he'd found a wife. He knew right away that this was true love. And when I saw Anneli for the first time, I didn't wonder why."

Kari Suurluoto's parents had owned a farmhouse in Juankoski, and the entire family was there to help. That's where Keijo had brought Anneli to meet the family for the first time. Anneli, although on her way to becoming a teacher, was from Tuusniemi and a farm girl, so she quickly learned her way around the house, moving hay with a pitchfork and brewing coffee. Her work ethic had charmed her future in-laws, who had been a tad suspicious about a girl who wanted to be a teacher, thinking she held herself in higher regard than farm folks.

"My parents had only finished grade school, and so did Keijo's parents. But Anneli was an angel. It was easy to see how kids would love her. She was my first serious crush, although I knew she wouldn't look at a boy five years younger, and besides, she was dating Keijo. But I kept dreaming about her. Anneli was so nice—she didn't ignore me, and she wouldn't let Keijo tease me. She was protective."

A lynx, I almost said. In New York I had learned about Native American totem animal theories, and in these mythologies lynx were protectors and carriers of secrets. I remembered how Mom had tried to shield me from my father until the very end, how she'd told me to crawl away and hide.

"Keijo was jealous about Anneli, even when it came to me, a teenage boy. We all witnessed it at the wedding. I danced too close to Anneli and for too long, and Keijo saw how happy I was to be near her. He almost hit both of us but didn't thanks to Anneli's brother. That Jari was a really nice man."

Kari Suurluoto hadn't been surprised when Keijo murdered Anneli. He was shocked, sad, and furious, but not surprised. They'd seen it coming, all the Suurluotos had said, but they'd been divided looking for a reason why he did it. Keijo's father had died the summer Hilja was born, so he wasn't around to take sides, but Keijo's mother thought that Anneli had been asking for it, always shaking her ass and fluttering her eyelids at men.

"Did she do that? Be honest with me. I can take it," I said.

"Depends on the person, really. I dreamed of Anneli's smiles and hugs meaning something more than just friendship, but I don't think they did. Anneli was a joyful being and so transparent with her feelings. She had Vyborg blood in her veins. That's where her mom came from when she escaped the war. I felt so bad for your grandmother at the funeral. Didn't she pass soon after?"

"She lived a few more years, but she was never the same again. I was quickly moved from her custody to Uncle Jari's."

"Was that good for you? My mom didn't want you to stay with us. I think she was afraid of Keijo. And she had a reason to be. He escaped from prison twice."

My world came to a halt. The shadow from the tree stopped swaying on the living room walls.

"Are you saying my father, these days using the name Keijo Kurkimäki, has escaped prison?"

"Yeah, from the psychiatric ward. His first attempt was cut pretty short. I think it lasted only a couple of hours. The second time they found him after four days. It was never publicized, but Keijo's mom received a call, warning her that Keijo might try to come see her in Tuusniemi. They finally caught him in Kuopio, where he was drunk out of his mind in the middle of the market square, throwing herring at seagulls. At the time my wife and I lived in Brussels, and I took care of the kids at home, so I don't know the details of what really happened. If I remember right, your dad pretty severely injured a guard and some girl, but I'm not sure. It was some ten years ago."

Because I had never heard of this, it must have happened while I was in New York. The last time my father called me was a couple of years ago. I'd made sure none of the pictures of Sans Nom showed my face—although my father was locked up securely behind bars and concrete and electronic locks, surely he was allowed to use a phone. I hated the powerful effect his voice had on me. The last time I'd seen him, he held my mother in his arms and begged her for forgiveness. I don't know if my mother would've forgiven him. I would never be able to.

14

I chatted with Kari Suurluoto for another twenty minutes. He worked in the Leppävaara suburb of Helsinki as a department head for a large household appliance store. He said he'd gladly meet up with me if I ever felt like it. He wanted to know if I looked like Anneli. I assured him that he'd be disappointed; I'd inherited Keijo's features.

Why hadn't anyone told me Keijo had been on the run? Sure, I had been in New York at the time, but come on. This was my father, even if he had lost custody of me as soon as he was locked up. I went back online to look for more information about him. Websites had archived public hearings and scanned newspaper articles. There was even a picture of my father. The only mention of me was how Keijo Suurluoto had a four-year-old child. A couple of articles showed a picture of our home in Lappeenranta at the time. I remembered how the stairwell in the building often smelled of fresh sticky buns, thanks to a neighbor who was an active baker. Was that the reason Mrs. Voutilainen's pies had made me feel safe, sending me back to early childhood, where I hadn't experienced enormous loss yet?

The only motivation I could think of for the murder was jealousy. I might never know if my father had any real reason to be jealous, and even if Mom had had sex with all the men in the neighboring apartments, that didn't give my father the right to kill her. I didn't remember her bringing over any strange men, but then again, I was too young to remember.

On Wednesday the restaurant was pretty empty, so I had some free time in the early evening. I tried my luck with Päivi Väänänen-Huttunen who lived in Kuopio. A woman warily answered the phone. She muttered her name, as if she didn't want me to hear it.

"It's Hilja Ilveskero. I was wondering if you went to high school with my mother, Anneli Suurluoto, formerly Karttunen?"

The woman didn't reply. There was a heated debate in the background in English. It stopped abruptly—she'd turned the television off.

"Who did you say you were again?"

"Anneli Karttunen's daughter, Hilja."

The woman sighed. "Is there any way you can prove it? Your number doesn't show up on my phone, and you could be anyone."

"I saw your picture in my mother's funeral album. Päivi Väänänen was written behind the photo. You wore a black bell-shaped dress, pearls, and large, gold-rimmed glasses," I said.

"Yes, I went to school with Anneli. It was just such a long time ago I had almost forgotten about her. Or wanted to. What do you want?"

"I just want mementos, memories. I hardly know anything about her. And if it's at all possible, I'd like to get in touch with Tarja Kinnunen and Tiina Turpeinen if you have their contact information. They were at the funeral, too."

"We were all tight in high school. We made an oath that we'd keep in touch until the day we died. Tiina studied in Joensuu like your mother, I was in Kuopio, and Tarja stayed in Tuusniemi. But when Anneli died, it all fell apart. I haven't seen Tarja or Tiina except randomly." It sounded like she was crying. "That's what death does to you. It doesn't erase just that one person—it has an effect on many people and through them, many more." Now she was clearly sobbing. "Our Hanne—I mean, my daughter is married to a man who reminds me of Keijo, and I'm so afraid—"

"Please report it to the police if he's beating her. Right now." Great. I was becoming a counselor.

"But then he'll kill us all. The police can't do a thing."

"They can if you give them a chance."

"Where do you live?"

"Helsinki."

"I can't right now." Her voice was interrupted by a sob. She blew her nose. "I have my high school diary somewhere. I used to write a lot. I can't promise anything, but I'll go through them and see if I can find something about your mother. Didn't Jari die recently? I saw his obituary in the papers."

I confirmed this, and Päivi promised to call back later. Her call kept on tugging at me. Not because of my mother or the friends she had lost, but because of this Hanne I didn't even know, who was about to make a classic mistake.

I'd decided to disregard my own mistakes as I waited for Yuri Trankov in front of Hotel Torni on Thursday. The weather had turned bitingly cold, and the air smelled of sleet. Right as a sleek black Jaguar stopped in front of me, a snowflake or two landed in my hair. Trankov got out of the car. Once again he'd dressed up in his mobster outfit, sunglasses included. At least this time he hadn't used hair gel. Kissing my cheeks brought him close enough for me to smell the sea in his cologne. Goddamn it, really? I had clearly been without a man for too long, and I wanted Trankov to touch me more.

I'd dressed up as neutrally as possible. I wore simple jeans, combat boots, a loose gray sweater that came down to my hips, and a puffy jacket. I looked like I was going hiking.

I had told Mrs. Voutilainen that I was meeting Trankov. I'd left Monika a note in the kitchen, telling her I was out and about with Mrs. Voutilainen. It wasn't much of a security system, so I had also packed my Glock and a box of ammo in a pocket inside my large purse. It felt suspiciously heavy, and I hoped Trankov wouldn't offer to carry it.

He opened the door for me, disregarding the traffic jam he was causing. When a car honked at him, he waved his hand in a pompous gesture. The Jaguar didn't have Syrjänen's plates, so I memorized the number. The car smelled new; I doubted it had been driven more than a few thousand miles. The interior was dark-red leather, and the rear windows were tinted. When Trankov started the car, the GPS came on and began to speak in Finnish. Trankov turned it off.

"We don't need that," he said. "I know the way. Do you like my car?"

I looked at the shiny metallic parts and dark-red upholstery. Trankov turned the wheel, also covered in leather. I decided to keep my gloves on for now, although the car was warm. I should have worn a hat; that way I'd have had less of a chance of shedding in the car. Although, maybe it was for the best if I left some traces in the Jag, which was either a rental, leased, or bought with stolen money.

Trankov lead us out of Kamppi toward Länsiväylä Highway and sped up when the lights turned yellow, then weaved between lanes. The car could go up to 174 mph. Could Trankov even handle such speeds? Where did he think he could try it out? On Länsiväylä he was over the limit driving eighty. I didn't say a word. He'd be the one to pay for the ticket or lose his license. Perhaps he didn't care, because he had guardian angels in high places, people who could erase his ticket from the database as easily as his reentrance to Finland.

"Is Långvik Syrjänen's permanent home these days?" I asked. "What happened to that villa in Kotka's Hiidenniemi? Wasn't it supposed to become a holiday resort for the rich?"

"That's old hat. Syrjänen sold the property a year ago this spring. He got a good price for it, too. Turned out it wasn't all that easy to make the area into a resort the way he had planned—he would have needed more land, which would've meant building fake islands. Neighboring landowners weren't selling and were opposed to the plans. They told Syrjänen he wouldn't get permits or that it would take years to happen."

"Is he going to take the project to Långvik then?"

"Why are we talking about Syrjänen? Are you interested in him? If you are, I have news you won't like. Syrjänen is not in Långvik. He went to Tallinn to meet a potential business partner. It'll be just you and me. We can concentrate entirely on art."

Right after the intersection at Ring 3 Highway, Trankov got off on a road heading south. The intersection was confusing. Repair crews were making turning difficult, and Trankov was cursing at the slowpoke in front of us. I'd traveled plenty to Kirkkonummi and Inkoo, but I'd never been to nearby Långvik. We passed the Hirsala golf course, which was completely devoid of golfers. Sometimes we were in the middle of nowhere, driving inside an untouched forest, and occasionally we saw houses in villagelike groups. Then two people on horseback came toward us—finally something that slowed the Jaguar.

"Do you ride?" Trankov asked.

"I can ride," I told him. The last time I rode a horse was in Canada during a ten-day trip with my Queens academy classmate

Benoit to see the horse ranch his parents owned. We also went to Montreal, where we got acquainted with the security arrangements at a local hockey stadium. While we were at the ranch, I was woken up late one night by a phone call. I'd forgotten to turn the cell phone off, as if I'd felt I might receive an important message. I quickly stepped out of the room and walked outside to take the call under the stars. It was Chief Constable Niilo Rämä from the Kuopio police. He'd expressed his condolences and told me they'd found Uncle Jari's body. Most likely he'd drowned and been in the water for days; they'd have more specific information after the autopsy. I still remember walking into the stables and crying against Bessie, the horse I'd ridden the day before. I felt animals could comfort me better than humans. Ever since then, I associated horses with sorrow. I had to leave Montreal before the others. I didn't go for my things in New York but instead flew to Helsinki from Toronto.

"That's what I thought." Trankov's voice brought me back.

"What?"

"That you can ride. A horse would've made a great addition to the painting, but unfortunately I don't have one. Good thing I have something better. Something you'll surely like." Trankov smiled in a way that couldn't be interpreted as anything but sexual. I looked at his slim, long-fingered hands turning the steering wheel in the narrow bends in the road. They made me think of David; for a man well over six feet tall, he had strangely small hands and feet. Trankov was only a couple of inches taller than me, and his fingers were those of a pianist. They could have easily reached around my throat, and though his fingers were thin, I'm sure his hands were strong.

We turned onto a side road and drove a few yards before reaching a six-and-a-half-foot-tall brick wall. The gate was forged iron. Trankov pulled a remote control out of his breast pocket and pressed in the code. The gate began to open slowly. Three two three one; I was pretty sure that was the code. If Trankov noticed that I had snooped on the code, he didn't care. He drove into the garden behind the wall. The garden was landscaped in French fashion: low, shaped bushes; gravel pathways; a couple of ornamental junipers; no tall trees. The main building was only a few years old, although whoever built it had tried to make it look neoclassical. The garage fit three cars, and there was another building in the yard with large windows. I caught glimpses of the sea behind a small hill, and a staircase led down to the sauna on the shore.

"Does Syrjänen own this?" I asked.

"He's renting. The owners are on a three-year work assignment in Shanghai. Some people Syrjänen knows through his business. And the wife is into painting. I lucked out."

Now Trankov pushed in the code for the garage, and I didn't have a chance to look at it. One of the security cameras was at the garage door, and I grimaced at it as Trankov drove the car in. The pompous SUV was there.

I let Trankov get out and open the door for me. He acted like the perfect gentleman. I held my purse tight against me.

"Let's go to the studio. Nobody else is using it right now," Trankov said.

"Where did you learn how to paint?" I asked while I made a mental map of the buildings and security cameras.

"In Vorkuta. That's where I spent my childhood." I remembered how Trankov had told Mrs. Voutilainen that he hailed from Murmansk, and Laitio had mentioned the years Trankov had spent in a Siberian foster home.

"Did Paskevich live there, too?" I hit a sore spot with that question.

"He never lived with me and my mother. They were never married." His eyes flashed with anger, and I didn't know if it was because of me, the memories of a reluctant father, or anger toward his father.

We all have our weaknesses. You better know your own and those of your enemies. Use them wisely, Mike Virtue had said. I'd located one of Trankov's Achilles' heels with Laitio's help.

Trankov opened the studio door with a key. The wall facing the sea was all glass, and two of the narrower walls were half-covered in windows, too. The skylights near the door let the light from the north side of the building seep in. The northern wall had a couple of doors, probably leading to a powder room and a bathroom, and a small kitchen occupied the corner with a fridge and hot plates. Next to the kitchen was a bar with two tall stools.

"Can I get you something before we start working?"

I didn't trust him, so I just asked for tap water and got a glassful for myself. Trankov gave me a crooked smile as if he'd read my thoughts.

"There's also some sparkling water and beer in the fridge. They're Finnish, and I guarantee they're unopened," Trankov said.

"Water is fine for now, thanks."

The walls had been plastered white. The little I could see of the floor between protective papers and various piles was white rock tile, and it could handle paint thinners and removers. There were three stands that held tightly stretched canvases, and two of them were covered. The largest stand held a primed canvas about six and a half feet tall and four feet wide. Mary Higgins had taught me how to prime canvas; when her chemically induced creation project began, she could fill three canvases in a row and then rest for days before she finished the paintings.

The studio was warm, so I removed my jacket, and Trankov rushed over to take it and hung it on a small coatrack. Was he going to paint me in his mobster clothes? His black suit was spotless, and

I wanted to smear it with my lipstick, but I only wore a touch of mascara. I remembered what Paskevich's brothel room had looked like in Bromarf, covered in makeup, wigs, and clothes for his female companions. I made it out of that pickle without a scratch, so I figured I'd do fine here, too.

"Take your time and look around," Trankov said. "I'll go change."

He disappeared behind a door. I looked for a CCTV in the corners and found it between the skylights. It looked like it could record the entire room. Whatever I'd do here Trankov would find out later. So all I did was walk to the panorama window and watch the scenery by the bay. The sleet had turned into a drizzle, and the tiny droplets began to move the surface of the sea. I saw three swans gliding toward the shore; one of them looked like a baby from the previous spring, as it was still covered in fluffy gray feathers. Uncle Jari had read me the story of the ugly duckling when I was a child, and he had to stop whenever I cried at the discrimination the poor duckling had to endure. I wanted to go into the story to show those ducks. Uncle tried to convince me that there was a happy ending, but I didn't believe him. I didn't finish the story until later in my teens, and I still wanted to avenge the poor duck's suffering, abandoned by his parents.

"What are you thinking about?" Trankov appeared next to me, now wearing white rubber-soled sneakers covered in drops of paint. He'd switched into light-blue jeans and a roomy jacket down to his knees. He wore a white T-shirt underneath. This man really knew how to dress for his roles. I understood where he was coming from.

"Ducks and swans," I told him.

"I bet you were never a duck," he said.

"Of course not."

Trankov already knew one of my soft spots—Stahl—and I wouldn't reveal any others.

"So, shall we? You've seen one of my paintings, so I thought I'd use a similar theme. It could become a sort of Diana, the goddess of hunting. Surely they teach Greek mythology in school here? And look what I found for you."

Trankov walked a few steps toward the veiled pile in the middle of the room and pulled the sheet away. I almost screamed when I saw the familiar tufted ears and spotted fur. The lynx was stuffed in a seated pose, its posture regal and whiskers thick. The taxidermist had wanted to display the animal in an alert state, yet benign, which is why its mouth was closed. Only the eyes looked wrong: they were made of glass and looked dead.

"What do you think?" Trankov asked.

"It's dead."

"What, you wanted a live one? We need to go to Russia for those. You can get anything in Russia. Or did you want the kind of fur coat Anita Nuutinen wore? Maybe a lynx pelt to stretch out on? I thought about that, too."

"Yuri, I don't want to see a dead lynx. Where did you find it?"

"I found this taxidermist online. This lynx was hit by a car somewhere in Juva. I had to drive hundreds of miles to get it just for this painting. It will be gorgeous. I'll lift it up on the pedestal a bit so you can lean your arm on it." Trankov got on his knees next to the animal and wrapped his arms around it. "I'll paint you two on a cliff so your posture looks natural. It's the lynx princess throne in the midst of majestic scenery. You two rule the world from high above."

Laitio was right to warn me about Trankov. He wasn't just dangerous; he was also deranged.

"I've dreamed of this painting for years. Ever since I heard how passionate you were about lynx. Here. Take this robe. You can wear it when we have a break. Now go take your clothes off. This studio is warm enough to keep you comfortable."

15

I stared at Trankov. I couldn't believe what I was hearing. We hadn't talked about nudity. Then again, I only had myself to blame for not asking questions. I had followed my instincts, and they told me Trankov would have some useful information. I had behaved like a lynx that jumps after a deer and doesn't notice a hunter in the bushes.

"All right, just hold your horses, Yuri," I told him in Finnish.

"I wasn't going to take anything off. Only you." I both despised and liked Trankov's smile. "Look at these sketches. They're just simple pencil drawings."

I'm not very well versed in the visual arts, but Mary Higgins had taught me a thing or two while I lived with her. Trankov's work was definitely old-fashioned and not abstract. It depicted a woman and a lynx high up on a cliff. The model could have been any woman.

"Can't you use your imagination? You could paint anyone. You don't need a model," I told him.

"I want to see how the light moves on your skin. You can't imagine that."

I had had enough of this. This lynx would take a leap and narrowly escape the bullet. I tried to assess whether Trankov was armed. His white smock didn't have a bulge.

"I'm surprised you're this shy. Based on your performance at the Bromarf villa, I had thought the opposite. You wouldn't be the first woman I've seen naked."

"I'm not interested in hearing about that." I yanked the bathrobe from his hands and disappeared behind the same door where he had changed clothes. It was a combination changing room and sleeping alcove and had a wide bed and a closet where Trankov's suit was. I went through his pockets, but all I found was a crumpled gas receipt. It looked like driving a Jaguar was getting expensive.

I didn't even know what I was expecting from him. Did he really want to paint me with no ulterior motives? I wasn't naïve. I had humiliated him, and he was biding his time before taking revenge. I'd knocked him unconscious and rescued the woman he'd planned on giving Paskevich as an offering.

I wasn't afraid of nudity. I had modeled for plenty of Mary's friends back in New York, and under their gazes I had felt just as comfortable as if I'd been dressed. What I worried about was the vulnerability of being naked. I couldn't hide anything. Still, I took off all my clothes except for my panties. Then I threw the bathrobe on and grabbed all my things before returning to the studio.

Trankov was setting the stuffed lynx on a sawhorse.

"How did you know lynx are important to me?" I asked. "You sold my neighbor a painting a couple of years ago, and it was meant as a message to me."

"When Valentin was planning his revenge on Anita Nuutinen, he looked into everything. Do you remember Mika Siiskonen, the bodyguard who worked for Nuutinen before you? Valentin's brother had some connections in Florida. Siiskonen badly injured his ankle and couldn't get back to work. Boris arranged a job for him at a gym in Fort Lauderdale. Siiskonen didn't mind going from sleet to sunshine."

"So you're saying there was nothing wrong with his ankle?"

Trankov propped up the lynx. He grabbed my shoulders and walked me next to the stuffed beast.

"Well, the ankle's not completely healed. Tougher men than him would break if their ankles were repeatedly hit with a metal bar. His ankle can't support his weight for more than a few feet."

"And who did the hitting?" I asked, although I didn't really want to hear the answer. A smile slowly spread across his face.

"This'll be good. Really good. Too bad your hair is so short. I'd like it to wave in the wind. Never mind. I can always paint it how I want. I can paint *you* the way I want." Trankov moved my right hand onto the lynx's coat. It didn't feel at all like Frida. This animal had had no name; it was just one of many pieces of roadkill. What time of year had it died? In the fall and winter, males traveled alone and would only search for mating companions in the spring.

"Siiskonen was extremely cooperative. He got us the keys to Nuutinen's house in Lehtisaari. The room for the new bodyguard had a lynx poster on the wall, and since it was the only personal item left behind, I thought it was important. The new bodyguard seemed smarter than Siiskonen—she changed all the locks and security cameras in the house. Of course we heard about that whole fur coat incident in Moscow. Valentin had informants everywhere. Even some of the people who worked for Vasiliev were loyal to Valentin. They didn't keep all their eggs in one basket." Trankov began squeezing oil paint out of the tubes and onto a mixing plate. "Then, when we finally found out your last name, the rest was easy. But let's not dwell on the past. We're friends now, aren't we?"

"And friends won't be clobbered with metal bars."

"I would never hit a woman." Trankov's hurt yelp was so exaggerated it made me relax. So this guy liked to brag about his exploits? Another weakness.

I knew a large oil painting took longer than a single afternoon, so I let Trankov get on with it. He moved the brush around the canvas, probably creating an outline. I recalled how Frida's bones had felt under her fur and how quickly she'd transformed from a relaxed feline into a nimble beast. This stuffed lynx didn't even smell like the real thing. I switched positions a couple of times, and it took at least half an hour before Trankov made his request.

"All right. You can take your robe off now. I'll get a better feel for the outlines."

I took the robe off and hung it on the sawhorse. The room was warm, not a single draft coming from the gigantic windows. Still, I felt goose bumps on my skin under Trankov's gaze. Maybe I was trusting too much in Trankov being like his father, who hadn't been able to resist women. I suppose Trankov hadn't been blind to the damage it had done to his father, many times over.

"Tell me, why were you allowed back into Finland again? Who told you about it?" I asked.

"It would be better if you didn't speak," Trankov said while dabbing a thin brush into light-brown paint. He took a look at me, then looked at the canvas and began to paint a thin line. "The Russian militia called me and said I could apply for a visa again. Despite that, Valentin doesn't feel comfortable coming back. He's worried about getting arrested. He doesn't have the same kind of friends that I do."

I didn't ask which friends. Trankov asked me to lift my chin a little and look into the distance, as if there were something interesting on the horizon.

"Look alert. You're the lynx princess observing her queendom. Enemies lurk everywhere."

I held my tongue and didn't criticize Trankov's artistic view, although it was hilarious. I guessed he was serious with this lynx princess business. I was also relieved that he didn't ask me to take my panties off. He was concentrating on his work, and the setting felt entirely professional. After an hour and a half of posing, I asked to step out of the pose. I was starting to cramp.

"Oh, yes, of course. Should I make some tea?"

"I can put the kettle on," I offered.

I would drink only what I made. I pulled on the bathrobe and walked into the small kitchen. I found cups in the cabinet along with an unopened box of black tea and a jar of honey. I wouldn't have any honey unless I saw Trankov taste it.

I turned the water boiler on after I made sure it was clean inside. Outside, I saw swans come out of the water and walk onto the shore. I wondered about Trankov's friends in high places. When did he look into getting hired by Syrjänen? They got along well, considering Trankov lived in Syrjänen's house.

After the water boiled I poured it into the cups and let it cool before I dropped in the tea bags. Trankov was transfixed by the painting; after some pondering he added a dot of dark brown. I wanted to ask him what he knew about David Stahl. David had laughed when I'd told him about my adventures in Bromarf; he'd asked me to tell the story again and again when we were in Spain. The memory made me teary eyed—good thing Trankov was still focused on the painting and didn't see my face.

I asked Trankov if he wanted honey in his tea. He didn't even turn his head when I poured some into his cup. I brought the teacup over to him and took a look at the painting. It was definitely just a starting point, and you could barely make out figures on the canvas. There was no need for me to be naked at this point, but because Trankov had painted with care, I didn't question it; he seemed to know what he was doing.

"Don't look at it just yet," Trankov said, looking embarrassed.

I went back to the kitchen and added honey to my tea, too. As a cub, Frida had stalked a swan that had ended up in our yard. She'd circled closer to the swan, but as soon as the swan spread its wings and hissed, Frida ran off. I'd watched them from afar and laughed. Later I'd regretted laughing at her. I don't think Frida had ever heard a bird hiss like a cat before.

"I turned up the heat so you won't get cold. I didn't even dream of using nude models back in Vorkuta, and as a young kid I don't think I would've dared to ask them to take their clothes off. We had just one room, and I used it for painting when Mom was at work. I had to be careful not to make a mess. The art school had plenty of light, but they had no heat. I had to wear fingerless gloves and heat my hands over a candle. Once, my glove caught on fire. I still have a burn mark on my left hand. Look." Trankov lifted the back of his hand to my face. An irregularly shaped red mark about the size of a quarter sat between his thumb and index finger.

"I was lucky. I had a teacup nearby and dipped my hand in it." Trankov toasted me with his cup.

"Does your mother still live in Vorkuta?"

Trankov turned serious and looked at the floor—another Achilles' heel. "No. She's dead."

"So is my mother."

"I know. Your father killed your mother. Maybe the same could be said about my mother."

"Are you saying Paskevich had her killed?"

Trankov walked to the window. The swans noticed his movements and rushed back to the shore.

"You can kill in so many ways. You don't need guns or poison to do it. But enough about my mother. Are you ready to continue?"

I downed my tea and asked if the powder room was behind the second door. I took my bag with me and looked in the mirror. I didn't like the way my eyes looked. I tried to bring out their glow.

Trankov had already begun to paint when I returned, but he stopped to pose me again. Even his gentlest touch felt heavy, and when he helped me take the robe off, my brain signaled, *Alert! Alert! Retreat immediately!* I didn't listen. I just posed. Luckily Trankov kept quiet. Brushes of all sizes flew over the canvas, and another hour went by quickly. It was almost four in the afternoon. I could see the dusk slowly creeping in from the sea. How long was he going to keep me here? I hadn't found out half of what I wanted to know. I had to find out more about Syrjänen's business plans.

Trankov painted for another half hour, then took a while to stretch. I was hungry, and although I had learned how to control feelings of hunger, those feelings often came out as anger. I always kept a couple of energy bars in my bag, so I had to rely on them.

"So you have no idea where David Stahl is?" Trankov's question startled me.

"Stahl has nothing to do with this," I said as I dug for my energy bars. I could feel the hard leather of my gun holster inside the bag. I peeled the wrapper off the bar and ate a third of it in one bite.

"Are you hungry? There's fish soup in the main building. All we need to do is heat it up. Let's take a break," Trankov suggested.

"I think I better get going. Can you take me to Kirkkonummi? I'll catch a train from there."

"Stay for dinner with me, and we'll also need to arrange to meet again. You can get dressed."

I was curious to see where Usko Syrjänen was living these days. The headquarters for his businesses was somewhere in Vantaa. The previously prepared fish soup sounded suspicious. I decided to take the risk while I walked to the changing room. Trankov's question about David bothered me. How much did he know about our relationship? Trankov had claimed that he could tell me things about David that neither I nor Stahl's so-called employers had a clue about. Were these scraps of information the reason I was standing here naked on the shores of Långvik?

"Did you want to take a look? The painting is not even remotely done, but I think you'll get the idea." Trankov pulled me by my wrist to the front of the stand.

Now the lynx looked like more than just a sketch; it was more alive on the canvas than the stuffed model. Trankov had worked quite a lot on my body as well; my painted version wore a wreath of flowers around her hips to hide the pubic area, and although my breasts were exposed, he'd managed to make me look demure rather than sexual. My face was only a sketch, as was the background, but the spirit had been captured. The image was neither menacing nor endearing; I would've called it dignified. I decided not to start making guesses as to why Trankov had wanted to paint it. I certainly wasn't an irresistible siren, and I doubted Trankov had chosen me because of a vendetta. I felt like he was waiting for feedback.

"Interesting," I said. "I just don't know what you're trying to say with this."

"Does art need to have a message? This is a portrait. Isn't that enough?"

I didn't want to argue. What did I know? I was just the model. I walked out of the room behind Trankov. He locked the studio door and took out the remote control to open the doors to the main building. The security camera for the main building was above those doors, and I flashed a smile at it. Once in, Trankov took my jacket and hung it in the foyer closet that was covered in full-length mirrors. I held on to my bag. This building, too, had large windows looking at the sea: the largest was the size of the entire wall in the living room. I could see the swans swimming again. There was movement on the shore across the bay. It looked like a tall man with binoculars around his neck. A bird watcher, I supposed. The shape slipped back into the dusk, and I felt cold all over. He had moved just like David. But he couldn't have been David, could he? I wanted to pull the shades to hide the view.

"So you live with Syrjänen. It's interesting how close you two are. You're not his secretary or a bodyguard. You're just his architect," I told Trankov.

"It's just temporary. Usko needs to travel a lot, so he needs a house sitter. When he goes to Russia, I'm his interpreter. His language skills aren't that great—he can barely speak English. I suppose that's why he and Vasiliev had some . . . misunderstandings."

"How did you end up working for Syrjänen?"

"The pieces just fell into place. Besides, I liked staying in Finland. It's so much safer here than Russia. You don't get thrown in jail or shot at your front door because you've criticized some politician."

"You just have your ankles smashed with an iron bar."

Trankov blushed. "Siiskonen was paid well for his services, and he got a one-way ticket to Florida to enjoy the sunshine. Should we eat? I'm hungry, too. It's easy to forget everything when you paint."

The table was already set in the kitchen: bowls, spoons, and a basket of bread covered with linen. The soup waited on the pristine ceramic stove top, and Trankov turned on the burner.

"Who's been cooking?" I asked.

"I have . . . or well, not really. I bought this soup from a restaurant in Helsinki."

I barely held back a sudden attack of the giggles. Trankov was multitalented, that was for sure; besides being a master painter, he was a great actor, too. But I still hadn't found out the plot for this vaudeville act. I'd be fine with that as long as it didn't turn out to be a tragedy.

Trankov stirred the soup. Then he asked me what I'd like to drink. I would've been fine with just tap water again, but he insisted I drink at least sparkling water.

"We have wine, too, you know," he said, but I refused. I kept a close eye on him. The pockets in his smock looked empty, but I wouldn't be sure unless I actually felt them. And he better taste the soup first. I peeked into the bread basket. The Russian black bread was already sliced, and I switched some slices around, just in case. If Trankov noticed what I was doing, he didn't comment on it. He brought the soup and a tray of butter to the table. By now my stomach was really grumbling. I stirred the soup in the pot and ladled some onto my plate. Then I opened my bottle of sparkling water. It made a safe hissing noise. I reached over to pour some for Trankov, who was serving soup for himself. The table was really narrow and bare, except for the place mats.

"Enjoy," Trankov said in Finnish. I raised my spoon, but I didn't taste the soup despite the combination of the creamy fish broth and pickled cucumber making my mouth salivate. Trankov's eyes were laughing at me.

"You really don't trust me, do you?" He spooned some soup into his mouth, smacked his lips, and swallowed. "This soup is excellent. Vasili is a great chef. You know, there are other great cooks in town, besides your staff."

Trankov ate another spoonful. I hadn't come up with a way he could've slipped tranquilizers into my bowl, so I started eating. The soup was spiced well and very buttery. I pulled a piece of bread out of the basket. Uncle Jari had called it Russki bread, but he hadn't meant it to be derogatory.

Once my energy was restored, I asked Trankov whether Syrjänen had plans to find a replacement for his holiday resort now that the Hiidenniemi plan had gone haywire.

Trankov gave me a sideways glance. "Still interested in Syrjänen? 'Easy does it,' Syrjänen says. He learned a lot from Hiidenniemi. You have to be patient and proceed based on possibilities. Syrjänen wants to see who gets a seat in the next election, then he'll know whom to contact for negotiations. All your journalists talk about is election funding. Isn't it obvious those on your side will be supported?"

I had had this conversation with Helena before, and I completely agreed with him, so I just nodded and poured some more soup.

"This has been my favorite dish since I was a child. I used to fish, although old ladies next door warned me that the fish in the river all had three eyes because of the pollution. But life is full of risks, right, Hilja?" The frenzy brought on by painting was now gone, and Trankov seemed relaxed. I couldn't allow myself to let my attention slip, although the warm soup had definitely calmed me.

"Stahl should be happy he's not behind bars," Trankov said, surprising me again so much that I almost choked on a piece of bread.

"What do you mean?" I asked between coughs. Even a sip of water didn't help. Trankov got up quickly and began to beat my back, slightly harder than necessary, but I could feel the piece of bread move. Trankov remained standing behind me. I could see his reflection in the window. I was half expecting his hands to slowly rise to my neck, and I was ready to bite and kick.

"He was a middleman. He didn't follow Europol orders. There was a warrant out on him, and he was finally located. Someone always leaks information when enough money is offered. He'd apparently had a long list of excuses, and some dumb people believed them."

"How do you know all this?"

"I'm still in touch with the source I used to find out about Stahl for Paskevich. Then it looked like Stahl was a double agent. Now he seems more like a triple or quadruple agent. Or maybe he's in it for himself. He's aware of the risks." Trankov's shrug was duplicated in the window. It was almost pitch-black now, and all I could see outside were the yard lights that had turned on automatically.

"Do you know where Stahl is?" I asked.

"How much are you willing to pay to know?" He placed his hand on my shoulder.

"Nothing. I'm not interested anymore."

"And why not?" Trankov asked while he slowly moved his hand along my shoulder to my neck, stroking my hair. I got up and pushed him away.

"I think it's time you take me to Helsinki—or at least to Kirkkonummi."

"Why such a hurry? Let the food settle, and let's relax on the couch. Then we can continue painting."

I had to admit that Trankov was a handsome young man whose smile was absolutely charming when he wanted it to be. I had no complaints about his slim body, either. I could just imagine the toned abs the smock and T-shirt were hiding. I stepped toward Trankov, and before I knew it my arms were around him. I pushed my cheek against his; he felt smooth and warm. How lonely I had been since April, with no one to touch me. Trankov was no David—nobody else would ever be—but why should he be replaced? Couldn't I just start over? I let Trankov kiss me, first cautiously and exploring, as if he thought I'd bite him if he got too rough. I smelled him, tasted him, and wondered whether it was right to feel this way. My eyes closed, as if they were protecting me from seeing who I was really kissing, who I was letting touch my butt, who I allowed to slide his lips along my neck and down to my collarbone. The man was Yuri Trankov. The man Laitio had warned me about numerous times.

16

The thought of Laitio brought me back to reality. I pushed away from Trankov and asked if he would take me somewhere or if I should call a cab. I was slightly surprised that he didn't try to convince me to stay; instead, he said he'd give me a ride all the way to Helsinki. I repeated that Kirkkonummi would be fine—there were plenty of buses and trains I could catch.

Trankov was awfully quiet in the car. Only after we'd gotten to Hirsala Road did he suddenly ask how "that politician" was doing.

"You mean Helena Lehmusvuo? How would I know? I'm sure she's busy with the election."

"She looked so startled when she saw me at the opening," Trankov said.

"For good reason! You drugged and kidnapped her. Or did that somehow slip your mind?"

"It wasn't personal," Trankov said. "We just wanted to find out how much she knew. If you see her, tell her I'm sorry. If you hadn't interfered we would have taken her back home safely."

Interesting. So if Trankov decided to, say, drug me or smack me in the head with an iron bar, I shouldn't take it personally—he had to do it, and I shouldn't be offended. Mike Virtue had lectured us about the ethics of various mafias, but it sounded like Trankov had his own Vorkuta-Moscow definition of what means were necessary.

"When can you come model for me again?" he asked. "I can always work on the background whenever, but I need you for another session."

"I don't remember when I have a day off, but I'll call you when I know."

"And don't forget. Otherwise, I'll come get you." Trankov took his hand off the steering wheel and stroked my thigh. I grabbed his hand and reminded him that he was under the watchful eyes of the Finnish police, so he better concentrate on driving. He just laughed.

He left me at the Kirkkonummi station. The next express train from Turku would stop in five minutes. Trankov made sure I got on the train and kissed me on both cheeks. I took the first available seat next to a window and saw Trankov still at the station, waiting. When the train began to move he blew me kisses.

Once I got home I locked my gun in its case and wondered how quickly I would lose my license now that my job didn't require a gun, and I didn't exactly use it for sport, either. I needed to get back to the shooting range.

Monika was still closing at Sans Nom. So far there had been no incidents: no annoying customers, no angry phone calls, and no anonymous threats. No one had appeared asking for protection money or to claim her food had gone bad. I knew I would soon be itching to get out of this boring job. The only exciting thing in my life right now was Yuri Trankov, and he wasn't enough.

I went back to Kari Suurluoto's story about my father having escaped twice from prison. Why had nobody told me? Sure, my father had lost custody as soon as he was behind bars, and his rights to me ended when I turned eighteen. I was a complete stranger to him.

Yrjö Street had a luxury bathtub, so I took a long, hot soak. Monika's environmentally conscious cousin apparently never used it, but I didn't give a thought to dying polar bear cubs when I let the hot water flow. I thought about how dirty I would have felt if I'd let myself have sex with Trankov just because of a childish desire for revenge against David. I'd never held myself back sexually, nor did I ever swear loyalty to another person—I had never promised David anything, and he hadn't asked me to. But Trankov certainly wasn't the solution for my emotional emptiness.

I thought of everything I knew about David. He hadn't been working for Europol that long and specialized in energy issues. He'd never been one to follow the rules. It had taken him three months to contact me after he blew up the boat. He'd claimed he spent the time healing and had gotten nasty frostbite from swimming in the sea. I wasn't supposed to ask him anything else—this was his way of keeping me safe.

I couldn't come up with anything that would have proved Trankov's claims about David to be false. I could see David Stahl suddenly changing teams and working for the criminals, especially if his former bosses were threatening him with jail time. David had never been good with authority.

"Often a clear chain of command makes our jobs easier. Do not rebel against your foremen just to prove a point. Sometimes you have to swallow your pride and give in. You need to learn how to tell what is appropriate in each moment." Mike Virtue's soft, low voice was inside my head as I added more hot water to the tub. Oh, Mike. I don't think you would have allowed David Stahl to attend the security academy. Money didn't buy placement in the academy; we all had to go through tests to see if we were a fit for the profession. I'd taken the cheapest possible flight with two layovers, in Stockholm and Amsterdam. Once I arrived in New York, I stayed three nights at a one-star hostel in the sketchiest-looking corner of Queens. The interview seemed more like an interrogation and had focused on my background, and I was sure my father's crime would prevent me from moving forward. Mike Virtue had given individual feedback about the test to every applicant. I remembered vividly how my pulse was beating in my wrists as I waited for my turn in the hallway. I didn't know how many had applied, but I knew they took only twenty. The African American man who had gone in before me came out looking pissed off and kicked the wall. Clearly he wasn't a fit for bodyguard work. Mike waited for me behind his desk with a pile of papers stacked in front of him. Our tests. He'd devised the questions.

"Sit down please," he told me, a phrase I was familiar with from classroom English, but his accent was different than my teacher's back in Outokumpu. I wanted to remain standing; I could then make a quick getaway before Mike saw how disappointed I was in the results.

"I've never had a student from Finland. We had a Dane a few years back, but I don't think you guys are culturally similar. Are you Finns more like Russians?"

I felt like passing or failing hung on this question.

"We aren't like anybody else. We're used to being in between others. Our national poet, Runeberg, said we're not Swedes, we won't become Russians, so let us be Finns."

"That's interesting," Mike said. "You're the first Finn to be accepted to the academy. Welcome." He got up and extended his hand.

I shook it with a broad smile on my face. Only later did I thank my lucky stars for Mike not knowing much about Finnish history—the quote I'd given him was actually from A. I. Arwidsson, a man who promoted Finnish cultural identity.

Even the bath wasn't calming. I thought about biking to meet Monika on her way home from work but decided to use my computer instead. I used Laitio's login information to access the Bureau's website. I wasn't sure what I was doing there, so I typed in David Stahl's name. There was no information about him, nor about Daniel Lanotte. I wished I could get my hands on Rytkönen's computer; he must have had access to all sorts of information. Next I typed in Carlo Dolfini's name. The shoeless man was bothering me six months after the incident.

Bingo! There was an entire report. "Dolfini, Carlo Pietro Giovanni. Born April 4, 1969, in Rome. Moved to Abruzzo County in Lago di Scanno in 2005. Profession: baker. He has run bakeries in Trastevere and Scanno. Family includes wife Rosa, no children. (Not at least with Rosa; no information on possible children outside of this marriage.) Has connections to the mafia in Rome, moved to Lago di Scanno to hide from them? (Not confirmed.) Wife alleges he traveled to the United States last spring, and according to the neighbors the wife followed him later. There is no immigration information for either of them ever arriving in the country."

The sentences that followed made my heart stop.

"A partially decomposed body was found during an effort to dry out a marsh in Maremma on October 18, and the body was identified as Carlo Dolfini. He was shot in the back of the head. Mrs. Dolfini has not been found. Relatives have no information. The local police are investigating (or claiming to investigate!!!) Dolfini's death. Most likely they aren't."

Based on these last sentences, the writer had been Laitio. Had he just gotten the information from Caruso in Italy? Why else wouldn't he have told me about Dolfini? I knew the reason. Laitio wanted to protect me. He wanted me to forget about Stahl. Whoever had left Dolfini's body in Montemassi must have found out that someone stayed there with Stahl. I was allowed to come back to Finland without incident and was left alone because either I hadn't seen anything the murderer would have considered worrisome for his or her security or the killer was David. That didn't explain why his cell phone was in Dolfini's pocket, though.

None of this speculation was helping. *Just accept it and move on. You'll never find out*, my logical side tried to tell me. Too bad that voice had never been particularly strong.

Monika had come back and was rummaging around in the kitchen, so I turned the computer off. She asked how my day was, and I gave her a vague answer about walking in the woods, although my ears were burning with this lie. I went to bed and closed my eyes, but the image of bare feet sticking out of a swamp kept me awake. I heard a female voice in my ears, "Where are you, Carlo? With some woman?" How soon after the call had Rosa Dolfini "traveled to the US"? I didn't know these people, and if Carlo Dolfini had really worked for the mob, he would have known the risks he was taking.

I loathed myself, lying there under my blanket and wondering if David was alive to see the nearly full moon whose bright light was forcing its way into my room. I had to get up to close the curtains. I saw a man making his way down the street. He was small and wide, and once he reached my window, he turned so I could see his face. It was Martti Rytkönen.

I woke up calm even though I'd seen Rytkönen the previous night. Why wouldn't a man stroll over to the intersection of Yrjö and Eerikki in the middle of the night? Why did I assume it had to be about me? Still, I had a hard time concentrating at work. While I drove to Veikkola for a load of organic root veggies, I kept thinking about David's family and whether they knew anything. David had told me about them often: his father, who was half-Russian and half-Estonian, and his mother, who was from Finland's Tammisaari and had gone to study Russian in Tartu, Estonia. He'd told me about his sisters who were about ten years older than him. One of them was married, the other wasn't, but all of them still lived in Tartu. Surely David would have told them he was still alive? I thought about getting in touch with them and claiming to be a close friend who was worried about David's disappearance. I remembered his parents' names: Anton and Eva. The sisters were Sofia and Johanna. I didn't know whether Sofia had taken her husband's last name. Johanna was single.

My other option was Brother Gianni. He might know something. The monastery must have had a phone, if not Internet, and I knew Brother Gianni would keep his mouth shut. Whatever I decided to do, I had to do it quickly—I felt like David was more in my life than ever before, urging me to find him.

Damned Stahl and this goddamned obsession! I was so lost in thought that I didn't notice the Mercedes-Benz that had ignored the yield sign on a side road. I slammed on the brakes and drove off the road. I managed to stop the car before it went into the ditch, and the Mercedes kept on its merry way. It took me a bit of revving to get the van out of the mud and back on the road.

When I got back to the restaurant, I spotted Veikko sitting on the back patio with his buddies, having coffee and leftover Karelian pasties from the day before.

"What's up, girl?" they hollered when I hopped out of the van to unload the vegetables.

"Rutabaga, turnips, carrots, and beets—that's what's up," I told them.

"You're planning on making a *rosolli* salad?" asked Veikko.

"It's not the season for Christmas foods yet, right?" Veikko's friend asked me. When I nodded he said, "So you're kind of the security woman of this restaurant?"

"Well, sort of, if there's even a need for one," I told him.

"Seems like there is a need. Last night some strange guy was creeping around. I didn't want to tell the girl who served us our coffee in the morning—she's so fragile she would've gotten scared."

"I don't get spooked easily. Tell me more about the guy."

Veikko's friend finished his pasty. The mixture of smashed boiled eggs and butter fell off the pasty onto his shirt, and the man wiped it off with a handkerchief. "I had to get up in the night when—"

"Don't use foul language! A woman's present!" Veikko interrupted and shoved his cup toward the man, showering coffee onto the street.

"Take it easy. I had to take care of business. I saw a man circling the patio and taking pictures of the building. It looked like he was avoiding the security cameras."

"What did he look like?"

"I only saw him from behind. He was pretty short but wide. He wore a dark coat, no hat. His shoes looked expensive."

This sounded familiar. A gentleman fitting this description had been lurking below my window the night before, too. I just had to confirm my suspicions from the security cameras.

"Do you think he was going to break into the restaurant?"

"Not sure, but he definitely knew about the security cameras."

"Thanks." I dug for a twenty in my wallet and gave it to Veikko's friend.

As soon as I was done unloading the van, I walked into the office to check out the CCTV monitors. I made sure all files from the previous evening were saved and brought the cameras back online. Then I viewed the files.

This character had definitely known how to avoid the cameras. Still, there were a couple of glimpses that didn't completely crush my theory about it being Rytkönen. I just wondered what he was up to. Why would an officer from the Bureau show interest in the security system at a restaurant in Ruoholahti? Not to steal our booze. I had a bad feeling he was here for me. Had Rytkönen found out that I was the one calling him from Stahl's phone?

Jouni called for me from the kitchen, saying we had an emergency. Two of the kitchen staff had caught the flu. So for the next week, I worked in the kitchen as a sous chef while each staff member took a turn getting the flu, including Monika and Jouni, but luckily they were off at different times. I remained healthy. I checked the security cameras daily for new signs of Rytkönen slinking around, but he was nowhere to be seen.

Päivi Väänänen-Huttunen kept her promise and called me when I was on my way to work the evening shift. She sounded agitated.

"I couldn't keep reading those diaries. They just seemed so childish," she said. "The things a high schooler worries about. Apparently getting a *B* on an English test was the end of the world. But I did find something about Anneli. She was always very happy. In my diary I wondered how she could be in such a good mood all the time. I guess I was envious of her, too. Boys liked her because she was so easygoing."

"Was she a flirt?"

"Not more than others. In the early seventies, girls had to pretend to be much more prudish than girls these days, and we had to wait for the boys to make the first move. Anyway, the diaries aren't actually that important. I called Tiina Turpeinen, her last name is Mäkelä now. She told me the police had dropped by to talk with her about your mother's murder early last year. Tiina couldn't figure out why they had opened the case again. Your father had been convicted, and that was the end of it. The police officer who came by was pretty strange, too, but he had a valid-looking international badge."

"An international badge? Do you have Tiina Mäkelä's phone number? Where does she live?"

Päivi gave me a phone number and mentioned that Tiina Mäkelä lived across from the Siuntio church. I thanked her and typed in Tiina's number so hastily that I mistyped it twice. I called, but she didn't pick up. I left her a voice mail, and it took only a couple of minutes for her to call back.

"Sorry, I don't answer unknown numbers," she said. "So nice to hear from you, Hilja. I've thought of you often, especially since that police officer visited me in the spring. How are you?"

I really didn't have the patience for small talk, so I told Tiina that I was working at a restaurant in Helsinki and lived downtown. Then I asked her to tell me more about the police officer.

"He was tall. Had an accent when he spoke Finnish."

"Do you remember his name?"

"I may have written it down somewhere. He didn't give me a business card. Let's see . . ." I heard the phone hit the table. "Here we go. I can't really tell from the handwriting . . . Looks like the last name begins with an 's,' and only the first letter of the first name is legible. I'm thinking 'p'?"

I was pretty sure it was a 'd.' I asked Tiina if she would have time to meet tomorrow morning. It was my day off.

"I'd love to, but I'm working in the morning. School's out at three. Can you come then?"

I said okay but that I had to make some arrangements. We agreed to meet at Tiina's place at three thirty.

When I got to Sans Nom, chaos was still in full swing. Monika, who was rarely upset, had a fit when I told her I was going to Siuntio the following afternoon.

"But we have a private event until three. We can't manage without you. Mohammed and Alex are sick, and Helinä's nose is so runny I can't let the customers see her."

"Well, you'll just have to manage."

"Monika, don't let Hilja always get her way," Jouni roared out of eyesight.

"And you shut the hell up! Can't I go to Veikkola for the vegetable pickup tomorrow instead of the day after tomorrow? They're not in the ground anymore, right?"

"I need fresh produce for Friday," Jouni growled.

Monika found a compromise. I was only allowed to meet with Tiina Mäkelä for thirty minutes, then I had to hurry back.

As soon as I got off work, I looked through my things for the best picture of David I could find. It had been taken near the mountains in Seville in the spring, about one and a half years ago. David's hair was blond and short, and he looked straight into the camera. His eyes smiled, but his lips didn't. That's why I had liked this picture the most: it looked like David was revealing to the photographer—me—what he really thought with his eyes. But perhaps the laughter in his eyes was aimed *at* me. David had told me in Montemassi multiple times that he couldn't risk coming back to Finland since he left on the *I Believe*. Now it seemed clearer than ever that he had lied to me.

The empty van shook in the wind as I drove the Turku motorway toward Veikkola. I blasted *Musta Humppa*, a Led Zeppelin cover by the band Eläkeläiset, in the car stereo. In Veikkola I threw the root vegetables and other veggies into the van so carelessly that Jouni would have told me off. He went to extremes to make sure his ingredients were clean and high quality, and this occasionally unnerved Monika, who didn't want to waste food by throwing it away. I took the route to Siuntio through Lapinkylä and was soon stuck behind a tractor pulling a load of chopped wood. No matter how I flashed my lights, the driver didn't let me pass. It was twenty to four when I finally pulled into Tiina Mäkelä's yard. She opened the door before I even rang the bell. A dachshund jumped out from behind her and started barking at me, showing Tiina how alert he was.

"Onni really wants to go for a walk, but he'll just have to wait until we're done. Come on in," Tiina said.

I walked along the maze of a hallway to the dining room. Tiina was only familiar to me from pictures. Her soap-opera hairstyle had turned into a light-gray bob, and her square black glasses gave her a sharp expression.

She took a good look at me, then bluntly said, "You don't look much like Anneli. More like your father." It sounded like she had just given me a prison sentence. "Want some coffee?"

"First tell me about that police officer. Why did he come to see you, and what did he want?"

"See, that's what I was wondering, too. He even called me a couple of times and made sure I was the same person who had attended high school and the classroom-teacher program with Anneli Karttunen, later known as Anneli Suurluoto. I asked him why they were interested in the case thirty years after Anneli's death. The officer said he was doing research on spousal murder characteristics across Finland, Estonia, and Germany. He said it was a project for some European police force, and Anneli's murder case had been chosen as one of the sources. When he first called me, I told him I didn't want to even think about what happened. He gave me a few days to mull it over, and of course the predictable happened when I was forced to return to my past. Anneli began to haunt me."

"How?"

"She appeared in my dreams. You were there once, too, walking along the church aisle, crying. As if Anneli was demanding to be remembered and that I needed to talk to the police officer. Like I somehow owed it to her. So I finally agreed to meet with him, just like I agreed to meet you."

The man had come over and asked Tiina to tell him everything she remembered about Anneli and to look for any old photos she might have. When I heard this I got goose bumps.

"Do you happen to have a picture where my mother is smiling and wearing a ruby ring on her ring finger? The picture we displayed at her memorial?"

"Yes, I do. Do you want to see it? The man asked to take that one and a couple of others for making copies, and he returned the originals like he promised."

"First, let me show you a picture." I pulled a photo of David from my purse. "Is this the police officer who visited you? David Stahl?"

Although David's hair was black when we'd met in Italy, I'd seen his Europol badge and I knew that he had a blond crew cut in it.

Tiina barely glanced at the photo. "Yeah, that's him. And you're right, the name was Stahl. I have to say, he looks a lot scarier in this picture than in real life. He made me feel somehow guilty for Anneli's death. And I'll tell you straight, too, I never liked Keijo, and that's why your mother and I didn't stay in touch. Anneli followed Keijo to Lappeenranta and dropped out of school when you were born. She said she'd finish her studies later, although Keijo didn't want her to."

While I was fascinated by these memories of my mother, I interrupted and asked Tiina for the exact date when David had seen her. She went to get a thick journal. The date was March 28, a couple of weeks before I'd gone to Italy. David had told me that he'd been in Italy since February.

My time was up, and I had to get back to Sans Nom. Tiina asked when we could meet again; she wanted to get to know Anneli's daughter better. I didn't want to promise anything. I was so humiliated and angry at David that I was determined to throw the ruby ring into the sea and tear up all his photos.

I worked for a week and a half before I had my next day off, a Monday. The last time Sans Nom had been closed, I'd spent it cleaning and prepping foods to compensate for the lack of staff. It was now November, and the days were even darker. I had always considered Helsinki a well-lit city, but now shady corners were everywhere, and the darkness ate all my energy. Nothing seemed to bring it back, not long jogs along the shore, dark chocolate, or even vitamins. Trankov called me at the restaurant a couple of times and persistently demanded to find out when we'd continue with his painting, but each time, my hands were tied with Sans Nom. The last time he called, it turned out he was pretty busy, too. He had to go to Moscow with Syrjänen. He said he'd call me when he got back, but he didn't know when that would be. When I hung up I felt like I had been released from under an oppressive weight. Maybe Trankov had finally had enough of me.

At six o'clock on Monday evening, I caved. I called the international number service to look up David's family members. There was a phone number for Anton Stahl in Tartu, no other relatives came up in the search. I asked for the address. David had told me how his family lived in the city center near a moat park. When I located a map of Tartu online, I saw that the address fit this description. While we'd been in Montemassi, David had planned on taking me to meet his family, as soon as it would have been safe for him to return to Estonia. I had really believed him.

I peeked out of my room to see what Monika was up to. On her evenings off she usually meditated, and when she was in that state, she didn't hear or see anything. I closed the doors between our rooms. I didn't want her to know how desperate I was. I prepared myself to find out that David was dead. Or that he was in Tartu with a wife. Or in a prison in Belarus. I tried to prepare myself for everything while I dialed the phone number. First the numbers for a nondomestic call, then Estonia's country code, and finally the land-line number for the Stahls. Cell phone information wasn't available.

A woman answered. It sounded like a TV was turned on to a sports channel—I could hear the excited commentator.

"Are you Eva Stahl, David's mother?" I asked in Swedish, knowing it was Eva's first language.

"Who is this?" Her tone dropped, and she sounded suspicious, then hissed something in Estonian. The TV was turned down. So there were other people around.

"I'm Hilja, David's friend." I knew David had been back to see his parents the year before, in the fall. Now I'd find out whether I was brought up during that trip.

"What friend? What is this about? What do you know about David? Are you from the police?"

"When was the last time you saw him?" Confusion might turn out to be the best weapon.

"A year ago. We haven't heard a single word, except what the Finnish police told us. And you're a Finn, too, aren't you? You speak Swedish like a Finn, and your name is Finnish."

"That's right. I'm Finnish. The police officer who called you was my colleague Martti Rytkönen, right? He's not on David's case anymore."

"Yes, Rytkönen. He was a nice man. You said you're David's friend. What's your name again?"

"Hilja . . . Karttunen. I also work with him in Europol."

If Rytkönen called David's parents again and found out that someone had called, he'd figure out it was me, but I had no time to hesitate.

"Do you have any news about David? Is he finally safe? Or was he thrown into jail for supposedly murdering that Italian man?" Eva Stahl's voice was anxious and hopeful.

"Unfortunately, we do not have that information. We've lost track of him."

The woman let out a little yelp. I wanted to stop lying and tell her I was just as desperate as she was to find out what had happened to her son. Only my pride prevented me from doing this.

"What did he tell you about Carlo Dolfini's murder?"

"Only that he was innocent. He is, isn't he?"

I didn't know what to say. David had lied to me, so I was sure he could do it to his mother, too.

"David said he had been staying with Jaan. Are you familiar with Jaan Rand? He's a monk at a monastery in Tuscany, goes by the name Brother Gianni. But even he doesn't know about David," Eva Stahl continued.

"Yes, I've met Jaan."

"They treated Jaan so poorly. They can't do the same to David. Can't you help him?"

I was curious to know what she meant by the poor treatment, but I couldn't ask. I would get in touch with Brother Gianni for details later.

"Listen, if you hear from David, anything at all, please get in touch with us. It might be important for his safety." I wasn't sure if giving my phone number to David's mother was wise, but I quickly came up with a better option and told her Teppo Laitio's number. I'd memorized it by now.

"This is my secretary's number. He's called Laitio. Tell him you have a message for Hilja. Remember to mention the first name, not just my last name, Karttunen," I advised.

Eva Stahl repeated the number. I felt like we both hung on to the phone call as if it were the last shred of hope, although neither of us could give the other information that would make us less anxious.

"I know David's been in sticky situations before. He would not have been able to tell you absolutely everything, and neither can I." My lukewarm words sounded hollow, and by the time they reached Tartu, they'd turned cold.

I'd never seen pictures of David's family—he never carried them around. If they were as careless as half of the Western world, I might find some images on the web or Facebook. I wanted to know whether David had his mother's eyes, as Eva Stahl's muffled voice betrayed the tears in them.

"I don't know what to believe anymore. That police officer, Rytkönen, told me that David had violated his contract and some laws, and he was going to prison. An Italian one?" she asked.

"Rytkönen doesn't know all the facts about this case. Call my secretary as soon as you hear from David. Good-bye." I hung up.

For a minute I sat with my mouth open. Then I began to gather my thoughts. Rytkönen must have been incredibly arrogant or a goddamned moron if he didn't think I would get in touch with the Stahls, too. There was only one way to find out. I browsed the Bureau's secured pages for a while, then got dressed. It would be safe to make a phone call among the crowds in the railway station, and I'd still have time to get a new phone card from the kiosk.

Eva Stahl's voice was still in my head when I walked down into the tunnel that went past Amos Anderson Art Museum. Eva and her husband had wanted to name their son after a benign king, but instead their offspring was a boy with multiple marks of Cain on his forehead. I recalled the desperate eyes of the statue of David. I wanted to believe that David Stahl had been forced to do the inevitable, but it was difficult.

There was a line at the kiosk, and the crowd gave my call the perfect protective layer. It took Rytkönen thirty seconds to answer. I tuned my voice all scratchy and unclear before I began to talk.

"Kassi, I think we should meet."

17

I had no plans of meeting Rytkönen as myself. It was time for Reiska Räsänen to come out of the closet. I knew it was a hell of a risk, but I was ready to take it. To make sure I'd have time to prepare, I arranged to meet with Rytkönen on Sunday, at eleven.

Rytkönen didn't seem stupid. Obviously he wanted to know how I'd found out his number, what my connection to David Stahl was, and how I knew his code name, Kassi. I promised to tell him. I wanted the meeting place to be perfect—poorly lit would be best. I ended up suggesting Ourit Island at the very end of the Hietaniemi beach. On a cold November Sunday evening, it shouldn't be a popular place to jog.

As far as I knew, Rytkönen had only seen me once for a few minutes at Laitio's apartment. Now he had probably seen pictures of me and maybe some camera footage. He'd maybe even studied the way I moved and walked. Or that's what I would've done.

I started getting ready and evoked Reiska early in the morning and the darkest hours of the night. Monika had never met him, and now wasn't the best time to explain why I needed to dress up as a man. I didn't dare smoke in the apartment, so Reiska wouldn't light up until he met Rytkönen.

I went through the Bureau files again. Rytkönen, Martti Kullervo was a lawyer from Iisalmi. He'd immediately recognize Reiska's dialect. They might even bond over it if I was lucky, although I doubted whether the bond would be tight enough to make Rytkönen spill the beans about Stahl.

Then there was the chance that Rytkönen was David's right-hand man and knew everything about me and my alter ego. In that case I had nothing to worry about.

I found Brother Gianni's aka Jaan Rand's contact information from the Sant'Antimo monastery website. I risked sending him an e-mail, although it could have been intercepted. If David was lying to me, why should I protect him? If I sent my message in Finnish, at least nobody else in the monastery would understand it. Although the website looked modern, I had a hard time imagining each monk having a computer in his little chamber.

Dear Brother Gianni, or Jaan Rand, It seems you forgot to mention that David had been in Finland only a couple of weeks before I arrived in Italy. David didn't tell me this either, but I found out. He's not quite as clever as he thinks he is. I also spoke with his mother. Sounds like there was a good reason for you to become a monk. Was it something to do with David? Best regards, Hilja Ilveskero

I drove Monika to work on Thursday in the pouring rain. We were fully staffed again, and everything ran like clockwork. On our way to the restaurant, Monika asked if I was satisfied with my life. I didn't know what to tell her.

"Why wouldn't I be?" I finally said. "Are you satisfied?"

"I don't know. I keep thinking about all sorts of stupid stuff. Like how empty the restaurant felt when Jouni was sick for days," Monika said and sighed.

"Are you obsessed with men whose names begin with Jo? First Joau, now Jouni. Who's next? Please don't tell me you're going to hire someone named Jorma."

"Shut up! I know Jouni is living with his girlfriend, who doesn't like his long days at the restaurant one bit. I guess that's why I'm interested in him—I can't have him! How about you? Are you ready to move on from David yet?"

"I can find men in bars if I want to. Hey, how about you and me go out one night and pick up some guys? I can go to his place or get a room at Hotel Torni, and you can bring yours to the apartment. How about . . ." I was going to suggest Sunday evening because I had Monday off, but then I remembered my plans with Rytkönen. We turned into Sans Nom's courtyard, and Jouni and Helinä were comforting Veikko, who was crying.

"What's going on here?" I jumped out of the car with the motor running.

"It's Ripa . . . he's gone to meet his maker. He died in the cold, right there at the back door. I wish he would've died in the warmth of the recycling container. Poor Ripa," Veikko said.

I turned to look at the back door, where an unrecognizable lump had been covered in a tablecloth under the marquee. I walked over and yanked off the colorful cloth. It looked like Veikko's friend had convulsed and choked on his own vomit. I grabbed his wrist and checked for a pulse, but it looked like he'd been dead for hours. It was strange that nobody in the apartments above had spotted the body. Maybe the marquee had hidden it. The office parking spaces were in front of the house, so the workers wouldn't have seen him when they arrived.

"I don't even know when he left the box. He must've felt sick and didn't want to puke in our bed. Wish he'd at least woken me up. I feel like I'm having a heart attack," Veikko said.

"Did you call the police?" I asked.

"What's the use? He died of booze like all of us." Veikko had now gone pale and was holding his chest. "Looks like it might be my time to go, too."

I immediately called the police and requested an ambulance. I moved the van out of the way and did some police work of my own. I checked the security cameras for clues of Ripa's time of death. Around 3:00 a.m. someone moved in the yard, but all I could see were Ripa's shoes. He didn't walk all the way to the door. I checked the front-facing cameras, too. Ripa had been walking in front of the restaurant, and I could clearly see him at 3:06 a.m. The next image showed another man's shoes, so Ripa had had company. I didn't want to give this material to the police, because I needed to investigate whether the shoes matched those of the stalker in the backyard the other day, and I suspected it was Rytkönen. It wasn't private property; anyone had the right to walk there, even in the middle of the night. That was no crime. Offering someone poisoned liquor, however, was.

I heard the police car arrive so I hastily copied the images to a USB stick. I couldn't hide the information from the police, nor could I delete it—they'd find out what happened. I just had to cross my fingers that the police didn't think of asking about the cameras.

The policeman named Miettinen was nearing retirement age, and the other one, Keronen, looked young enough to be a rookie. He tried to hide the nausea building up as he observed the body, whereas Miettinen seemed tired of alkies.

"Was the deceased very ill?" Miettinen asked Veikko, who was still clutching his chest. Where was the ambulance?

"His internal organs were shot to hell," Veikko said. "His doctor had told him to lay off the drinking because if he didn't, Ripa wouldn't live for long. And sure enough, he didn't. We had plans to go to rehab over Christmas."

"And the deceased's name is?"

"Risto Antero Haapala."

"Do you remember his date of birth?"

"He was born in midsummer. You know, the *real* midsummer. I can't remember the year. He was over sixty."

"Any close relatives?" Miettinen managed to ask before the ambulance screeched in with its siren on.

Veikko went even paler when he saw the ambulance.

While the first responders took care of Veikko, other paramedics loaded Ripa into the ambulance. I was hoping the police would take off without further investigation. When the ambulance took Veikko away, I wondered if I'd ever see him again. And who would arrange Ripa's funeral? Did he have an estranged wife and a couple of kids who were ashamed of him? And would they be happy he'd taken a job in the great air force in the sky? I might never know.

I asked the police if they knew Veikko's last name, and they cursed simultaneously. In all that commotion they'd forgotten to ask. Nobody in the restaurant knew, either. The police would find it out from the hospital. They wrote down information about Sans Nom's staff and asked them routine questions about the kind of life the homeless alcoholics were leading in the recycling container out back. Even if Ripa's autopsy showed signs of poisonous booze, only Veikko would be interrogated. If he had bought that bottle for his friend he could be accused of manslaughter.

"If you find it out, could you let us know Veikko's last name? I just feel so bad for the poor guy. I want to know what happens to him," Monika said as the police were leaving. Jouni had already gone back into the kitchen.

"Are you a relative?"

"No, just a friend."

"Well, that's not enough," Miettinen said. Keronen scratched his ear and didn't say a word, just looked down at his notepad where he'd scribbled Monika's phone number. Later in the afternoon Monika told me that Veikko's last name was Vuorinen and that he was recovering from a heart attack. He still needed immediate surgery. That's all Keronen had found out.

Now that we were all running behind schedule, I didn't have a chance to look more closely at the CCTV images until later in the afternoon. I compared the shots of the weird character Ripa had reported lurking about and the man who had been with Ripa the night before. The shoes weren't the same, and although the pant legs seemed to match, there were probably thousands of pairs of dark wool pants in the city. The creep was short, although Ripa was not tall, and his knees were much higher than the mystery man's. Whoever it was hadn't bothered to change his walking style, either. The man in both of the camera shots moved in a bit of a waddle, like someone with really thick thighs. It seemed to point to Rytkönen, making me even more curious to meet him. Maybe he had found out that the raspy voice on the other end of the line was me. Still, it didn't make sense for him to sneak around my place and the restaurant when he could have just picked me up in a police car and taken me to headquarters for interrogation. Maybe Rytkönen knew David's phone had been in Carlo Dolfini's pocket. I tried not to panic. When Dolfini's body had emerged from the marsh in Maremma, it meant someone hadn't done their job well.

Jouni went to see Veikko at the hospital the next day. Veikko was going to be taken to a rehab clinic in Ridasjärvi, where he could take time to heal from his bypass surgery.

"He was pretty shaken up, and I'm not surprised. He's a man who's used to freedom. He did say he had already spent a few winters in Ridasjärvi with Ripa and then left the clinic when summer rolled around to roam the shores of Helsinki, boozing. Looks like Veikko has to give up those summers now," Jouni said.

I had never had such a romanticized view of the life of a homeless alcoholic. Working as a security guard, I'd seen enough of them going from one bottle to another. Some of my colleagues had considered them less than human, and they used all possible chances to humiliate them and beat them up. The homeless men wouldn't talk to the police. I'd followed the antics of Veikko and Ripa the entire summer when we were fixing up the restaurant, and suddenly it was strange to not see them peeking out of the recycling container or drinking at the shore. Because the cause of death seemed obvious, the police probably weren't in a hurry to do Ripa's autopsy. Maybe there were only two of us in this world who wanted to see the report: I, who suspected foul play, and the person who had committed the crime and hoped nobody would ever find out.

I took all week to prepare for my role as Reiska. Petter had decided to take his sister to the Haikko spa on Sunday night, saying that Monika was overworked and in need of some pampering. This suited me fine; I got to be home alone, and I had plenty of time to transform into Reiska. On my way to the Ourit Island, I could smoke a couple of cigarettes to shroud myself in Reiska's usual scent.

Reiska wasn't an attention seeker. He dressed like an average Finnish man, except the T-shirt thanking Winter War veterans usually drew some attention. This late in the year, it wasn't warm enough, so I left it at home. I wore thermal underwear under the jeans and stuffed the crotch with a hair roller. Reiska's worn-out combat boots were a size too large for me, but a thick pair of wool socks helped them feel tighter. Reiska wore a checked collared shirt and a wool shirt from the Prisma market under his brown leather jacket. He decided to wear a baseball cap to hide the eyes.

Reiska Räsänen didn't have a license to carry a gun, unlike Hilja Ilveskero, so the gun had to stay behind. I wasn't planning on getting shot by a police officer. Reiska didn't carry much in his wallet. He had an old library card for Kaavi library that even a grade-schooler could've forged, a couple of business cards, and a photo I had found at a secondhand store. It was taken in the early 1980s, and the mustachioed man holding a baby boy dressed in colorful terry-cloth coveralls could have easily been Reiska's dad. I looked a couple of years older as a man than as a woman, which Reiska had to remember when he chatted with other men in bars about Finland's greatest accomplishments, such as winning the hockey world championship or Mika Häkkinen's victories on the racetrack.

I fumbled around with the fake mustache for a while—I hadn't practiced enough. The mustache was made by a costume assistant at a theater in New York. She'd wanted to know whether my father had had a mustache, but all I had been able to tell her was that his hair was light brown. I didn't recall seeing Keijo Suurluoto with a mustache or a beard, and I had no clue whether his body hair was thick and black or wispy and light, like Uncle Jari's. I was glad I had forgotten. Reiska's mustache was slightly lighter than his hair, which was a wig. It made sense to let the impostor hair poke out from underneath his baseball cap.

As a medium-sized man, I was less noticeable than as a tall woman. Unfortunately, I was more susceptible to getting into fights in the wee hours at a hot dog stand or a cab station. Women in the same situations would have to just fend off unwanted attention.

Reiska did his best to keep a low profile and stay out of trouble, although this meeting with Rytkönen wasn't a careful gig.

I left the apartment after ten to make sure I'd arrive on time. I was smoking as I walked, and I tried to suppress my cough when the smoke entered my lungs. *David, for you I'm willing to get cancer,* some pathetic creature squeaked inside Reiska's head. He shooed Hilja away quickly.

Hietalahti Street was completely empty. The cemetery was already closed. As a kid I had believed skeletons really climbed out of their coffins during a full moon and made a racket with their dancing. Or at least the remaining skeletons would have—my mother had gone to space in a space capsule. I had to admit I still wasn't entirely convinced there were no ghosts. I occasionally saw people who had already passed on: my mother, Uncle Jari, sometimes even a child who hadn't grown any more than an inch. The ghost ride inside my brain was alive and kicking.

Along the shore I saw an old white-haired man approach me with two large brown dogs that jumped around energetically, seeming to enjoy the nippy weather. The puddles on the road weren't frozen over yet, but the sky was full of bright stars, and the strips of clouds were thinning before my eyes. Sunglasses were a ridiculous accessory in this weather, but I still put on my aviators when I hid behind a large spruce to wait for Rytkönen. The glasses would turn darker in sunlight, so right now they were fairly light—but at least they covered my eyes a little.

The island was surrounded by docked boats, packed away for winter. I could always hide among the boats if the situation got sticky. I looked for security cameras, but I couldn't locate any.

Rytkönen arrived a few minutes before our meeting time and parked in the one remaining spot in the lot. I'd told him over the phone that he had to come alone, but there was no way I could verify that he'd actually followed my orders. The entire Hietaniemi beach could be littered with police, and Rytkönen could have carried at least a recorder or a video camera, but I had taken risks like this before, too. And like I had once confessed to David, I actually enjoyed danger. Mike Virtue considered this the worst mistake a bodyguard could make. Danger should be nothing to get excited about, and if it was, you were in the wrong line of work. This time, though, I was ready to defy Mike. Jumping into the frying pan wasn't an option right now.

I observed Rytkönen for a few moments before I stepped out of the shadows. He looked confident, as if he had the situation under control. I on the other hand could feel my unease growing.

Just march ahead and forget about Hilja, I told myself. *You are Reiska, who knows something important about David. You have the upper hand. You'll be fine.*

"Evening, Rytkönen." Reiska's tone was practically boastful. He walked over to Rytkönen but didn't shake his hand, and Rytkönen didn't extend his hand, either. He just nodded.

"And who might you be?" he asked after eyeing Reiska up and down.

"My name doesn't matter," Reiska tried to say in their common language, but his Savonian lilt slipped out.

"As you know, I'm a police officer. I can force you to tell me your name."

"Your work buddies might not like it if I told them your name is Kassi. Or that you claim to be by phone."

"What do you know about Kassi?" Rytkönen stepped away after realizing he was right under the glare of the streetlight.

Reiska felt like a lynx balancing on a tree trunk, stalking a deer. One wrong move, and he'd scare his prey. However, if his risky move was successful, he wouldn't be hungry for days.

"You hear all sorts of things when you hang around with the right kind of people," Reiska said.

"You know our mutual friend Finnjävel. Or what's the name you use for him?"

Reiska backed up, too, although the cap shaded his face well.

"Finnjävel, Daniel Lanotte, Bengt Näkkäläjärvi. David Stahl has many names." Reiska made up Bengt just to throw Rytkönen off, but he didn't even look surprised. He wouldn't be easy to confuse.

"He probably doesn't remember who he is half the time, or whose side he's on. Who do you work for?" Rytkönen asked.

"The highest bidder. Just like Stahl."

"Did Stahl send you?"

Oops. My lynx claws were slipping off the angled tree trunk, and my tiny tail wasn't enough to keep my balance. Reiska noticed the man with the two dogs approaching again behind Rytkönen, and the dogs were off their leashes. Was this Rytkönen's backup? Did the dogs sniff out the lynx?

"I'm here on my own behalf," Reiska told Rytkönen.

The dogs ran over and sniffed at Rytkönen's dark-blue wool pants.

"Santtu, Pumba, come back here!" the owner yelled. He had to stroll over to put his dogs on their leashes. Rytkönen did his best to ignore the dogs while one of them was still sniffing his shoes. Reiska was amused; maybe Rytkönen had stepped in dog shit.

"They're fine. They wouldn't hurt a fly," the owner continued, but Rytkönen didn't pay any attention. When the man had finally leashed his dogs and pulled them away, Rytkönen walked closer to Reiska. Reiska had a hard time analyzing Rytkönen's features due to his sunglasses.

"You want money for your information?" Rytkönen asked. "Sorry, but our informant budget is empty—even that fund wasn't spared from the budget cuts. And how would I know if you have info I'd want? Do you know where Stahl is hiding?"

Obviously Rytkönen was clueless about Stahl's whereabouts. Reiska was annoyed.

"You can tell your employers that they're not the only ones who want Stahl. It sounds like your camp was behind Dolfini's murder because you have my number," Rytkönen said. "You're probably pissed off for letting Stahl get away. I don't know where he is, but you can't touch him. Of course you want revenge, but it won't work. The Belarusians know what they're doing, and once they've finished with Stahl, you'll have nothing left. Not even a scrap. Finnjävel has always overestimated himself, thinking he can juggle four balls when he can barely keep two in the air. Stahl's not dead yet, but I don't think he's going to live much longer. Guy thinks he's a cat, and soon his ninth life will be up. Don't waste your time on him. Just be happy someone will kill him for you."

18

With these words Rytkönen turned around and walked away. Reiska watched him go. Even I didn't understand what Rytkönen's little rant was about. Reiska took stock of the situation. Rytkönen was clearly shorter than him, but the man was pure muscle, and he didn't seem like the type who'd start talking after a couple of broken ribs. Besides, he was a cop.

Reiska walked back to the shore and lit a cigarette to calm down. So David had not been killed in Italy, or at least whoever had killed Dolfini hadn't killed Stahl. That was slightly comforting. Reiska began to kick a nearby tree. Fucking, fucking, fuck. He didn't know if Rytkönen was just putting on a show.

Although it was near midnight, traffic was still flowing on the Lauttasaari bridges. An ambulance howled its sirens, rushing toward Espoo, past the night shifters who occupied the brightly lit buses on their way home. Reiska started his walk toward downtown; the last number eight tram had already gone. A couple of dives had to be open somewhere near the city center, and he could use a beer, if not two. Reiska was both grumpy and feeling righteous, which wasn't a good combination.

Halfway toward downtown I felt Reiska come loose. Although I was still wearing his clothes, in my thoughts I was Hilja. And they weren't pretty, either. I felt humiliated, disappointed, and scared. David trusted Rytkönen more than he trusted me. Rytkönen knew where David was, and his news wasn't good. I marched Reiska to Yrjö Street to sleep, and he listened to me. He'd been back in the closet for so long he hadn't had a chance to strengthen his willpower. I could easily silence him.

Silencing myself was harder. I had to employ a couple of tequila shots to do the job. When I poured the third shot, I dug for David's pictures and the ring in my bag. I hadn't tried the ring on since I'd found it, but now I slipped it on my left ring finger and downed a shot. I yelled the worst words I could think of at David's pictures, shouting so hard that sweat started to bead on my brow. I took the pictures and the ring to the bathroom and held them over the toilet.

"Fucking Stahl, just see me get rid of you," I hissed, but I couldn't force my hand to throw in the pictures and the ring. That was the kind of softy David had molded me into. His pictures seemed to be winking at me and giving a victorious grin. I had a fourth shot of tequila.

I spent Monday in bed. I just didn't feel like getting up. Everything was wrong. Sans Nom was hit by the flu again, so I had to work around the clock for the rest of the week. Friday evening was the worst. A group of Finnish-Swedish ladies had come in for an early Christmas party, and despite some of them being Monika's old friends, they were demanding and gave the poor waiters the runaround. I fed root vegetables into the peeling machine and listened to their whining. I went to check on the security cameras to see whether the ladies were really behaving as poorly as it seemed. The monitor blinked; the memory card needed replacing, but I spotted a familiar face sitting near the group of women and forgot about it. Of course it was Martti "Mara" Rytkönen.

"What did that short jock order?" I asked Helinä.

"The man sitting alone? Tofu skewers."

"I'll take them out to him. Did he order anything else?"

"Yeah, another orange juice with sparkling water. He already finished one. I guess he was thirsty."

I collected Rytkönen's order and walked over to his table. The ladies whooped loudly at the table next to his, but he didn't seem to mind. He sat at his two-person table like a king.

"Good evening," I said, then pretended to be surprised. "My goodness, haven't we met? At Chief Constable Laitio's place?"

Rytkönen wasn't the least bit surprised to see me at Sans Nom, it seemed.

"Hilja Ilveskero, yes, I remember you. Laitio was the one who recommended this restaurant. I thought he was more into eating meat. So, what are you doing here? Have you quit the bodyguard gig?" he asked, staring at his plate as if trying to figure out what he ended up ordering. The hemp-infused tofu marinated in sesame oil and chili sauce was skewered with shallots and cubed peppers, served with a side of steamed millet and garlic corn gravy. Monika and I had picked the corn ourselves earlier in the fall at a farm in Pikkala, and the corn leaves had cut my fingers.

"Restaurant work suits me fine right now," I told Rytkönen. "The security business hasn't had much to offer recently."

"It sounds like you also screwed up your previous jobs a bit. Or well, a lot. One of your clients was killed, the other was kidnapped."

I eyed his drink, which was close enough for me to grab and pour onto his head.

"How's your boyfriend?" Rytkönen asked smiling.

"Which one?"

"That half Estonian, David Stahl. Or is he your ex now?"

"I don't talk about my current or ex-boyfriends," I said and turned toward the kitchen. I was startled when Rytkönen grabbed my wrist. His grip was like a vise, just like when we'd met at Laitio's.

"You know what? I could take you for a little chat at the Bureau's headquarters anytime. I could even arrest you for harboring an international criminal. If you know where Stahl's staying, it's in your best interest to let me in on it real soon. Or do you prefer charges for abetting a murderer?"

His face was flushed with anger, which had also made him slip back to his Savonian dialect. I calmly placed my available hand over his and sunk my nails in. Although I kept my nails short, the pinch was painful enough. Rytkönen grunted and let me go. The ladies nearby were giving us curious stares. They hadn't been prepared to see a proper show at Sans Nom tonight. Once again I, the leading lady, didn't know whether it was a farce or a tragedy.

"What murder? I have no idea what you're talking about," I told Rytkönen.

"Stop lying. Your lover is wanted for murdering Carlo Dolfini and dumping his body into a marsh. You were in Italy when Dolfini disappeared. His wife supposedly left for the United States, but she's probably deep in some other marsh, because she hasn't been found."

"Why would Stahl kill this Dolfini?"

"He worked for Gezolian and could have recognized Stahl. The Russian and Italian mobsters are entangled. Teppo Laitio has been trusting you quite a lot, and that Stahl character. He ought to retire when he can't tell a crook from an honest man."

Although I wasn't sure where the script would go next, I could at least change the way I played. I walked away from Rytkönen. On my way to the kitchen, I told Helinä that she should take care of table four's dessert orders and bill. I'd just dropped by to say hi. Rytkönen could very well take me in for interrogation and even arrest me. He could always make up an excuse. Come to think of it, I hadn't been in a real jail yet, although we'd practiced tolerating the conditions at the security academy in Queens. I'd been held for forty-eight hours, and I knew it was just a test, but I was still on the brink of getting badly claustrophobic. Lynx didn't belong in a cage.

Because I wasn't needed any longer in the kitchen, I went to swap out the memory card in the camera monitors. The red light was still blinking. Once done, I checked the monitors to see how Rytkönen's appetite was doing. I had to do a double take when I saw that Rytkönen was no longer alone. Yuri Trankov had joined him.

Luckily Helinä was picking up orders from the kitchen. I stopped her.

"That guy who joined the bodybuilder at table four, were they on the same reservation?"

Helinä gave me a broad smile.

"It's your fan again. The place is full, so I asked him if he minded sitting with the other gentleman. Do you want to serve him?"

"No. And if he asks for me, send him to the kitchen. Or rather, the surveillance room."

I went back to the room and turned the camera from the table of women to focus on Rytkönen and Trankov. Rytkönen had to know who he was sitting with, or he hadn't done his homework.

Trankov wore his silly mobster outfit again: a black three-piece suit and a dark tie. He looked even paler than before with his face framed in his five o'clock shadow. I wondered whether Syrjänen's trip to Moscow had gone downhill, or was Trankov experiencing an artistic crisis? I caught myself feeling slightly disappointed when he hadn't asked anyone if I was working. Our painting was still unfinished.

Rytkönen was in no hurry to finish his meal. I saw Helinä take Trankov's order while she handed Rytkönen a menu—looked like he was going to get dessert. Trankov flirted with Helinä, and she flirted back. My fault; I'd told her at the grand opening that he was all hers, so why was I was so annoyed by this? Suddenly everything pissed me off, including Jouni, who had walked into the monitor room to scream at me that I was needed in the kitchen to chop parsley and oregano. I followed him without protest.

I slaved away in the kitchen, filling dishwashers and wiping floors. As I got up with a soiled rag in my hand, I felt a touch on my shoulder. Then hands covered my eyes. I heard Jouni say that outsiders weren't allowed in the kitchen. The cologne and the wool I felt on me revealed who the intruder was.

"Yuri!" I quickly turned to face him, and he put his hands back on my shoulders, as if he were going to embrace me. "You're back from Moscow."

"Are you happy to see me?" Trankov asked without a smile, but his eyes gave me a look that would have melted even the weakest soul. Not me, though.

"Of course I am. When should we continue with the painting?"

"Whenever's good for you. Do you work tomorrow?"

"Unfortunately yes, but I'm off Sunday night. Would that work?" I pretended to be as excited as he was.

"Syrjänen will be around then, too. I'll introduce you to him. Should I give you a ride?"

"No need. I'll borrow the van, and I remember how to get there. Is six a good time?"

Trankov nodded, now with a smile on his face. "It'll take a few more hours to finish the painting, but there's plenty of room in the villa. You can spend the night."

Artist Trankov didn't seem to be bothered at all by the fact that six in the evening in November meant it was pitch-black in Finland.

Either he had already finished figuring out the lighting on the painting or he wasn't as artistically ambitious as he claimed to be.

As soon as he left, Jouni came around muttering how I used his kitchen for dating and was carrying around a gross rag full of bacteria. I went to the monitor room and wound the tape back to watch Trankov and Rytkönen eating. They seemed to exchange only a few words. Trankov spent most of the time staring at his plate of cabbage rolls. Only when Helinä brought Rytkönen his bill did Trankov smile, but the smile was aimed at Helinä. When Rytkönen took off, the men shook hands.

I kept on thinking about Rytkönen and his contradicting words. He had told Reiska that David was a prisoner of the Belarusian mafia, but he'd asked me where David was. What a schizo.

Laitio hadn't told me that David was wanted for Dolfini's murder. He should have known about it, unless Rytkönen was just trying to fool me. I couldn't wait to get home and go through the Bureau database again. Monika was dragging her feet; she kept checking her list of fresh ingredients to pick up from the outlet on Saturday and how much cash was in the register. The loud ladies had spent almost three thousand euros, so tolerating their mood swings had definitely been worth it.

At home I took a shower and pulled on my pajamas, a sweater, and knitted socks. Then I used Laitio's login information to browse the Bureau's database. I looked up the Dolfini file Rytkönen had originally saved. There were more details now.

"Italian police have a warrant on Daniel Lanotte for the murder of Dolfini. Those boys are a bit slow."

I looked up Daniel Lanotte's file. It was in English, so Rytkönen hadn't created it. The information was marked as highly classified. Daniel Lanotte's real name was noted as David Stahl, and according to the file he had also appeared as Anton Kallas. Stahl was a

Finnish citizen, Lanotte had a Swedish passport, and Kallas came from Estonia.

According to the Italian police, Lanotte had been a double agent who had defected from Europol during the delivery of Strontium 90 and had killed Boris Vasiliev and his three minions in the boat explosion. Then he returned only a portion of the isotope to Europol, although he had claimed to have returned all of it. Europol intelligence found out what the quantity was supposed to be, but by then the Belarusian businessman Ivan Gezolian, who had been the source for the isotope, had sent his representative, Carlo Dolfini, after Stahl. Stahl had killed Dolfini and disappeared.

The Italian police had received an anonymous tip about Dolfini's body, but they didn't find it in the apartment Lanotte had been renting. Dolfini surfaced six months later a couple of miles away from Montemassi in a marsh. Lanotte is suspected to have killed Dolfini's wife as well. An international warrant is still out on him. He should be apprehended if possible. There were suspicions that Stahl might come back to Finland to see his girlfriend, whose part in the events in Italy is unclear.

A note had been added to the end of the memo: "A tip we have just received reveals that Stahl has one more fake identity, that of Bengt Näkkäläjärvi. The last name sounds Sami. The fugitive may have either a Finnish, Swedish, Estonian, or even Norwegian passport."

Despite everything, I started to laugh. Reiska had really pulled a fast one on Rytkönen. I just couldn't believe that Rytkönen would be so stupid, and he hadn't tried to figure out who Reiska was. Surely he had. Also, why was I still roaming free and not brought in for questioning? They knew I had been in Italy when Dolfini died. Was Laitio still influential enough to protect me, or was someone else vouching for me? The former prime minister?

It wasn't unlikely that David had killed Carlo Dolfini. It wouldn't have been his first murder, and Dolfini had worked for Gezolian, the man with the dirty bomb. I just didn't understand what had happened to Rosa Dolfini. I remembered her anxious voice over the phone. She may have been completely supportive of her husband, and David had had to get rid of her, too. Maybe David Stahl was a murderer many times over and only thought of himself.

That was the kind of David I had no desire to know. He deserved to meet his maker at the hands of Belarusian torturers. I turned my computer off and knew this night would never end. Even if I poured all the tequila in the world down my throat, I wouldn't be able to drown this sorrow.

The Sunday morning sun took a while to light up Helsinki. As I drove toward Långvik, the gray of November felt like a thick blanket that muffled my feelings. Maybe it was finally time to let go. I had been hanging off this loose noose with David as the rope, and it was time to take it off my neck and leave it behind. The most vivid memories of our relationship were disappointing: secrets and doubts, passion that wiped everything else away, two bodies physically and mentally naked, pressed against each other. I put on an Eläkeläiset album and hoped Reiska's favorite band would make me feel better.

My overnight bag contained my Glock. I'd also equipped myself with something less noticeable but just as deadly as a gun: a few slices of dried webcap. These mushrooms had accompanied me on my trips through customs in various countries, and no one had ever suspected they were lethal. Most recognized false morels and white amanitas as poisonous, but the webcaps were less recognizable. I'd claim them to be gypsy mushrooms should anyone ask. I wasn't entirely sure why I was carrying these mushrooms. I guess they could have worked like cyanide. Suicide by mushrooms didn't sound too tempting, though, knowing I'd suffer for days before dying.

Once I reached the gate, I called Trankov to open it. I didn't want to reveal I had memorized the code from our previous trip. Within seconds the gate began to move, and I barely made it in before it slid back into place. The yard in Syrjänen's rental villa was decked out in Christmas lights, although it was mid-November. LED light strings were thrown over trees and draped along gutters and window frames. The art studio was dark—no decorations there. When I parked the van, I saw Trankov appear at the studio door. Once I got in we went through the usual ceremony of kisses on the cheek, which didn't feel completely unappealing. A red foldout loveseat had appeared in the studio since my last visit, and there was a small table next to it. I was glad to see the stuffed lynx was gone. Paintings had been stacked out of the way against one wall, and only the canvas stretched tight in the easel remained. I rushed over to see it. Trankov followed so closely that I could smell him and feel his warmth.

The lynx looked even more alive. A sun was setting behind the mountaintops in the background, and it colored the fur in gold. Water roiled in the foreground, right below the woman and the lynx. I wasn't sure if the landscape existed somewhere or if Trankov had just used his imagination.

The woman wasn't finished. The flower wreath was still covering her hips and tops of her thighs. The roses in it were the same shade as the lynx fur, and the green vines waved in the wind. Both the lynx and the woman looked like they had just stopped running. The woman's thighs looked powerful, and her bare toes grasped hold of the moss beneath her. One of her hands was spread open as if in a greeting, while the other rested on the lynx's neck. The upper body and face were still just a sketch.

"I gave up on giving the lynx princess long hair. It has to be short, the same length as the lynx hair. Like your hair," Trankov explained. "Can you take your clothes off again? The upper body is enough, but do as you please. It should be warm enough."

Trankov's tone was practically humble. I took off my jacket, then the sweater, and finally my T-shirt. I had once felt a sudden attack of romance at an airport and bought myself a lynx shirt that matched the one I had given to David in Spain. I wore it now because it no longer had meaning for me.

Trankov helped me into the pose from before, but he didn't bring out the roadkill lynx.

"Where's my posing partner? Don't you need it anymore?"

He looked confused. "I thought you didn't like it, being dead and all. I gave it to a restaurateur I know."

"You're right. I didn't. And the lynx on the painting looks done. But I need something to rest my hand on. Do you have a prop that could help me look more natural?"

He walked to the pile against the wall and found a stool. He adjusted its height and set my hand on it. His touch gave me goose bumps and made my nipples hard. If Trankov noticed, he hid it well. He walked around turning all the lights on, then turning them off one by one, adjusting their brightness with a remote control. He looked concentrated, like a real professional. I had always admired people who were good at what they did, which almost made me forget about how I'd originally met him. I gave myself a quick reminder.

"Is everything all right? You're not too cold or thirsty?" Trankov asked when he was finally pleased with the lighting.

"Everything's okay."

"We can start then. Remember, you're alert. You know enemies lurk nearby. You two know that hounds have almost caught up with you, but you're not afraid. You're more cunning than they are."

The way Trankov was evoking this imaginary world brought back weird memories from Mike Virtue's classes in Queens. I didn't even want to think about what he'd say if he saw me now. Instead, I thought about Frida. I had seen the way she'd reacted when she detected dogs nearby. Her eyes widened, her hackles stood up, and her tiny nub of a tail began to whisk furiously like a domestic cat. I let Frida enter me, and I saw the shores of Hevonpersiinsaari and the islands across. The hot rock smelled like summer, and the patches of moss were soft under my feet.

Trankov glanced at me occasionally, but he didn't actually see me. He only saw the subject of his painting. Sometimes he stopped to mix colors, wipe a thin strand of hair off his forehead, marking it with brown paint. He'd switch between slow, concentrated brush strokes and quick slaps on the canvas.

Out of the corner of my eye, I saw movement on the shore outside. This brightly lit room enclosed by large windows was like an aquarium, and anyone could see inside. I wasn't particularly turned on by the thought that Usko Syrjänen could be roaming the yard, staring at my tits, but I was willing to pay that price if I found out how he was planning on acquiring the land he needed for his recreational villas. And I wanted to know how David tied into it.

Trankov painted for an hour and a half before he stopped. His forehead beaded with sweat, and his eyes glistened like Frida's when she'd caught a rabbit.

"Time for a break. Want some tea or something to eat?" he asked.

"Tea's fine." I threw on my lynx shirt, took off my shoes, and went to the restroom. Only then did I remember I should've kept an eye on Trankov brewing the tea. When I returned I inspected my empty teacup carefully and waited for Yuri to pour the tea. I let him scoop honey for himself first and took my tea and walked over to the couch. Trankov followed, and we sat down.

"So how have you been?" he asked, like an old friend. "Looks like the restaurant's keeping you busy."

"Yeah, but it's just the right amount of activity." This may have been a suitable time to ask about Trankov's impressions of his dinner buddy, Rytkönen, on Friday, but he started talking again.

"Do you still miss David Stahl?"

I lowered my eyes from his investigating gaze.

"Why should we talk about Stahl?" I had to muster all my acting skills to sound bored with the topic. I stared at Trankov's wrists that were covered in paint splatters. The bones jutted out sharply.

"Hm. Did Stahl ever tell you he has a son?"

I looked at Trankov wide-eyed. David had always been sad about not having kids. In Montemassi we'd dropped hints about the possibility of having a child together, and I had started liking the idea.

"No? I guess he found out about the child only recently," Trankov added.

"How do you know about this? Or are you just making this crap up?"

"Knowledge is power. Surely you've learned this by now. The more you know, the more intimidating you are. I happened to bump into a woman in Moscow I'd met before. She's from Lithuania, named Gintare. Once she was just as beautiful as you are, but now she's a fraction of her past beauty. In the early 2000s she was Stahl's lover and got pregnant. Gintare didn't want Stahl in her life. She had told Stahl about an abortion, and I guess she was planning on going through with it, but then she changed her mind. The child was born in the spring of 2002, and Gintare gave it away to an orphanage. I hear the kid is mentally disabled, thanks to Gintare's drug use during pregnancy. And an addict is easy to bribe. I got all this information from her for only one hit."

David had told me about Gintare, but he thought she went through with the abortion. Trankov moved closer and wrapped his arm around my shoulders.

"You see, Hilja, Stahl was a fool. They forced Gintare to tell Stahl there was a child after all, and that the kid was kept in terrible conditions in a Lithuanian orphanage. A clever way to lure Stahl into a trap. Stahl is gone. But don't worry, my dear. Let me help you forget."

19

I didn't resist when Trankov leaned in to kiss me. Actually, I kissed him back. It was a soft, searching kiss that was asking for permission for more. I set my teacup on the table and clamped my arms around him. His body felt fragile. I could feel his spine and the hard muscles of his shoulders. Trankov traced his hands on my cheeks and hair, but all his movements were light, as if he was prepared for me to pull away quickly, just like last time. I moved my hand down his back and under his smock, feeling for his belt, and I slid my fingers inside his pants, touching his skin. I located the vertebra and the dent where a lynx would have a tail. Trankov kissed my neck and began to pull my shirt off, but then stopped.

"Are you sure you want to do this?" he asked.

"I am, but not without a condom." I didn't want another incident like in New York. I didn't want a kid even if it would level the playing field with David. I hadn't checked the date on the condoms I always carried in my bag—maybe they hadn't expired.

Yuri kissed my lips, then went around dimming the room lights with his remote control and pressed a button that brought down the automatic shades. I could have still backed out of it, but I didn't want to. After all, I wasn't cheating on anyone; I belonged only to myself, and for a short while I could belong to Yuri and Yuri to me.

He returned, and we began to undress each other. Yuri was completely different from the self-assured, shameless David. He let me lead, made sure he wasn't hurting me. He wouldn't be leaving bite marks on me. I couldn't believe how horny I was, how much I had desired someone against me, on top of me, inside me. I wrestled myself on top of Yuri and had an orgasm. I came again when he was on top of me, whispering something in Russian into my ear. It was probably for the best that I didn't understand him. I couldn't think of a single word I wanted to tell him, not "love" or "dear." Words weren't needed now.

Finally his entire body arched, and he let out a moan. He opened his eyes, his large, dark-blue eyes surrounded by long lashes that beaded with drops of sweat. I closed my eyes when his shaking body fell over me. Hell no. Was Trankov one of those men who cried after he came? I was expecting to hear a confession about a wife and two kids in Moscow. I wouldn't stick around for that.

My heartbeat began to slow down, while Trankov's pulse was still fast. I felt his lips on my shoulder and his wet eyelashes on my neck. I was glad his body had stopped shaking. I finally dared to open my eyes. Trankov's eyes looked so sad, and he looked way too young. I didn't remember seeing his birthdate in the Bureau files. I would've remembered it; that's what I was trained to do.

I was thirsty. I reached for my now-cool tea while Trankov pressed his head against my chest. The room was way too warm, and the pale-red lighting made it look like a lukewarm hell.

"Is everything all right?" Trankov asked and hugged me tight.

"Yes. Just feeling a bit dehydrated," I quickly told him and pushed him off me. I got up and filled my teacup with water from the tap, drank, and poured some more. I took a third cupful over to Trankov and sat on the couch next to him.

"Want some?" I asked.

He grabbed the cup and drank. The condom was slowly, comically sliding off him. David had claimed that Gintare had broken their condom on purpose, and Rick, my landlady Mary's friend from her performance group in New York, hadn't bothered to check whether the condoms he'd been carrying in his pocket were still useable. They hadn't been. I didn't realize I was pregnant until I didn't get my second period in a row. The academy had beaten me up physically, so I'd just assumed the changes with my period were because of heightened exercise—it had happened to me before. But then my breasts began to swell, and the pepperoni pizzas I'd gorged on before began to nauseate me. I knew something was wrong, and I'm glad I went to see someone. I didn't second-guess my decision when my doctor asked me questions about my situation. The abortion was performed as soon as possible, and I missed only two days at the academy. I didn't even let Rick know what had happened, although I ran into him a couple of times at Mary's parties. I had asked the doctor to insert an IUD right after the abortion, but I didn't trust it. I hardly ever thought about the child; I hadn't wanted to see whatever had been taken out of me. It was my only choice. Whenever I saw news about antiabortion rallies in the United States, I told them to go screw themselves. These idiots had no idea what they were talking about.

Only now did I look at Trankov's body—before I'd only felt him against me. You could have almost called him skinny, but his strength couldn't be underestimated. His shoulders and arms were powerful, and his stomach was like a washboard. I wondered what sort of martial arts he was into. I remembered how easily I had knocked him out in Bromarf, but I had surprised him. I wouldn't be able to pull that again.

"Can you stay the night?" Trankov asked. "I should continue painting, and then I want to make you dinner. We'll stay up late."

I told him I could stay. Then I went to the restroom to pee and rinse myself. The room was so warm I didn't bother putting any clothes on, and the shades were still down. Trankov, however, got dressed and flashed me a bashful smile when I settled into my pose as a lynx princess. Now he worked slowly and deliberately and at times watched me for a while. His lover's eyes were gone, though; he was back to being an artist.

My lunch had been fairly substantive, but after another thirty minutes of posing I was feeling really hungry. This was one of my most unattractive features: being hungry like a wolf after sex. Many men had been thrown by it. I usually told them professional athletes had to eat after exercising, too. Chewing on a steak was often a convenient method of getting rid of men I didn't want to see again. It probably wouldn't work with Trankov, and besides, I still needed information from him.

"How old were you again, Yuri?" I asked when he was lost in thought, staring at the painting.

"Does it matter?" His blue eyes flashed.

"Not really. But you seem to know a lot about me, so it's only fair if you tell me this insignificant detail about yourself."

"Twenty-six. But I've seen more of the world than most," Trankov said boastfully, sounding younger than he was. We had less than ten years between us, so it wouldn't count.

I remained quiet until he finally set his brush down and wiped sweat off his hairline. I rolled my shoulders, realizing that at some point during our lovemaking, I'd held the weight of two bodies. My muscles would be sore tomorrow.

"Are you done?" I walked over to my clothes. I didn't feel like being intimate. I was just hungry.

"You're done for the evening. I'll work on this a bit longer," Trankov said.

I got dressed, then asked to see the painting. Trankov spread his arms as if to say, why not.

"Just remember two things. It's not completely finished yet, and it's not your portrait—I didn't try to make it look like you. I wanted to capture your soul, if that's even possible," he said.

I'd rather Trankov paint my face than my soul, but I doubted he had succeeded. Heck, even I didn't know who I really was half the time. Still, I approached the painting suspiciously. The woman in the painting had lynx spots in her hair, and her eyes were lined with black and white. Thankfully she didn't have long tufts of hair on her ears. That was me in the painting, and I was getting goose bumps. There it was, a piece of my soul, and there was no way I could take it back.

Trankov watched me. I appreciated how he didn't interrogate me for an opinion. I looked from another angle, backed away from the painting, glanced at it from left to right. The woman's gaze kept following me, and that was evidence of artistic skill. I could almost smell the lynx.

When I couldn't find words to describe what I felt, I gave Yuri a peck on his cheek. He responded with a relieved hug and asked if I was hungry. For once I could answer without lying.

"Syrjänen is in the building, along with Julia, his current girl-friend, and Hanna, the housekeeper. I told Syrjänen I was bringing a guest," Trankov said.

"Are we having dinner with them?" I asked.

"I'm not sure." He looked at his watch. "It's almost nine. I'm guessing they already ate."

Damn. I would've loved to get to know Syrjänen over dinner. Sharing an experience like that connected people and made them trust each other. But now I had to play it by ear. I had brought a change of clothes, so I wore them for dinner: a flowery tunic with a plunging neckline that showed off the lace of my bra, turquoise earrings Monika had brought from Africa, and purple knee-high boots. The leather on the boots was so thin I couldn't walk long distances, but they worked fine as indoor shoes. Trankov changed out of his smock to a gray zip-up knit jacket. His white jeans had speckles of paint on them, but he didn't seem to mind.

I brought my purse along. The Glock was weighing it down, so I couldn't let Trankov carry it. He slipped his arm into the crook of mine as we walked together through the brightly lit yard.

I'd only seen the foyer, the kitchen, and the dining area in the house. We followed the smell of cheese into the kitchen.

"Hanna?" Trankov called out and knocked on the door at the end of the kitchen hallway. A woman in her forties peeked out. Her hair was up in a bun, and she wore a red-and-white gingham apron. Trankov gave her a kiss on both cheeks.

"Can we still eat something?" he asked, like a little kid. "Did Usko and Julia eat already?"

"Two hours ago. They're watching a movie. They wanted fondue. Would you like some? It'll take a while to melt the cheese, but you can start with a salad." Hanna stared at me while she spoke. Her eyes seemed to classify me as an easy girl. Whatever.

"This is Hilja. She's been modeling for me," Trankov said. "When do I finally get a chance to paint you, Hanna?" Trankov flirted with the housekeeper, who was obviously pleased.

"When hell freezes over," Hanna said.

"But that's already happened, Hanna. You forget that I'm from Siberia."

If Hanna had been equipped with a dishcloth or a duster, she probably would've taken a swing at Trankov. Now she just scooted us over to the kitchen, muttering to herself in a Tampere dialect.

"Let's go see Usko and Julia," Trankov suggested, and I followed him, although I would've preferred gorging on Hanna's salad.

Trankov took me by the hand and walked me through a ginormous living room. It was lit only by a couple of dim spots of light, but the yard and the seashore were lit with bright lights, like it was still daylight. Syrjänen—or rather the owner of the house—had probably never heard of climate change.

I heard shooting and a woman screaming behind the door at the other end of the living room. Trankov knocked on the door and pulled me in.

"We just wanted to say hello," Trankov said in English with a Russian accent that was much thicker than minutes before. "This is Hilja."

The room was a home theater, and the screen was so huge you could barely watch it comfortably. They were watching a Western from the fifties. Syrjänen sat in a large armchair but got up to shake my hand. The woman remained splayed on the couch. She appeared to be as tall as I was, but that's where the similarities ended; she was all legs and breasts. Her C-cups were the result of obvious plastic surgery, like the glossy plumpness of her lips. Her hair cascaded down her back in a black river, and her face was layered in too much makeup.

"Syrjänen—or rather—Yuri's friend should call me Usko." Syrjänen's amicability had been well rehearsed and was almost genuine. "How's the art making going?"

Instead of responding, Yuri blushed and said a few words in Russian to Julia. She shrugged and said, "*Ne hotsit,*" not feeling like it, which made Trankov blush even more.

"It's great to have Yuri here as my interpreter. You see, I was never good with languages, and I dropped out of school at fourteen.

But hey, I've done pretty well for myself, right? Are you a professional model?" Syrjänen asked me.

"No. I work at a restaurant."

I'm sure the ministers had told their buddy and financer Usko Syrjänen about the reasons why his boat had been blown up, but I suspected I was just a minor character for Syrjänen, not the lover of the man who destroyed his boat.

"Good, good. You know, we sometimes have these big parties, and we could use some additional staff. Give Hanna your phone number." Syrjänen was acting like a good guy.

Julia paused the DVD, freezing the cowboys and women clad in corsets as they rode away from the Indians.

"Let's go eat," I told Trankov as I slipped my arm around his waist and gave him a kiss on the cheek. I felt like he was expecting me to behave this way. Syrjänen said something under his breath about us meeting again later, but the movie was in full swing again before we'd left the room.

Hanna had set the table with salad, bread, and wineglasses. The cheese smelled stronger now, mixing with the fragrance of the white wine. I was pretty sure I was drooling by the time Trankov pulled out a chair for me and began to uncork the bottle of wine. The bread looked homemade, and besides the usual fixings the salad had avocado, mushrooms, and roasted cashews in it. I decided to trust that the oil and vinegar bottles weren't spiked with something while I piled my plate high. Hanna appeared in front of us like a homely hostess straight out of the old black-and-white movies I used to watch with our neighbor, Maija Hakkarainen. These were exactly the types of people I had to keep an eye on. My classmate Edgardo had gotten himself into big trouble when his client, an oil millionaire from Miami, hired a friendly looking gray-haired lady to help around the house. She had worked for his ex-wife and turned out to be the best blackmailer around. Edgardo had been so upset that he wanted to share this information with all of us, and of course Mike Virtue told him off for breaching confidentiality.

The wine was chilled and tasted like currants. The mushrooms were freshly picked, and the avocados were just ripe enough.

"I hope you're better company than that man in Sans Nom last Friday," I told Trankov as I finished my plate. "We were so booked that Helinä had to seat you two together."

"What man?" Trankov looked confused. "Oh, that man. No, I didn't mind him."

"Helinä said he was being rude."

"I don't know. We didn't really talk."

I remembered seeing a heated exchange of words on the security cameras, but I didn't say anything. All I needed to know was that Trankov wouldn't tell me everything.

"It looks like you enjoy working for Syrjänen," I said. "At least the perks are great," I continued as Hanna brought over the pot of fondue and cubed pieces of bread.

"Usko genuinely appreciates me and trusts my skills," Trankov said.

"So what are you two working on now?" I asked while I stabbed a piece of bread with my fork and spun it in the bubbling cheese. I'd once tried making fondue, but I had burned it so badly I had to throw away the pot.

"Sorry, my dear. It's a secret. But it'll be huge and something you've never seen before. We're marching straight into the future, the 2100s. I get to use my imagination to the fullest in the designs."

"Is it in Finland?"

"Yes. And not too far from where we're sitting," Trankov said.

I wondered how much I had to tease and seduce him to find out more. How stupid could I pretend to be, and how thick could I lay it on before Trankov realized something was up? Back in the bar Ateljée at Hotel Torni, he had been boasting about designing zoning plans and artwork he'd paint directly on the walls.

The fondue filled me up quickly, and I had to start pacing myself after a couple of forkfuls. Trankov had finished his glass of wine and poured me some, too, although I had managed to take only a few sips. I raised my glass and smiled at him. I didn't know who this act was more for: myself or Trankov. Pretty boys like him had never been my favorites. David had never been a nice-looking man, and he didn't take good care of his skin, but he was still damned sexy. I told myself to stop making these comparisons. Trankov was easy to spend time with and was just a source for information and occasional fun.

"Why do you like lynx?" he asked.

I'd only told my closest friends and lovers about Frida. That information was just too intimate to share.

"I just do. Native Americans believe in totem animals. Maybe the lynx is mine."

Trankov extended his hand to touch mine, still gripping the stem of the wineglass.

"They're fine animals. I saw them a couple of times near Vorkuta," he said.

"Is that right? They usually stay out of sight."

"I used to ski late on winter evenings and would go deep into the forest to watch the stars. I'd sit silently as long as I could. I saw all kinds of things. When you're cold enough, you can even see angels. I only caught a glimpse of ears and a tail when one sniffed me out and turned away. The other one I saw was standing near a cliff before it went after its prey. That's the one in the painting with you."

I was just about to launch into Frida's story when Hanna walked in to check on the fondue and make sure the contents hadn't burned. Once she was gone, Trankov asked about my training. I told him the kind of details about the academy in Queens that wouldn't have made Mike Virtue pull his hair out.

"I've never been to New York. Will you go there with me and show me around?" Trankov asked.

I was about to answer when I heard steps approaching the kitchen. Usko Syrjänen appeared in the dining room, rolling his shoulders.

"Oh, I'm sorry. You're still having dinner. I'll join you for a glass of wine. Julia won't want any—she says it makes her fat." Syrjänen poured himself a glass and sat next to me at the table. Trankov blushed again, and I couldn't tell whether he was annoyed or pleased.

Syrjänen started talking about the weather, pondering whether there'd be a lot of snow this winter or if he could take the boat out all year. I wanted to ask him about *I Believe 2*, but I remained quiet. I was at Trankov's mercy here; if he'd told his host I was somehow connected with the man who had blown up his boat, I would've been in trouble. Maybe Trankov enjoyed having his own little secrets.

"Is your boat out somewhere?" I asked Syrjänen.

"It's in Helsinki. I'll bring it over when I have some time, or Yuri can do it. Do you like boating?"

"I only row, and I'm more of a camping person." I sipped my wine and calculated my risks. "Speaking of which, there are surprisingly nice spots for hiking and mushroom hunting here near Helsinki. Nuuksio and Porkkalanniemi are fairly populated, but when I get to Kopparnäs, I'm hardly bothered by other people," I said.

Syrjänen wrinkled his brow at the mention of Kopparnäs, but I couldn't draw any conclusions from that.

"I used to have a cabin near Kopparnäs, and I went there often. I got to know many of the mushroom-hunting grounds," I kept on babbling. "Are you familiar with that area? I know there were plans to build a nuclear power plant there about forty years ago. Quite a safety issue so close to the capital."

Trankov looked embarrassed. Syrjänen, on the other hand, smiled at me.

"Kopparnäs. I've been there a couple of times. Nice place. So you know it well, you're saying? Hey, Yuri, what do you say we bring Hilja along when we're out there enjoying the view? We could use an experienced guide who knows where the best mushrooms are hiding. Those mushrooms might turn out to be a key player," Syrjänen said.

"A key player for what?" I asked. "Are you planning on starting a business for nature lovers?"

"We'll see about that." Syrjänen's smile was even wider than before. "A rolling rock gathers no moss. No venture, no gain. You need to have ballsy ideas that others think are impossible. Those are the ideas that bring innovation into this stale world. And when you have good connections, you can do anything. Right, Yuri? Do you think this young lady has local knowledge we could use?"

Trankov was practically squirming in his seat and quickly changed the topic to his painting, asking if Syrjänen wanted to see it. He obviously didn't want me to talk with Syrjänen about Kopparnäs. Once we were finished with the fondue, we all went to the studio.

"Did you draw those sketches we talked about?" Syrjänen asked Trankov as he opened the door.

"Yes, I did. Let's look at them some other time. I don't want to bore Hilja with business," Trankov said and turned on the lights. In the glow the painting looked hyperrealistic and cheap, nothing like what I had seen. But Syrjänen seemed pleased.

"Perfect. Just think about it. What an amazing idea these unique, customized wall paintings are. We can negotiate with customers about them while we are building for them. Can we use this painting as an example of what we are capable of?" Syrjänen asked.

"As an example of what?" I asked, but Trankov interrupted me.

"This painting belongs to Hilja. I already promised it to her. I'll paint you another example."

I couldn't quite read Syrjänen's face. He walked around the studio lifting sheets and looking at tubes of paint. Trankov put his arm around me. His embrace felt like shackles. The idea of staying in the studio for the night with Trankov didn't seem nearly as appealing as before. Had I had too much wine to hop behind the wheel and drive away?

"Do Russians like this sort of figurative art?" Syrjänen had pulled out a framed canvas that featured a man wearing a fur hat, driving a horse and buggy.

"Russians like all sorts of art. Don't worry. I can handle all styles, even iconic painting. We just have to have them blessed in a church."

An expert in painting and an architect. Pretty good for a twenty-six-year-old, especially as Trankov had worked some of his life under his father, Paskevich. I felt his arms and wished Syrjänen would go away. The wind picked up outside, and the skylights reflected the swaying strands of light inside.

"Hilja is not just a model and a restaurateur," Trankov suddenly said. "She's also graduated from a security academy in New York as a bodyguard. You told me once you didn't want Julia to walk alone in public. She'd have a good bodyguard in Hilja."

I shoved Trankov away, and he grunted.

"That was years ago. These days I'm exclusively working for the restaurant," I said.

Syrjänen looked curious.

"My, you're a multitalented woman," Syrjänen said. "And you know what? I have been thinking about Julia's safety. She still has some unfinished business back in St. Petersburg, and it's not that far from Finland. Should we talk about this a bit further? We could really use you in my company, Uskon Asia. I can offer a competitive salary. Maybe we could work out a contract?"

20

I was about to say something when Syrjänen's cell phone rang. He had Queen's "We Are the Champions" as a ringtone.

"That's right. I'll be right there," Syrjänen said in English, hung up, and then cursed in Finnish. "That Julia is so goddamned jealous, but you might get along if you get to know her. I have to go now. Maybe we'll go on a trip together later, perhaps in Kopparnäs. We could take *I Believe 2*."

I Believe 2 was about three feet longer than the boat David had destroyed. I didn't even know where a long boat like that could moor in Kopparnäs. He must've dragged along a motorboat that allowed him to reach shallow shores.

"I'll get in touch with you, Hilja," Syrjänen said and walked away.

I waited for a minute before I yelled at Trankov. "What the hell was that about? You blabbing to him about my past? Those days are over!"

"But are they, Hilja? I don't think you're satisfied working as an errand girl for a restaurant. Just think about all the fun we could have working together—and outside of work." Trankov tried to hug me again, but I shook him off and went to the restroom.

Behind the locked door I thought of how many glasses of wine I had finished and realized I shouldn't drive. Trankov had kept filling my glass at dinner.

Trankov had put on music, and I didn't recognize the melancholy instrumental waltz. It sounded very Russian. He'd dimmed the lights and sat on the couch with his head hanging off the back, eyes closed. I sat next to him and rested my head on his shoulder. We didn't speak. The waltz changed into another, and then to a melody with an accordion. Trankov quietly hummed the melody into my ear.

"Are you sad?" he asked when the accordion changed into a cello.

"Why would I be?"

"Because of Stahl."

"Why do you keep talking about him? Forget about him already," I snapped and kissed Yuri. Since the grand opening at Sans Nom, I had felt this desire for revenge ooze out of him. Maybe this was his way of getting back at me for my beating him up in Bromarf—seduce me and forever twist the knife in the wound David had opened.

Our kiss ended when Yuri moved positions on the couch and rested his head on my lap. I waited for his next move, but nothing happened. I closed my eyes and tried to clear my mind of everything but the music. The minor notes comforted me. Yuri's head felt warm against my thighs, and sitting like this, silently, felt more intimate than having sex.

"Have you ever been in prison?" Yuri's question surprised me. He'd turned onto his back and petted my cheek.

"No. I don't think I'd like it."

"I've been told that prisons here in Finland are a piece of cake. You get your personal television set and everything. I was worried

I'd be jailed for that kidnapping, and that's why we left with Fath—Paskevich so quickly. Then we realized we could've just as easily sued you."

"And that's why you were allowed to enter the country again? Were you talking with lawyers?"

"Valentin called one day and said the militia reported we were safe to travel to Finland again."

He was right. My intrusion to the villa in Bromarf could've earned me a charge or two, although my endgame had been to release Helena Lehmusvuo, but that case was already closed. According to Laitio, Paskevich had not crossed the border between Finland and Russia since then, and the Bromarf villa had been sold.

"How about you? Do you have any experience with prisons?"

"It was just a misunderstanding. And I learned from it." Trankov's face was grave, although he was the one who'd brought up the subject. "There was this demonstration, and I was accidentally a part of it. I was so naïve I didn't think it was dangerous. The next thing I knew, the militia was clubbing me and dragging me away in handcuffs." He shuddered.

"What was the demonstration about?" I asked.

"Against Putin. It was during his first term as president. We were kept in prison for almost two weeks. I was allowed one phone call. Valentin refused to help me. He admires Putin. He thought it served me right to pay a heavy price for my own stupidity. I was eventually released, with a fine of a thousand rubles. I didn't even ask Valentin for the money. I sold my phone and painted a couple of quick paintings that I sold at the subway stations. If I hadn't paid the fine, I would've been thrown in jail."

Trankov sounded bitter. Laitio had told me about Trankov's childhood in a Russian orphanage, and from what I had heard, they were pretty close to prisons, too. I had to be careful. I didn't want to know everything about Yuri.

"I never want to live in Russia again. They broke two of my ribs in jail. The police claimed I had stumbled when they arrested me. Syrjänen promised to help me with a resident permit, and when I've been in Finland long enough, I'll apply for citizenship. I'm pretty sure I'll get it, seeing how much work I have to do here," Trankov said.

"Do you still keep in touch with your father?" I asked.

"No. He never acknowledged me as his son, never gave me his name."

When I let out a laugh, Yuri looked hurt. "I assume nobody told you what your father's name means in Finnish?" I translated it into English—"shit joke"—and explained what sort of association any Finn who heard the name would have.

Yuri smiled. I couldn't help but lean over and kiss him. Then I began to undress him, turning him on, pulling him into my lips, inside me, underneath me, above me. We fell off the couch, and the floor felt warm. Yuri let out that strange weeping sound again, and I bit him on his chest and wouldn't let go until I came. Then I let myself relax completely. I would've fallen asleep on the couch if it hadn't been so hard. Yuri folded out the couch and found us a sheet, blankets, and pillows. We fell asleep next to each other, my back against his belly, arms wrapped around each other, his lips against my neck. I don't remember dreaming.

When I woke up in the morning, Yuri was already awake. He stood naked next to the bed and pointed a gun at me. My gun.

"Why did you bring this with you? Don't you trust me?" His eyes looked like they did at the grand opening, brimming with hatred.

I pulled the blanket tighter around me, although it wouldn't have protected me from bullets.

"I don't trust anyone," I said.

"But you'll sleep with someone you don't trust?"

"Don't give me lectures about morals! Are you telling me you don't have a gun or two in this studio and a few more in the main building? I doubt Syrjänen's business partners are innocent and pure, so I'm sure you must be prepared for them. No?"

"I'm an architect and an artist, not a bodyguard. My days of carrying guns and roofies around are over. I'm an honest man now, and I don't want anyone else to lie, either." The gun was shaking in Trankov's hand. The Glock hadn't been loaded—only an idiot would walk around with a loaded gun in her purse—but I couldn't tell whether Trankov had put bullets in it or not.

"Why were you digging in my purse anyway? How dare you talk about trust!"

Trankov blushed. "I wasn't really going through it. I was just going to drop in a surprise that you'd find later."

"Give me the gun. The butt facing me." I stood up slowly. In physical conflict whoever has the most strength doesn't necessarily have the upper hand; it's the person who has the most guts. Mike Virtue had stressed this to us time and again. Trankov had been careless. He'd shown me his soft, vulnerable belly, and now I would dig my claws and teeth into it if I had to.

"I trusted you," Trankov said quietly, his gaze with less anger now. He shook his head. "I don't trust people that easily, either. I did trust you, though." When he handed me my gun, I saw that it wasn't loaded. I placed it beside me on the bed. I saw my purse next to the restroom door; Trankov had wanted to go through it in another room. I was mad at how careless I'd been.

The room smelled of coffee, and now I saw a couple of sand-wiches, cups of yogurt, and some juice on the kitchen table near the coffeemaker. Trankov made sure I never went hungry. I began to dress, and I would leave as soon as I'd had breakfast. Trankov could keep his painting.

He turned his back to me and walked into the dressing room. I rinsed the cup I'd used the day before and poured some coffee into it with a splash of milk from an unopened container I had found in the fridge. I grabbed the blueberry yogurt and an open-faced rye sandwich with cheese and shoved the bedding away from the couch so I could sit on it without getting bread crumbs everywhere.

Trankov took a while in the dressing room, and when he came back he wore a dark-purple suede suit with a matching tie and an off-white shirt. He looked like some Russian czar who had escaped a painting from the 1800s. I almost couldn't stop myself from reaching out to him. If I really needed pretty boys like him, I'd find them in bars.

Trankov didn't eat; he just had a cup of coffee and didn't speak. I looked outside, where the weather had turned cold, but not cold enough for the trees and grass to be covered in frost. I wouldn't need to worry about starting a frozen van.

When I was finished with breakfast, I washed my face and brushed my teeth. When I came back Trankov was standing in front of the painting.

"I can't hand this over yet. It's not finished," he said.

"No rush. I live in a furnished apartment, and I wouldn't have room for it anyway."

"I suppose you don't want to give me your phone number?" He wasn't looking at me. He still had his eyes on the painting, his face like a grumpy little boy.

"No, I don't. And what would you do with it anyway? You'll always find me at Sans Nom. You can call there." I pushed my way between him and the painting. "Yuri, don't be so childish. Don't take it personally if I'm carrying a gun. I always do that."

"Even with Stahl?" he asked.

"I already told you, we need to stop talking about Stahl! I have to go now. Thanks for everything." I kissed him on his cheeks and touched his hair. Then I was gone.

I heard nothing from Trankov for the rest of November. Syrjänen's dreams about boating all year round didn't come true; the weather cooled down dramatically and snow covered most of the ground by late November. I went to check out the conditions in Kopparnäs on a day off. In some places there was enough snow to ski on, and I saw some people on their kicksleds. I dragged my feet in the snow along the seashore and looked at the tracks that accompanied mine where a fox had run. There were a lot of deer tracks, and when I followed them into the forest, I saw familiar paw prints: a lynx had been after the deer. The snowbanks weren't strong enough for me to walk over to see whether the lynx had caught its prey. I needed a pair of skis or snowshoes.

I'd brought the files David had left for me, and once again I was comparing my surroundings with the plans on the map. Syrjänen wanted to own Kopparnäs, but why would David be so interested in it? There had to be more than their connection from the Hiidenniemi case before. Maybe it had to do with Syrjänen's new, influential business partners that Trankov had hinted at. Or perhaps it was all about that storage for the military; it was completely out of place in the middle of a recreational area. Who knows what was hiding behind the chain-link fence and the warning signs? If there had been plans for a new nuclear power plant in the seventies, they would've strictly investigated its environmental impact. This place couldn't hold hazards from the Soviet-era rental times, could it? I had no opinion on nuclear power, but I also didn't quite trust something humans had come up with. Mike Virtue had once told me over coffee that nuclear power had been a genius invention—as long as the power plants and uranium stayed in the right hands. I could see that Mike wasn't sure who had the right hands, and I wanted to know that, too.

Three deer darted off as I returned to the path they'd made to the shore. I slipped on the cliff and hurt my ankle and slowly hobbled back to the Kestikievari inn for a hot chocolate and a sandwich. Nothing had changed since the last time I was there. I felt like an alcoholic, forcing myself to appear at her regular haunts to drink only juice. This inn was strongly connected with David, and that's why I had to be there. I had to cauterize the memory from my mind, make the man irrelevant to me. It probably couldn't be done with just one visit.

I didn't realize I was covered in sweat until I was back in the van, turning the ignition. The radio played the same Bach piece that the violinist had played at the Turku book fair. By the time I reached the Hanko Road intersection, I had to pull over. My tears were blinding me, and the music slipped into my soul like medicine, and this time the tears cleansed me. Damn you, Bach. Listening to him made me suspect that there may be a god somewhere.

The Sans Nom staff had been informed that Veikko's heart surgery had gone well. Jouni and Monika took some time off to see him at the hospital, but I couldn't get over my fear of hospitals to see him, although Mike Virtue's voice in my head reminded me how bodyguards couldn't have phobias about places. I squealed back at him, *I'm no longer a bodyguard*. I was just a dishwasher and vegetable-peeling-machine operator. People like that were allowed to have weaknesses.

The police returned to the restaurant in early December. This time they weren't just cops on the beat; they were from the Bureau and were investigating the death of Risto Antero Haapala. They arrived on a Thursday an hour before we opened and wanted to talk to the entire staff.

"You are not accused of anything. We just need to find out how Haapala obtained a mixture of alcohol and windshield wiper fluid that contained methanol. Do you have any idea who usually supplied him?" the officer asked.

"How should we know? Talk to his friend, Veikko Vuorinen. They bought their drinks together," Monika said.

"Vuorinen claims he has no clue. When he and Haapala went to sleep, neither one of them was carrying any alcohol. They'd run out of beer by nine," the older officer told us. He wore a beard and looked bored with death.

Monika looked through her planner. "So he passed away during the night between November 3 and 4. Our kitchen closed at eleven that evening, and by one we had the place cleared out and closed. Does anyone here remember anything out of the ordinary about that night?" Monika asked the staff.

Of course nobody did. Except me, who had seen a pant leg and a shoe in the security camera footage. The police hadn't asked for the tapes, but the officers from the Bureau were more thorough. The younger officer, Chief Constable Sutinen, asked where the cameras were located. Everyone looked at me.

"I deal with the surveillance here, not that there has been much to deal with." I told them where the cameras were and complained how I stupidly deleted events older than a week. The police were of course free to double-check. The USB stick I'd used to save the images from the evening Ripa had died was safely locked away on Yrjö Street with my gun and the items I'd found in David's drawers.

"Do you recall seeing anything suspicious on the tapes from that night?" Sutinen asked me, and Jouni took that as permission to get back to work. He took off, trailed by curse words and the rest of the staff. Only Monika and I remained.

"I would've brought them to the police if I'd seen someone offering a drink to Ripa. He'd fallen over where the cameras couldn't see him, so his death wasn't recorded." I acted shocked, although my mind was blinded with rage. Why weren't the police wondering why they hadn't found a bottle of poisoned alcohol anywhere near Ripa? Had Rytkönen just coolly watched while Ripa drank enough to kill himself and then taken the bottle with him, leaving the man to choke on his own vomit? The pant leg and the shoe weren't enough evidence against a police officer of his status, and besides, I couldn't think of a reason why Rytkönen would've wanted Ripa dead. That's what his colleagues would wonder, too, so I kept my mouth shut and didn't volunteer to help the police. The bearded man was smart enough to ask whether any of us had found the bottle, and my answer in the negative wasn't a lie.

The police visit gave me another excuse to chat with the staff about Ripa's death, but no one had any information. Veikko and Ripa had been part of the restaurant, acting as a sort of a human compost, helping with our leftovers, and now we grieved for them. Jouni guessed that come spring, the newspaper-recycling container would host new tenants. I wondered what would be the best time to reveal to Rytkönen that I knew he was a killer. I decided to remain calm; this information could be valuable one day. I copied the security camera tape onto two more USB sticks and hid them in different locations in our apartment. Monika's cousin was about to come back home, and I needed to find another place to stay. If I had a car, I could move back to Torbacka, if that cabin was available. I'd be close enough to Kopparnäs, the area Usko Syrjänen coveted.

A tabloid headline caught my eye on my way to work the next day: "Usko Syrjänen and Beautiful Julia: Engaged!" I pulled the paper from the display and leafed through it. Syrjänen smiled sweetly in the image, whereas Julia pouted. The paper wrote that Julia Gerbolt, twenty-eight, had been married once before. Syrjänen had left his current wife for Julia, although he wasn't technically divorced yet. Now Syrjänen's wife was demanding half of his fortune. No wonder he was renting at Långvik. The story didn't mention anything else about Syrjänen's business background except that he owned construction and shopping-center companies that had been expanding rapidly and that he was a good friend to many important politicians. The story mentioned how Syrjänen had become friends with a slightly shady Russian businessman Boris Vasiliev, who had died when Syrjänen's boat exploded.

Julia Gerbolt was from Moscow and had been a model in Russia. Her first husband was over thirty years older, an oil kingpin who had died of a heart attack the year before. Julia and Syrjänen had met in St. Petersburg at a party hosted by mutual friends. The future Mrs. Syrjänen seemed to be one of those people who could sniff out money. I got a whiff of blood from the money she had inherited from her rich, dead husband. I didn't know whether I'd be able to say no if Syrjänen offered me a job as Julia's bodyguard. That would be my shot at the inner circle, where David had once been.

On the Friday before Independence Day, I was just about to head out to the tram stop when a pile of envelopes fell through the mail slot. One of the envelopes was for me. I'd already gotten a few Christmas cards from former classmates across the Atlantic, thanks to the secured e-mail list. This envelope had a stamp: "Forwarded Mail." Inside was another envelope. I opened it to reveal a Christmas card. It wasn't just an ordinary card, either; it depicted two lynx curled together. I'd seen these cards in Huelva, Spain. My name had been marked on the envelope under "c/o Mrs. Voutilainen." The sender was someone named A. Lusis. There was no writing on the card, but the envelope contained a piece of paper folded in half twice.

Merry Christmas, Hilja my dear. I knew I could count on you to secure the contents of the locked drawer. Have you already figured out the meaning of that ring? I had it made for you and would have slipped it on your finger, but I had to escape. I trusted you would take care of yourself, and I was right. Remember to keep on taking care of yourself and the contents of the drawer.

I still cannot tell you where I am. It's too risky, and I don't want you in danger because of me. I'll return when I can, if I can. I wanted you to know that I'm innocent. Things just didn't go as I had planned. I couldn't do anything else. I don't expect you to wait for me, but I still hope for it. I pray for it. I don't care if you have others in your life.

There was no signature, but David's wobbly handwriting was easy to recognize, and the name Lusis referred to him, of course.

I was boiling inside. Who did Stahl think he was? Did he really think he could just waltz back into my life whenever it suited him, then disappear again for who knows how long? I was no Penelope who would sit around waiting for her man and decline all others. I wanted to call Trankov right then and set up a date. Instead, when I picked up the phone, I called Teppo Laitio. I had to talk to someone. No, not talk. Scream. It was snowing hard outside. The snow that had fallen in November had never melted, and old ladies slipped their way down Yrjö Street below.

"What do you know, Ilveskero! To what do I owe this pleasure?" Laitio said.

"Are you at home or at the headquarters in Jokiniemi? Is Rytkönen around?" I asked.

"Thank heavens, no. I'm in my office on Urheilu Street."

"And you're sure your phone isn't bugged? We need to meet. I just received a card from Stahl, and I think Rytkönen poisoned a homeless alcoholic who had been living behind Sans Nom."

By the sound of it, Laitio's cigar had dropped out of his mouth. I tried to recall all the things I hadn't shared with him, and I could imagine the fire and brimstone he'd pour on my head once I told him I had met Rytkönen while disguised as Reiska. Laitio had always been a bit unsettled by him. But I could no longer keep secrets from Laitio. I may have been a local champion in lying, but I didn't have a chance with the pros, and I'd never have a chance to represent Finland internationally. Laitio was at least a judge on the national level.

"What are you talking about? Who did Rytkönen murder and where was the card from?"

I hadn't even thought about looking at the stamp. The stamp was Lithuanian, and the envelope was postmarked in Kaunas. This supported Trankov's story about Gintare's child. David was trying to find the child that had been left at a Lithuanian orphanage.

"It was stamped in Kaunas on November 23. It was first sent to Mrs. Voutilainen on Untamo Street, because David knew the card would reach me eventually, even if he didn't know where I was at the moment." My voice had begun to waver, and I could've used a cigar or a shot of tequila.

"Get your butt over here then. I have something to tell you about my new best friend Rytkönen, too. I believe he's capable of anything—even murder," Laitio said.

"I can't come now. I have to work, but I'll try to leave before closing. Could I come after ten?"

"The missus has a bridge gathering. I could claim I have diarrhea to get out of it, but then she'll sulk for weeks."

We arranged to meet at his place the following morning, and I'd find someone to sub for me at work. Before leaving I read David's message over and over. I didn't understand why he was talking about just one locked drawer. He should've remembered there were two, and I had broken both. Who had gone in to check that the drawers had been broken into when the police hadn't even noticed it at first?

Another thought came to mind. Why did David mention just the ring but nothing about the kaleidoscope or the USB stick? Maybe it was a cover in case the letter ended up in the wrong hands. I now regretted having been so careless when I'd opened it without inspecting the envelope well. Someone could have steamed the envelope open before me.

I snorted. Was I really going to believe that David had enemies among the Lithuanian and Finnish mail carriers? When it came to David, I shouldn't have been surprised about anything anymore. He'd made his way to Finland undetected last March like a lynx to his hiding place, and reports about someone creeping around Sans Nom in the fall seemed to indicate suspicion that David was in Finland with me. I suddenly recalled the shadowlike figure on the seashore when I had visited Yuri at the studio the first time. That couldn't have been David. Then again, it would've served him right to see me make love to Yuri Trankov and fall asleep next to him. Served him damned right.

I almost broke the peeler when I accidentally threw in a spoon, and I also managed to spill tomato soup on one of our regulars. I was angry at myself, letting David Stahl have such an effect on me. I could see his light-blue eyes gazing at me as if he were standing right there.

"Screw you, David Stahl. I don't care about you one bit," I whispered when I did my routine check of the security cameras. All I saw was an empty field of snow. I had lost my status as local lying champion when I couldn't even fool myself anymore.

21

Only when I was sitting back in the tram did I wonder if I was a complete moron. Stahl was wanted for Dolfini's murder, I'd been hiding information from the Helsinki Bureau officers, and Laitio was their colleague. He was surely obliged to relay the information about this fugitive who had been in Kaunas a couple of weeks earlier, or else he was guilty of misconduct. Why did I feel like someone had to protect David? He should be caught, that bastard.

The snowplow was pushing fluffy snow along Urheilu Street, and the heated grass on the soccer field looked unrealistically green. I took a deep breath before I buzzed Laitio. He growled unintelligibly into the speaker and was already waiting for me at the door when I climbed the stairs. We hadn't seen each other for one and a half months, and I was startled by the change in him: his skin was gray, his hair was visibly thinner on the crown, his mustache drooped, his eyes were double-bagged underneath, and his jowls drooped like a hound's. I detected three sets of chins. Laitio had lost weight. The familiar mustard-yellow cardigan was now baggy on him.

"Hi. Come and take a seat. Want a smoke? I made some coffee."

I didn't light the cigar. I just watched Laitio go through the ritual of cutting the end of his cigar and taking a drag before tasting the coffee. He'd fixed a mug for both of us, and Laitio had apparently used some sort of an espresso roast, because the amount of caffeine would make me climb walls and give me a heart attack.

"How are you, Hilja?" he asked. "They want to get rid of me. Early retirement and blah, blah, blah. All sorts of bullshit. Rytkönen has convinced the bosses that this is a good idea, but upper management is not sure. I've worked as a cop since that guy was still pooping his pants. If you have any information that puts him in a bad light, I'll buy you cigars for the rest of your life. But first, let's talk Stahl. Did you bring the card?"

I pulled out the card from my bag and handed it over.

"And you're sure this came from Stahl?"

"That handwriting is his, and these are the cards we used to buy together in Huelva. The last name is also a hint—it means lynx."

"So this man has been carrying a card all over the world just to tell you at an opportune time that he's still alive? How romantic." I hadn't thought of the card from that angle, and I had to fight against the fuzzy feeling slowly spreading inside me. Laitio turned his computer on.

"I don't know who orchestrated this whole story and made the Italian police believe Stahl was responsible for Dolfini's murder. It has to be someone with good connections to the local police."

"And you don't believe he's guilty?"

"No, and neither does Caruso. Someone wants to catch Stahl because he knows too much. This means at least one man in Europol has been paid off—if that man isn't Stahl. Furthermore, some Belarusian is after Stahl. Our intelligence found out that some of the money Vasiliev handed over to Gezolian was forged."

"Do you think Stahl stole from them?"

"How do you think he's been able to feed himself all these years?"

I, too, had been treated to meals and enjoying life, renting cars, and joyriding around Andalusia and Tuscany with the dirty bomb money. I got immediate heartburn from the coffee.

"I guess it's better that Stahl has the money and not Gezolian. He's hiding in Belarus, and no one can find him. Under the protection of the president and who knows what other crooks. But what on earth is Stahl doing in Lithuania?" Laitio asked.

"He's looking for his child." He listened carefully and asked whether Stahl had told me this.

"No, it wasn't Stahl. I heard he didn't know about the kid until earlier this year."

"So who told you then?"

"Yuri Trankov."

"Trankov? That weasel and Rytkönen's minion? Don't believe a single word that comes out of that man. He's less trustworthy than ten Savonians altogether," Laitio yelled.

I felt my cheeks flush, but I tried to remain calm.

"Rytkönen's minion. What does that mean? I thought they didn't know each other."

"Shit always finds its way to another pile. Did you think Syrjänen's involvement with Vasiliev wasn't investigated at the Bureau? Ever since then he's been under the foreign department's surveillance. First he was under my jurisdiction, but later Rytkönen demanded to handle the case. What would be more beneficial than having his own snitch as Syrjänen's right-hand man? Paskevich got knocked over on his head—or perhaps some other body parts would be more appropriate—during that botched Lehmusvuo kidnapping, so he doesn't dare return to Finland, even now that he's no longer banned. His bastard son, however, is another story. Who do you think was behind allowing him back in? Rytkönen, of course."

My heart wasn't racing just because of the espresso. In my mind I replayed the tape showing Trankov and Rytkönen sitting at the same table. So it hadn't been a coincidence, and although outsiders wouldn't have gotten much out of their conversation, I'm sure it had been filled with coded language.

"When did you chat with Trankov? I told you to stay away from him."

"At the villa Syrjänen is renting in Långvik. I was modeling for him."

Laitio sighed heavily. He made futile attempts at wiping the partly dried flecks of coffee off his cardigan. When his phone rang he took a look at the screen, then answered it.

"What is it? I'm working." I couldn't hear what the other person was saying, but a smile began to slowly manifest. "Yes, that's fine by me. Like I said, I'm busy. You and Irmeli just have your lunch in peace. I'll find something for myself. And I won't forget to feed Kokki. Kiss, kiss, my little bunny." Then a confused expression came over Laitio's face. I wanted to have the upper hand, so I flashed a rude smile and blew a kiss to him. That didn't save me from his attack. He still wanted to know what the hell I had been thinking, agreeing to model for Trankov. What an idiot. I told him a condensed version: I'd modeled for Trankov until the painting was finished. Then I switched subjects.

"There has to be a connection between Syrjänen and Stahl, right? Why else would that USB stick containing the Kopparnäs papers be in David's drawer all the way in Montemassi?" I asked.

"And what was the reason he left it for you to find? Based on the message inside the kaleidoscope and his letter to you, he knew you'd rummage through the place before you'd take off. And you did exactly as he expected. Stahl really has you wrapped around his finger," Laitio huffed, and I wanted to smack him. "If those papers had anything worth hiding, Stahl put you in terrible danger when he gave them to you. What a selfish prick."

I was kind of flattered by this. David believed I could take care of myself and the information that was important to him. I switched topics again.

"Rytkönen has been stalking me. Recently he came in to Sans Nom and threatened me. He accused me of hiding Stahl somewhere in Finland and said he'd throw me in jail. Not only that, he's been spying on me at my apartment and at Sans Nom. Look. Isn't this Rytkönen?"

I pulled the USB stick out of my breast pocket and inserted it into Laitio's computer. I showed him the images from the security cameras, both from the night Ripa had seen an odd character lurking about when Sans Nom was broken into and from the night Ripa was killed.

"See? Isn't this the same man? And I bet it's Rytkönen," I told Laitio.

First he nodded, but then he shook his head.

"I recognize those shoes and that gait, but all you need is a second-year law student to convince the judges that these tapes have no standing, especially when you've hidden them from the police. And why would Rytkönen have killed a homeless man?"

Veikko and Ripa had lived out of the recycling container behind Sans Nom, so they were probably just protecting their home and questioned what Rytkönen was looking for. Maybe Rytkönen had been afraid Ripa would recognize him and let me know it was him, although Rytkönen hadn't really committed any crime at that point. He had just been looking for David. I thought about the break-in before the restaurant had opened. Veikko had seen men who looked like bodybuilders, but Rytkönen was much shorter than those guys. Maybe they were Rytkönen's buddies. Usually burglars kept on doing it and would eventually get caught, but this break-in was unsolved.

"Why is Rytkönen so obsessed with David anyway? He's Kassi after all. David trusts him."

Laitio sighed again. "That's what I wanted to talk to you about. I've looked into Rytkönen and found that he came from Europol, from the same intelligence department where Stahl works. They used to work together."

"And that's why Rytkönen is Kassi, David's trusted man?" I asked.

"Hold your horses. Returning to Finland and joining the Bureau was practically a demotion for him. I happen to know he wanted Stahl's position in Europol, but Europol didn't want Rytkönen in the Gezolian operation, because he has no official training as a police officer, which worked against him. So Rytkönen actually has reasons for holding a grudge against Stahl. I'm sure he'd love to see the man with a tarnished reputation rotting in jail for murder, although it looks like Stahl is doing a pretty good job of screwing up his reputation with this solo career he's leading."

"So you're saying Rytkönen is a trusted man who turned out to be a traitor?"

"Rytkönen is most definitely not the original Kassi. It's that Estonian police officer, Jaan Rand."

"Jaan Rand? But that's Brother Gianni, the monk over at Sant'Antimo monastery. I met him there. He told me he and David were classmates in Tartu."

"They were classmates, but Rand was also a cop. Stahl's colleague in Europol. But then there was that ugly incident. He shouldn't have felt the need to retreat to a monastery because of it, though."

"Which ugly incident?"

Laitio looked like he was in pain. "We all have our weaknesses. Rand's was very young women."

"How young?"

"Too young. I don't know the details. Twelve, thirteen." Laitio lit a cigar. "Really disgusting."

"I'm sure I've heard worse."

Laitio puffed a couple of times before he launched into the story of how Rand had not just been protecting an Estonian-Russian child prostitution ring but also used their services. Once the ring was busted, Rand helped his colleagues catch the people behind the operation, and this had been deemed as a mitigating circumstance. Rand got off with probation and had to resign. Then Rand became riddled with guilt. He converted to Catholicism and took off to live the life of a monk in Italy. Stahl demanded that this childhood friend remain as his contact. He didn't accept anyone else. For some reason people followed these orders, or at least in the beginning they did.

I recalled Brother Gianni's curly blond hair and his ascetic, thin body. His white shroud had been spotless like a bride's wedding dress. David had told me to seek him out. I was a grown woman, so I doubted Brother Gianni could've been a sexual threat to me. I imagined him lurking in the monastery shadows, peeping at little girls who kneeled in front of saintly images. But what had Eva Stahl told me over the phone? Something about Jaan Rand being mistreated. Surely she didn't believe Rand was innocent. Or maybe David told his mother something even Laitio didn't know. Or he had tried his best to protect his mother from the terrifying truth that her son's long-time friend was a sexual criminal.

Laitio continued. "Rytkönen finally convinced the big boys that Rand could no longer be trusted because he could be led astray with little Lolitas. Stahl became Rytkönen's responsibility."

"So you're saying Rytkönen thinks he knows everything about Stahl?"

"I suppose so."

"But he doesn't. He doesn't know that Stahl has never used an alias called Bengt Näkkäläjärvi. Still he believed in it enough to enter the information into the Bureau database. I'm sorry, Teppo—one time you left your login information out in the open when you went to check on Kokki. I couldn't resist."

I predicted I'd get another lecture, but instead Laitio burst out laughing. Finally, his face gained some color and even his mustache seemed to perk up.

"Oh, dear Hilja. How stupid do you think I am? I know you. You'll pounce as soon as you can."

"Are you saying you left your login information on purpose?"

Laitio chuckled. "Hell yes, I did! I know you as well as Stahl does, if not better. But if you tell this to anyone I'll of course deny it."

"Who would I tell? Rytkönen? I wasn't planning on adding him to my Christmas card mailing list."

"Did you feed Rytkönen that bogus agent name? Bengt Näkkäläjärvi? What a goofy name."

"It's a Sami name. I thought pronouncing it would keep Europol cops busy for a while. To be honest, I didn't come up with it, Reiska did."

I let Laitio in on how Reiska and Rytkönen had met. I could've added my sexual exploits with Trankov—it couldn't have gotten worse. Laitio had a better curse word vocabulary than Captain Haddock. I listened to his screaming. I knew I was an idiot.

"Here I had been hoping you had fallen out of love with Stahl. The only future I wish for you two involves sending long letters to a jail cell or taking flowers to a grave, if they ever find his body.

But how the hell does Rytkönen know that Gezolian's men are after Stahl?"

"Maybe he just fooled me?" I suggested. We took a long, hard look at each other. Laitio finished his cigar, and I thought about everything I knew. Trankov's treachery wasn't hurtful—after all, I had been expecting it. It just wasn't the kind of treachery I had been waiting for.

"Rytkönen leaks information to the Belarusians. Most likely he gets payoffs from Gezolian. I can't think of any other reason," Laitio finally concluded.

"How can you prove that?" I got up, took my mug with me, and walked to Laitio's office restroom. The wall was painted in all shades of lingonberry; the toilet seat and the sink were both purple, and even the toilet paper matched with its red-rose print. I poured my coffee out, drew water from the faucet, and drank it all. I poured another mugful. Laitio had begun to type on his computer, looking defeated. Goddamn it, I wouldn't let Rytkönen do this to Laitio— or to me.

"Well, I have nothing to lose," Laitio said. "I'm going to get fired no matter what. Who cares if I'm charged with misconduct on top of that, as long as we catch Rytkönen."

"What are you saying?"

"We need to get him to confess that he's leaking information to Gezolian and his gang. I can't do it alone. I need you, or your crazy alter ego. I never thought I'd say this, but I need you to dress up as a man and arrange a meeting with Rytkönen."

We hatched the plan for a couple of weeks. I worked, as usual. Laitio dropped in a couple of times to eat and have plotting sessions. Trankov was nowhere to be found. I called him once, asking about the painting. Once we were done with Rytkönen, Trankov had hell to pay.

Laitio and I had come to the conclusion that Rytkönen wasn't aware of David's hiding place, at least not when he came over to Sans Nom to threaten me. Apparently he had really thought I was hiding Stahl somewhere. We couldn't guess how much Trankov had told him about my relationship with David, but we decided Hilja had to be set aside for now—Reiska would be the key player. If Rytkönen had believed his lies about Bengt Näkkäläjärvi, he could believe other fairy tales, too. He seemed to think Reiska was an outlier for the Italian mafia.

Finding the perfect meeting place was problematic. It had to be a well-lit place out of the public eye. We decided to use the Kopparnäs inn's dance gazebo on the Monday before Christmas. I called the hostess for a table reservation, and she informed me the restaurant was closed. I asked how many guests she may have had in the inn, but she just vaguely responded that there was plenty of room. I had to risk that there might be witnesses.

"I'm sorry, but you'll have to slog through snow. We can't have two sets of footprints leading up to the gazebo," I told Laitio.

"Listen here, I'm an army and police academy man. Do you think I'm afraid of a snowbank?"

Maybe his heart was. Laitio was still gray in the face, although he was excited about our plans.

Two days before the meeting I went to the main post office and called Rytkönen's work number from a public phone.

"Hi there, Kassi. Are you interested in knowing where Stahl is these days?" I asked as Reiska.

"Who is this?"

"It's your old friend from the Ourit Island."

"Why would you tell me anything?"

"Let's just say I'm not too keen on my current employer anymore. I'm willing to cooperate with anyone who pays me more."

"I can't pay you."

"We can negotiate. I hear Stahl's head is worth its weight in gold to your employers—or should I say, its worth its weight in SR-90 isotope."

"How do I know this is legit?"

"You don't. Listen, this is all based on trust. I want to see Stahl in deep shit just as much as you do. He stole my woman back in Estonia."

Reiska could almost hear Rytkönen's gears turning.

"All right, we'll meet. But I'm not paying you a cent. Where and when?"

"At the Kopparnäs inn dance gazebo on Monday evening, at ten. That's twenty-two hours."

"And where's this Kopparnäs exactly?"

"You're a cop. Find out yourself." Reiska hung up.

Laitio went ahead to get ready a couple of hours earlier. He had time to locate a spot with a good view and hide his car without a trace. Thanks to the blizzard earlier in the day, he could rub snow onto the license plate, and it didn't look suspicious. I convinced Jouni to lend me his Dacia, because our van was too noticeable and could easily lead them back to me. I could've rented a car, but I didn't have the guts to do it while I was being Reiska. Finally Jouni agreed when I'd promised I'd never complain about the peeler machine shifts again and I'd always treat him with utmost respect.

Monika stayed in on Monday night, so I couldn't use our place for transforming into Reiska. Because I couldn't come up with another place, Laitio suggested I use his office. He'd tell the missus I was an IT guy helping him out with his computer.

Luckily I wasn't interrupted. Reiska wore the same clothes as the previous time, except the hat. I switched the baseball cap to Uncle Jari's old fur hat that I'd brought with me from Hevonpersiinsaari the winter before. It was made of sheepskin, and it had flaps that could be drawn over the ears with strings you tied under your chin. The bill shaded Reiska's face perfectly. I decided Reiska had recently become shortsighted, so I wore the ugliest glasses I could find from a secondhand store. I trimmed the mustache to look slightly more unkempt, and for the finishing touch I sprinkled some fake dandruff on my head. Good luck getting a DNA sample from that.

Of course I was nervous as hell as I started driving toward Kopparnäs. I'd brought my Glock along, but I could never quickly pull it out from under a thick, wool winter coat. Laitio had his gun with him, too. We both carried a recording device, and Laitio had a video camera on him.

There were no more streetlights on the roadsides after the intersection at Siuntio, and it was snowing hard enough that I wasn't sure whether regular lights or high beams were better. The Dacia was luckily equipped with decent winter tires. In the darkness of winter, the scenery around me looked unfamiliar; yards were sprinkled with Christmas lights, and the snowbanks glittered. I felt like a silly Christmas elf, and perhaps Laitio's role was to be evil Nuutti, who'd steal Rytkönen's gifts before he had a chance to open them.

I parked the Dacia off the road on the north side of the inn and walked back, trying to hide my footprints as best I could. The yellow wall of the dance gazebo glowed in the light, and the wreaths made of fake white roses that decorated the hall inside reminded me of a funeral. I muted my cell phone and messaged Laitio that I had arrived. As far as I knew, he had set up camp somewhere in the darkness between the gazebo fence and the forest. I had to put the phone away before receiving a confirmation from Laitio, because I heard a car approaching.

Rytkönen drove straight up to the gazebo. His dark-blue Volkswagen station wagon didn't exactly scream opulence. I backed up to the yellow wall to ensure my face was in the shadows, and I clicked the "Record" button on the tape recorder in my pocket.

"Howdy there, Kassi. How are the Christmas preparations goin'? Ready for your little gift?" Reiska was relaxed and self-assured, but I wasn't. My heart was beating so fast I expected it to jump out of my chest. I had to concentrate on my voice.

"Let's cut the bullshit. What do you have to tell me?" Rytkönen wasn't wearing a hat. His dark wool jacket and matching scarf were suitable for a winter evening; snow was crunching under his feet now that it was dipping well below freezing.

"That Finnish lady friend of Stahl's got a postcard from him sent from Kaunas, Lithuania. It was stamped at the end of November. The man's there, looking for his kid," Reiska said.

Rytkönen's mouth squeezed into a hard line.

"I already knew that. That's the precious piece of information you dragged me out here for? You're going to pay for my gas, that's for sure," Rytkönen said.

Reiska laughed. "Hold your horses. Stahl's on his little trip under the name of Bengt Näkkäläjärvi. He's a Swedish citizen with a Swedish passport. My intel says he's still hangin' about in Lithuania. I think it would be in your best interests to send someone after him," Reiska said.

"Who's your source?"

"The original Kassi. Brother Gianni. Jaan Rand."

"And he's ready to squeal on Stahl?"

"You gotta be careful when you're a monk, especially if you happen to like little girls. We both know that once you get a taste, you want more, even if you're supposedly protected by celibacy. Rand will need someone to guard him for the rest of his life, and a man in his situation can't afford to side with old friends like Stahl." Reiska was exaggerating. He had no idea whether Brother Gianni had gone off the beaten path during his monastery time, but a man like Reiska who had seen all sorts of things in his life did not believe that even God would help a man recover from his perversions.

"Sounds like you know why Rand had to leave Europol," said Rytkönen.

"I know a bunch of other things, too," Reiska said.

Rytkönen stepped closer. I saw how a vein was beating on his forehead, and his earlobes had turned red. The gust of wind made him squint, and for a moment it looked like the wind made his earlobes wiggle.

"You need to tell me who you're working for," Rytkönen said.

"It doesn't matter. Influential people. We have evidence that Stahl murdered Dolfini."

"You mean faked evidence?" Rytkönen spat. "Then we're on the same page."

Bingo. This is where Reiska had been trying to lead him. This would nail Rytkönen. Laitio must've been giggling out there.

"We have pictures of him dumping Dolfini into a marsh in Maremma. They're doctored so well even the experts can't tell they're fake. How much are you ready to pay for them?" Reiska asked.

"Let's see them first."

Reiska pulled the envelope out of his pocket. This was Laitio's queue to come out and reveal the next turn in this drama. Rytkönen stepped closer, then stared into my eyes as if he had recognized Hilja behind the glasses. We both tried not to blink.

"Here you go." I handed the envelope to Rytkönen, but I stayed still. If he wanted this gift, he had to move closer. He stopped and barely reached the envelope with his extended hand. Although it was freezing cold, I could see sweat beading on his brow.

Laitio and I had spent quite a while contemplating all the potential risks involved. The images were terrible, and Rytkönen wouldn't need to take more than two glances at them to realize it. The court wouldn't need it, but right now it was the only way to make Rytkönen reveal whose side he was on. I had asked Petter to help us; he was good at altering images, cutting and pasting seamlessly, but he had also been unreasonably curious about the purpose of these images. I had told him we were going to use them to get back at whoever had murdered Ripa, but I doubted he believed it. I told him he better not say a word about this to Monika.

Although Rytkönen had wanted to see the images before striking a deal, he didn't open the envelope. He just shoved it into his pocket. Warning bells flooded my mind too late, and before I was prepared I was staring down the barrel of a revolver. Rytkönen aimed directly at Reiska's head.

"Whoever you are, you know way too much about me. That could lead to unfortunate consequences."

Reiska was sweating now, too, and his only consolation was knowing that he wasn't alone and that the conversation was being recorded. Maybe Rytkönen had gotten sloppy after killing Ripa and thought killing was an easy business.

"What kind of an amateur are you, handing those photos off? You can be damned sure this is the only payment you're going to get." Rytkönen held his gun to Reiska's temple. The Grim Reaper stood only a few inches away.

"Goddamned Rytkönen, don't shoot!" Laitio was crashing through the trees like an entire cavalry. His pant legs were soaked, and he was slipping on the ice. Rytkönen turned his gun toward Laitio. In a split second Laitio was in front of Reiska, between death and me. He was panting heavily and hadn't drawn his own gun.

"What the hell is this?" Rytkönen's face was crimson, and he waved his gun around.

"Just admit you work for Gezolian and that you killed Risto Haapala." Laitio spoke on behalf of the both of us. The bravery in his voice sounded fake.

"Who's Risto Haapala?" Rytkönen asked.

"The homeless alcoholic you filled with poisonous alcohol." I had run out of energy to speak in Reiska's raspy voice, and Rytkönen looked up with a start when he heard me yelling. I lowered my eyes and hoped the bill of my hat would cover at least a bit of my face. Laitio's frame may have also covered me well, but would I be able to pull out my gun without Rytkönen noticing? I wished my hands were steadier and not like two brittle icicles.

"What is this nonsense? I have better things to do than chase homeless people around."

"Ripa just happened to be in your way when you were looking for David Stahl. First you hired goons to turn Sans Nom inside out, then you started to keep an eye on the place yourself," Laitio said.

"Take those hands out of your pockets, whoever the fuck you are," Rytkönen roared at me when he noticed me trying to feel for my gun. "Yuri, get over here," Rytkönen yelled into the forest. "Did you think I was stupid enough to come alone? Yuri, check their pockets."

Yuri appeared from behind the inn. His teeth were chattering, and he slid over with his thin indoor shoes.

"Well, what do we have here? The bastard son of Paskevich," Laitio said in English. "See? I was right. Shit always finds another pile."

Trankov looked like he was straining not to hit Laitio when he listened to his boss and frisked Laitio roughly. His gun was in his coat pocket, and Trankov handed it over to Rytkönen.

Then it was my turn. How could I have once been turned on by the touch of those hands? Trankov also knew I had a fake identity, a man called Reiska. Did he guess it was me behind this mustache? If he did, did it even matter at this point? Trankov didn't look at my face; he just went for the Glock. I realized he might recognize the gun. After all, he had held it in Långvik. But Trankov's face revealed nothing. He looked like a lifeless wax figure. He pulled out my gun and took a few steps back, but instead of handing it to Rytkönen, he removed the bullets and put the gun in his breast pocket.

"Are you sure they're clean?" Rytkönen asked in thick, stumbling English.

Trankov nodded. He looked nauseated.

Rytkönen weighed the two guns in his hands, then decided to go with Laitio's.

"It's best to take care of it with this one. It won't lead back to me," Rytkönen said.

"Do you have to?" Trankov's words came out as a sob.

"I've always hated that bastard," Rytkönen said, aiming at Laitio, who was still standing in front of me.

Acting on pure instinct Laitio dived, but the bullet hit him in the thigh. He fell down cursing, pulling me with him to the ground.

"And don't you try any funny business. This is the end." Rytkönen raised the gun again and walked close enough to Laitio that he could press the barrel of the gun against his head. I didn't dare move an inch, but Laitio rolled himself over me, as if he'd be able to protect me from Rytkönen's bullets.

"Stop it!" Trankov yelled. "Don't you recognize who that is?"

Rytkönen turned to look at Yuri while aiming the gun at Laitio. I propped myself up enough to see Trankov. He was holding a gun, and he was aiming it. At Rytkönen.

"Lower your weapon, Mara!" Trankov screamed. "Let them go! That's Hilja!"

"Hilja what? You mean Stahl's whore? What do you care?"

"Let them go, or I'll shoot you," Trankov said.

"You moron! Don't you know whose side you're on?" Rytkönen was now yelling at Trankov.

"No! I wanted to begin a new life and not kill people with you. Lower your weapon or . . ." I saw how Trankov closed his eyes for a moment, then opened them again. His face was completely void of color when he shot Rytkönen in the head. Rytkönen had no chance of surviving a shot like that.

I barely managed to pull myself and Laitio out of the way before Rytkönen fell. I don't know which one of us was screaming the loudest.

Trankov fell onto his knees in the snowbank and burst into tears. He muttered something in Russian and dropped the gun. I crawled away from Rytkönen's body so his blood wouldn't touch me, and I kept on yanking Laitio away, too. He was pale and breathed laboriously. I removed the mustard-yellow scarf from around his neck and used it as a tourniquet on his thigh.

22

Laitio lucked out—the bullet had only nicked him. After I'd bandaged the wound, I crawled over to Rytkönen to check his pulse, but I couldn't feel it through my gloves. Then I looked at the brain matter splattered on the ground and realized there was no point. I checked his pockets for the envelope that contained the doctored images, and I was startled by the warmth of his body. It was snowing harder now, and the wind had picked up, so the dead body would be soon covered in snow.

Trankov was still on his knees in the snow, crying. I took off my fur hat and the wig and ripped the mustache off, hurting my skin. I walked over to Trankov and put my hand on his shoulder.

"Yuri . . ." I didn't quite know what to say.

"I killed a man. I'm going to jail." Trankov had cleared his head enough to speak in English again. "I couldn't let him . . . Not you."

I wasn't sure who'd end up in jail from our little group. Trankov had shot Rytkönen, but Laitio and I were in quite a pickle. My next mailing address could very well be in the Hämeenlinna prison. Surely Laitio knew how we were supposed to deal with this, him being a cop and all. I knew the law, too, but following it seemed absurd at this point.

I walked back to Laitio. He was grimacing, but other than that he looked oddly pleased. Maybe he was in shock.

"I would've never in a million years expected Rytkönen to be the shooting kind. He's a bigger piece of shit than I even imagined. Are you okay, Hilja?" Laitio asked.

"I'm fine. How about you?"

"It hurts a bit, but I'll be all right. Did you get that gun from him?"

I kicked Yuri's gun over to Laitio, because I didn't want to touch it.

"Where's Rytkönen's blaster?"

"Probably under him."

"Let him have it then. That works."

"What do you mean *works*?" I asked. It was cold, so I pulled Reiska's fur hat back on.

"The plan I'm hatching right now. Listen here, kids. If someone gets in trouble, it should be me. Everyone at the Bureau knows how poorly Rytkönen and I got along. Apparently it escalated to a point where we drew guns. You two were never here. You'll leave Trankov's gun with me and get out of here."

"What are you trying to do?" It took me a moment before I understood. "But that won't work. You have no gunpowder residue from Yuri's gun. Ballistic experts will figure out in a second that you're trying to fool them."

"I'll use it to take another shot. Then, because of my heart condition, I'll have to be taken immediately to the hospital because I'm so damn shocked. I'll have plenty of time at the hospital to pretend I can't remember all the details and come up with a great story. I'm not the newborn cub you think I am, Hilja. This is incredibly awkward for the Bureau heads. One of the rising stars turned out to be a snitch for the bad guys." Laitio frowned as pain shot up his thigh. "Come on. Get out of here. I'll call the ambulance and the police. Share this information with Trankov in English. I guess I need to update my opinion of him now. Wasn't your car somewhere close? Take Trankov with you and tell him to shut the hell up. I'll give you about twenty minutes, and by that time you should be at Kirkkonummi."

"What about all these tracks and everything else? I'm telling you, this won't work," I argued.

"Don't underestimate me, girl. Make sure you take our guns. And destroy our recordings as soon as possible." Laitio handed me his video camera, which had been hidden under his bill like a headlamp. "Light me one more cigar, will you? It'll help me get through this."

I found the box of cigars and some matches in his breast pocket. I bit off the end of the cigar and lit it. When I turned to look at Trankov, I saw him standing, swaying like a drunk. I walked over to him and took him by the arm.

"Yuri, let's go. It's all over."

He looked at me in disbelief.

"But the police . . ."

"Laitio is going to take care of it. My car is close by. Come on."

I felt bad about leaving Laitio bleeding alone in the forest with Rytkönen's body. What if the police took their time and I hadn't dressed the wound well enough and he began to bleed profusely? I just had to trust that Laitio knew what he was doing. He had pushed between me and Rytkönen's gun and protected me with his body. I almost walked back to him.

Instead, I gave Trankov a slightly soiled handkerchief I'd found in Reiska's pocket and told him to stop sniveling. We trudged back on the snowy road to the Dacia, and luckily I got it running without problems. We drove in silence until we hit Hanko Road. Trankov sat with his eyes closed, his head back. I didn't know where

I should drop him off. If anyone else was staying in Långvik, they'd see immediately that Yuri was upset. If I brought him to our Yrjö Street apartment, I wouldn't hear the end of it.

"Yuri, listen to me carefully. If you'll do exactly like I say, you'll be fine. Laitio is going to take the fall. You weren't even near Kopparnäs tonight. Laitio shot Rytkönen. You and I weren't there."

He didn't seem to be listening. I repeated my message.

"Can you really pull this off in Finland?" he asked.

"We'll try."

"Hilja, I didn't want this. Rytkönen made me work with him. He said he could have me thrown in jail for kidnapping Helena Lehmusvuo if I didn't do exactly as he told me. And I was looking forward to starting a new, law-abiding life."

"So that's the reason why you became friends with me? To find out for Rytkönen where David Stahl might be?"

Trankov closed his eyes again and sighed.

"I wanted to pay you back for what you did to me in Bromarf. Believe me, I stopped feeling vengeful very quickly. I realized how lucky Lehmusvuo had been when you'd saved her from Paskevich. Maybe you had given me a chance at a new start in life. I seriously wanted to paint you, to be with you . . . But you're in love with Stahl."

"Yuri, even I'm not so sure about that. Does it really matter? You saved me and Laitio tonight, and I'll be forever indebted to you because of that." I let my right hand go off the steering wheel and tousled Yuri's hair like he was my little brother. "When did you realize it was me?"

"I know your features well, Hilja. I'm an artist, and I can see the bone structure underneath the mask of makeup. I couldn't let Rytkönen shoot you. I had to make a choice, and now I'm a murderer."

I was a murderer, too. Laitio and I had cooked up this plan, and now one man was dead. It didn't really matter who had pulled the trigger. We were all guilty. My father's blood flowed in my veins, and when it came down to it, I was no better than him. I looked at myself in the rearview mirror and saw Keijo Suurluoto's eyes staring back at me. I wanted to scream. I hit the brakes when the car in front of me suddenly slowed down and signaled left. The Dacia almost slid off the road. Trankov was muttering in Russian again, and I wondered if he was praying.

"Where should I take you?" I asked him once I had the car under control again.

"I left my car at the Kirkkonummi station. Rytkönen picked me up from there."

"Are you all right to drive?" I asked.

Trankov didn't answer, because he was crying again. We saw an ambulance approach us with its sirens screaming, followed by a police van. The blizzard had grown so thick I had no need to worry about my tracks in front of the dance gazebo at the inn.

We located Trankov's Jaguar in the parking lot at the station. I hoped I wouldn't be accused of neglect when I just dumped him out of the car and told him to drive home. I knew what the best medicine for death was, but I doubted Trankov would be much use for me in bed. I wasn't even sure if I wanted him anymore. I put him behind the steering wheel and made sure he fastened his seatbelt. I leaned over to kiss him and assured him that everything would be all right. Rytkönen wouldn't make him do anything anymore.

When Trankov finally took off, I felt drained. I had barely enough energy to open the car door, and once I got in I shook so hard that even the heater at full blast didn't make it stop. I didn't pity Rytkönen, but I knew I'd blame myself and Laitio for the rest of my life for having been such fools. Rytkönen played in the international field, whereas Laitio and I had a stake only in the municipality games.

I remained alert all Tuesday and checked my cell phone every few minutes, but there was no word from Laitio. Even the media and the Bureau's database remained quiet about the incident in Kopparnäs. As if it had never happened. Laitio was a real magician. Still, I wasn't able to sleep, and each time I heard a siren, I was startled to a point where Jouni asked if I had been speeding with his car and gotten into trouble with the police. I didn't throw a rutabaga at him; after all, I'd promised to show him my utmost respect.

Laitio let me wait until Thursday morning.

"Greetings from the hospital. They said I'll get out by Christmas."

I was about to say something careless before I realized I had to pretend to know nothing.

"Why are you at the hospital?" I asked innocently.

"A bullet scraped my thigh a bit, and it startled me enough to cause problems with my heart. My blood pressure is also too high. I could split it among three men of my age."

"Someone shot at you? What happened?" I asked.

"Rytkönen decided we should clear the air between us—with guns. A nasty situation, I tell you. But you know how he had never gone to the police academy? He didn't know how to aim, but I did. I know I'll get into a hell of a lot of trouble because of this. Will you come see me if they throw me in jail?"

"I'll be there." Tears welled up in my eyes.

"You can also come see me at the hospital. I have something to tell you. I almost forgot about it with all this hassle with Rytkönen. Let's just say it's sort of a Christmas present," Laitio said.

"Is it all right if I come in the morning? Jouni's calling me to peel the rutabagas. I owe him for borrowing his car."

"Sure, and bring some cigars. Damned wife, telling me I should quit. I'd rather quit the force."

The following day I walked into the best tobacco store in Helsinki and bought ten of Laitio's favorite cigars. I was curious to know whether his Christmas present was about David, but I wasn't sure if I was in need of such a gift.

Laitio lay in the hospital bed dressed in ugly pajamas. He looked ancient. Someone had cropped his mustache, and it looked oddly short. At least he smiled when he saw me come in.

"Teppo! What's all this about you fighting with Rytkönen? I haven't seen anything about it in the news," I said.

"I'm sure the story will come out after Christmas, but for now we'll keep it hush-hush. Sit down."

I pulled a chair next to the bed. Laitio was surrounded by that hospital smell, and I saw a large bruise on the back of his hand where the IV had been inserted.

"Rytkönen asked me to meet him in the sticks somewhere in Inkoo. He said we could talk privately there and find a solution to this situation we were stuck in. Besides, if we were outside I could smoke. Just to piss him off, I agreed to the plan, but he started to wave his gun around as soon as I got there. He shot me in the leg, but I was able to take him down. I had brought along a gun I usually use for recreation."

The gun license was a problem Laitio still needed to solve. If Trankov's weapon was illegal, it couldn't have been traced back to Laitio, but if it was legal, he had a lot of explaining to do. Even if Laitio could convince his colleagues that he'd bought the gun directly from Trankov and the license hadn't been transferred over yet, I didn't trust Yuri to keep his cool during interrogation. Maybe Trankov should leave the country for a while. He could always claim the gun was stolen from him when he was still living in Russia, and Laitio could come up with another story about how he had obtained it.

"Are they pressing charges?" I asked.

"Undoubtedly. This could turn into a huge mess, Hilja. I've been suspended for now, but before that I got in touch with Eini and asked her to start rooting through the files. That woman will do anything for me. Did you bring me those cigars?"

I took out the box, the cutter, and the lighter from my purse. "Here you go."

"Let's go up on the second-floor balcony. Hand me those crutches, will you?"

Laitio's thigh was wrapped in a thick layer of bandages, but I doubted his leg was the sole reason for his stay at the hospital. He limped slowly, cursing all the way to the elevator. Smoking wasn't allowed on the second-floor balcony, but Laitio lit up.

"I'm officially a bad guy now. Breaking the tobacco laws is the least of my concerns. Want some?" he asked.

"Thanks, but not this time. I'll have a smoke when I visit you on Urheilu Street."

Laitio took a few drags. I was surprised he wasn't freezing in his thin bathrobe that flapped in the wind. Suddenly he was coughing up a storm, bending at the waist. He straightened up and spat a disgusting, bloody lump off the balcony.

"My health might not be up to appearing in court. As if my heart failure wasn't enough, my lungs are shot to hell. So really, it wouldn't have mattered if Rytkönen had shot me. You just don't want crooks like him to decide if you live or not, you know? Then again, who knows if another type of a crook will come to power next, and maybe they're not as bad as they appear." Laitio winked. He had to be talking about Yuri Trankov, but we couldn't mention him in public.

"You never know whose team people are on. Sometimes a player is forced to make a move, even if they don't want to," I whispered. I was dying to be on the same team as David, but he didn't want me.

Laitio spat again off the balcony and took some time to clear his throat. Then he turned to me, his eyes looking sad. "I wanted to talk to you about Keijo Suurluoto, currently known as Keijo Kurkimäki," he said.

"What about him?" I grabbed the balcony because vertigo was washing over me.

"He's still in jail, and for good reason. Did anyone ever tell you he escaped about a decade ago?"

I told him I'd found out about it earlier in the fall, but I didn't really know what to do with the information.

"I think your father came after you. Or he was at least caught on the border between Tuusniemi and Kaavi. He managed to wreak some havoc on his way, too. He raped a seventeen-year-old girl from Tuusniemi."

"Holy shit! That man is more of a monster than I ever imagined!"

"The girl is the youngest child in a Laestadian family. She became pregnant, and her family didn't allow her to have an abortion."

I felt my skin tingle, and the hairs at the back of my neck stood up. I squeezed the handrail even tighter, and the cold iron made my hand ache.

"What are you trying to say?"

"Your sister—or rather your half sister, Vanamo Huttunen, was born at the Kuopio central hospital the following summer. As far as I know, she lives with her mother and her family in Tuusniemi. Eini found this information from the citizen registry."

"So Keijo Suurluoto has another child, and I have a half sister? Are you sure about this?"

"Her mother, Saara Huttunen, had been a virgin until the incident. And Keijo Suurluoto didn't deny it. On the contrary, he bragged about it. That part in the trial had been hidden from media due to the victim's age, but she never changed her name or her town of residence," Laitio said.

Laitio's voice was muffled. My legs gave in, and I had to let the handrails support my weight. The whole world was swinging, as if it were nudged off its course. For the past eight years, I had a half sister, and I knew nothing about her. Did she know about me? Did she or her mother even want to know about me? Maybe her mother had gotten married and Vanamo would be a member of this family, and she'd never be told how she was brought into this world.

"Give me that cigar," I told Laitio although I felt sick.

"Well, aren't cigars a way to celebrate a birth?" Laitio cut a cigar and gave me the lighter. "The wind here is a bit tricky—watch out."

I managed to light the cigar on my third try. Its smoke in my throat didn't stop my hands from shaking, and my knees from buckling.

"There are some other interesting facts in this story, too, although they're harder to prove," Laitio continued. "The police tried to reconstruct Keijo Suurluoto's movements during his escape. He was out for two days. The nurse who was watching over him received permanent skull fractures, and she'll never speak again. It's not a long way from the ward in Niuvanniemi to Kaavi and Outokumpu. Suurluoto stole a Skoda, only a couple of years old. They found tracks from a car like that on your uncle's yard in Hevonpersiinsaari."

"But Uncle Jari drowned . . . He was tangled up in his fishing net." I had a hard time breathing, but I kept on taking drags off the cigar.

"And he wasn't found until days later, which made it hard to pinpoint the exact time of death. Isn't it quite a coincidence that he would've died around the same time Suurluoto was on the run?"

I didn't need to answer that question. The view off the balcony had become blurry. I couldn't even distinguish the chimneys on the nearby roofs. My entire life I had run away from thinking about my father, doing my best to forget him. I hadn't realized how present he was in my life and what an effect he had on me. Not only had he taken my mother away from me, he may also have been responsible for Uncle Jari's death—he had just never been brought to justice for what he'd done to my uncle. My hatred toward Keijo Kurkimäki flamed red inside me, and now I knew why some people were able to kill.

"It's hard to investigate it, but it won't be impossible. I can come with you if I'm not convicted. You want to know the truth, don't you? To squeeze it from your father's lips if needed? I'm sure he can have visitors, even if he's in for life," Laitio said.

"Are you saying I should go see him?" I asked.

"When you're ready."

I wasn't sure if I'd ever be ready. Laitio's cigar had gone out, and he was shivering. I suggested we return to his room. I had just pulled the door to the hallway open when a male nurse ran over and began to lecture us about breaking the tobacco laws. I had to beg nicely for him to allow me to continue with my visit. When we were finally back in Laitio's room, he suddenly patted me on my hand.

"Don't worry, Hilja. Everything will be all right in the end. Right now I can't do anything about Stahl's warrant. We'll get together later to talk about what we know. Come to think of it, I could know everything Rytkönen told us. There were no witnesses to our conversation." Laitio chuckled. "If you hear from Stahl, let me know. Do you have any plans for Christmas?"

"The restaurant is open, and we'll have Monika's and some staff members' families there for dinner. On Christmas Day I'm moving to Alppila," I told him.

Jouni's sister had agreed to let me stay at her place while she was backpacking for a couple of months with her boyfriend. Monika would live with her cousin until the New Year, and then she'd move to her own place in Ruoholahti, a short walking distance from Sans Nom. It felt good to have temporary living arrangements. My life was in such turmoil that I didn't see a future in Sans Nom.

"Well, Merry Christmas then, and try not to worry yourself sick. You're not my daughter, but hell—blood is not always the thickest. I do like you quite a lot, Hilja," Laitio said. He patted my hand again.

I leaned over and gave him a peck on each of his cheeks, although his mustache was unbearably tickly.

I started my walk from Töölö to Sans Nom. Windows were shining with Christmas lights, and people rushed through the snow with their shopping bags. The world seemed strange and meaningless, like I was not a part of it. David, Trankov, Jaan Rand, and Rytkönen floated in my mind in an odd, painful mess that I couldn't solve with just a snap of my fingers. Rytkönen had been Gezolian's snitch, and he'd tried to locate David. So far he'd failed, so I assumed David was still alive. Rytkönen had been willing to let another interested party catch David for murdering Carlo Dolfini, even if it took fake evidence. Trankov claimed eyewitnesses had seen David in Kaunas, but Rytkönen had been looking for him in Helsinki on Yrjö Street and at Sans Nom. I recalled again the dark figure on the shore across the villa in Långvik. For a moment I had thought it was David. Then I remembered the letter where David claimed he didn't care if I had other men in my life. You don't see the lynx, but the lynx has already seen you. There was no point in me looking for David. I had not lied to Trankov. I honestly did not know anymore who I loved.

23

Kuopio was on a high enough latitude that it got pitch-black there by three. My train had been an hour late, and I'd spent some more time having lunch in the city before I turned my rental car east. It was negative five degrees, and the world seemed to have frozen. I'd asked the Hakkarainen couple to heat the Hevonpersiinsaari cabin for a couple of days before I'd get there, but I'd still brought a sleeping bag that was fit for the breeze on top of Mount Everest. No heating system could take away the chill inside me. I was afraid of what I might find.

It took only about an hour to drive from Kuopio to Tuusniemi—the roads were completely clear. I wasn't prepared to be at my destination so quickly. I turned onto a road leading to the village center and parked the car at the gas station, where I took some time to study the map. I could've included a GPS with my rental, but I wanted to keep my orienteering skills in check. I memorized all the intersections: take a left at the third turn, then a right at the second turn, then take the first turn on the right. It wasn't easy to read the signs in the dark, but I was able to find my way without stopping to take a better look. Even the smallest village roads had been well plowed, and the house I had been searching for looked like it had gotten a fresh coat of paint the previous summer. The farm was surrounded by three buildings. I left my car behind the barn, hidden away from the main building's view. The family could have still been inside, as it was not yet time to milk the cows.

I hadn't told anyone I was coming. What would I have said? I didn't want anyone to make a big deal out of this. I got out of the car, and the freezing air took my breath away. The air smelled like my childhood winters in Hevonpersiinsaari, and the snow crunched underneath my shoes like I was walking over Styrofoam. I expected a dog to lunge at me from the dog house, but all I saw was an empty leash. It was too cold even for a watchdog.

Then the door opened, and a small figure walked out. It was covered in so many layers it was hard to tell which sex it was. This person stumbled down the steps to the path in the yard and didn't notice me, only concentrating on the task at hand. The person was carrying candles and a gas lighter. The path was lined with five frozen ice lanterns. When the person walked closer, I could see it was a girl. A long blond braid fell out from under her beanie, and her nose was red. She was about eight years old, and she was testing the lanterns out. She first removed the old candles and tossed them onto a pile, then placed the new candles under the lanterns and lit them. The flames began to glow in the dark. Only after she was done did the girl turn to look at me.

It felt as if someone had turned my childhood mirror image upside down. I recognized her eyes and the determined yet curious expression on her face. She wiped her straight nose with her mitten, then looked at me fearlessly and smiled a little.

"I thought you were Laura from next door. Who are you? My name is Vanamo."

I couldn't say a word. I stepped closer and hugged her. Until this day my only sister had been a lynx. Now I had a human sister.

ABOUT THE AUTHOR

Finland's bestselling female crime author, Leena Lehtolainen first rose to fame with her series starring feisty detective Maria Kallio. She won the Finnish Whodunnit Society's annual prize for the best Finnish crime novel twice and was nominated for the prestigious Glass Key Award for the best Nordic crime novel. Her books have been translated into twenty-nine languages and sold over two million copies. Lehtolainen currently lives in Finland with her husband and two sons.

ABOUT THE TRANSLATOR

Photo © Kochun Hu

Jenni Salmi is a translator and localizer living in Seattle. She was born and raised in Eastern Finland near the Russian border, where she learned English, Swedish, German, and Russian. After mostly forgetting the other languages, she earned her master's degree in English literature at the University of Joensuu. She has also translated the first novel in Leena Lehtolainen's The Bodyguard Series, *The Bodyguard*.